LIVING on AIR

LIVING *on* AIR

a novel

ANNA
SHAPIRO

Published by
Soho Press, Inc.
853 Broadway
New York, N.Y. 10003

Library of Congress Cataloging-in-Publication Data
Shapiro, Anna.
Living on air : a novel / Anna Shapiro.
p. cm.
ISBN 1-56947-431-1
1. Teenage girls—Fiction. 2. Levittown (N.Y.)—Fiction.
3. Identity (psychology)—Fiction.
I. Title.

PS3569.H3383L58 2006
813'.54—dc22
2005056240

10 9 8 7 6 5 4 3 2 1

Designed by India Amos

Author's Note

My father was an artist, but my father is not Milt. I understand why people who didn't know my father would be tempted to think so, but no one who knew him could: the character and the man are as different as they could be, both in their aesthetic and childrearing practices. Neither is Nina my mother (though I wished my own had long braids), nor Maude me. Or they're all me. Of my friends, none is Weesie. Of boyfriends, none was Danny. I have no brother. If, however, people I've never met feel that they recognize something of themselves in my characters, then fiction is doing its job.

LIVING *on* AIR

PART I

1.

ONLY ONCE, WHEN she was very little, he asked her to pose for him—asked her to be part of that endless source of their pride and distinction, his art. She stayed in the specified spot on the studio floor, where she sat listening to the scratching of his brush against the canvas and watching his legs in a color-splotched chinoed dance as he leaned to this or that part of the easel, stepped to the side for a more piercing look at her, stepped forward, back.

The rough plywood of the floor made her shiver with aversion. Through the plain sheet of glass that formed the north wall, she could see the neighborhood children below—her best friend wheeling on a tricycle; a toddler in dumb amazement watching two boys in striped tee shirts tussling on the grass—and hear their faint calls and taunts. Then the twelve o'clock whistle blew and they threw down their bikes and toys and disappeared, the toddler dragged off by his puffy fist. The scritch-scratching of the brush went on, as did Maude's high sense of mission. A symphony began playing dimly on the classical music station.

"Can I look?"

"Just a minute. Just another minute. Sit still."

It was more than a minute before she was allowed to stand to see herself revealed.

But the image on the canvas was indecipherable, as in all his pictures—not an image at all. A bunch of bristly black lines.

Seeing the disorder of her face, he pulled out of his customary dreamy, helpless self-absorption. Years later, he would recognize this expression of hers when he stopped on a country road and called to some cattle grazing by its side: rolling their heads away to look at him as if the sight were too horrible to bear head-on. It was a look of pure distrust. He should have explained to her he just needed her perpendiculars; he just needed a human proportion: she was simply the one available. She should have known, he felt. She knew his work.

Even if she were capable of knowing, however, there was a picture he had done in art school that looked exactly like him, and there were shaded renderings of naked ladies carefully referred to as models or nudes, as if it made them less naked, tossed on the dustheap of history under the studio eaves, where she played. "It doesn't look like me, Daddy."

"It's an abstraction, sweetie."

She was three.

That look. It was the end of something. Neither of them knew what. Within a year, she had decided *she* would be an artist; she would deliver what Milt so rejectingly refused. In the meantime, they stood, the half-irascible, half indifferent 1950s daddy, the mollusklike little girl—not in being happy as a clam but in her self-protectiveness and knowledge that whatever she felt, short of cheerful acquiescence, was unwelcome where Daddy was concerned—as, she felt, was she. Her big dark eyes fixed on him as some kind of danger to herself, as if he canceled her out. If she moved just as carefully as she'd stayed still to pose, she'd be okay.

2.

"YOU'RE SO LUCKY. That's so cool. An artist!"

Everything was different at her paradise of a new school except this attitude, it seemed: whether the urchins of plumbers and line workers of her elementary school or these bright, cosseted teenagers, people were either awestricken or spitefully jealous about the artist in the family—though here the balance shifted, and both the awe and spite were tempered by sophistication and privilege. Not in Weesie's case, however. All the fathers Weesie knew were lawyers or businessmen or didn't bother having jobs, they had so much money. For both girls, being able to make art seemed more valuable than making money, though to each, it was the other who came from an exotic, unknown world.

"It's not such a big deal. He's just your typical failure," said Maude, who knew nothing about it but was at the age where it felt important to seem to. She felt all the danger of disloyalty and a strange relief. She had never said it, dared it to its face before: failure.

"But he's a professional. He's had shows and stuff."

"Oh, yeah," said Maude, flipping some hair back over her shoulder. Family pride took over, and she named his gallery, which was a good one, if not the best—Madison Avenue, not 57th Street. But the gallery had closed a few years before. It was the family outrage, recited in set form like Homeric epithets, that his single one-man show there had not drawn a review in *The New York Times*. "But it's not as if he, you know, makes his living by it. He teaches."

"Where?"

There were universities where an artist could teach and feel good about it.

"Out of his studio," said Maude. In the afternoons, children from their subdivision trooped in for lessons; in the evening, housewives.

But Weesie said, "I'd really like to see his, you know, 'work.'" She had a way of putting words into aural quotes that Maude greatly admired. She seemed always to be implying a great, high distance between herself and anything ordinary, including, in this case, her own well-meaning curiosity or the conventions governing art terminology.

Maude, aping the ironic style, said, "'It can be arranged.'"

The way it was arranged was that, instead of their taking the school van that delivered children who weren't picked up or didn't yet have their own cars, they both went in the car that came for Weesie every day, but which this time offered its suave tinted presence to the strip development along Hempstead Avenue and delivered itself to the astounded precincts of the Pughs' development, nosing among the Fords and Chevys.

"I've never been in a chauffeured car."

"Ernie's not a *chauffeur*," said Weesie, trying to minimize her family's humiliating wealth. "It's just a livery car."

Not that Maude knew what that was. Weesie, for her part, was embarrassed that anyone would attribute to her family so much side.

"I have to warn you," said Maude as they purred along.

Weesie, who knew from the name, Levittown, that this

was not the Long Island she had grown up in—not the estates of the North Shore but the ugly rash of new houses that her mother moaned about but that her father said were good for labor—thought Maude was going to make an excuse for where she lived, an unnecessary apology, and was set to forestall it. So she was surprised.

"The whole house is black."

"Black?"

"The walls are black. It 'brings out the colors.' In the pictures." Maude rolled her eyes. It was as if Milt's art were like Weesie's own father's piles of money—gross. But Maude intended to be an artist too, whereas Weesie intended to be poor, if at all possible. Maude's eyes were dark as Niçoise olives, dark like the hair in a straight bang above them and dangling in back over her belt.

"Not *your* room." Even Weesie thought a black bedroom a bit much.

"Oh yeah. I used to beg, *beg* them to paint it yellow. They promised . . ."

"What?"

"If I would keep it neat for a month, they'd paint it." Maude looked away, out the tinted window that mercifully subdued the Dunkin' Donuts, the modeled figures of a ship-shaped restaurant called The Jolly Roger, the car dealerships, the garish colors, the Esso station, and dimmed as well the lovely red Pegasus, inside a circle, of the Flying A.

"But you couldn't?"

Maude turned back. "It's been completely neat for about the last eleven *years*." She seemed to remember the gift and relief of Weesie's distancing abilities: "Wait till you see. Even the floor! There's gray carpeting in the living room, but everywhere else, it's this black, I'm not kidding. Even the kitchen. We even have a black *couch*."

"Maude, you just don't appreciate how lucky you are." This would always be Weesie's note.

The house, when they pulled up to it, not only did not look like anything special; it looked exactly like all the houses that stretched away down the calculatedly curved street in one direction and up it in the other and at precisely equal intervals across the street. Boxy little houses with peaked roofs, each with the same apple tree in front and the same reddish pricker bush, as the neighborhood children called them, at the side of the walk. It was, famously, the town where children coming home from school went into the wrong house, indistinguishable by them from their own. One of the first explosions of mass-produced housing after the war and the biggest such ever. To Milton Pugh, it represented a realization, or at least a stab at the realization, of Bauhaus principles—perhaps not better living through design, exactly, but rationalization of the distribution of the world's goods through the intelligent application of technologies created for other purposes. To most adults with his kind of knowledge or discernment, it represented an aesthetic abomination.

As they left the car, Weesie took in this effect of patterned sameness, which was softened by trees that had had fifteen or twenty years by this time to grow, and also by years of owner diversification—the closed-in stoop next door, dark ugly siding on the other side, the Pughs' distinctive half-story, where the slope of the roof had been cut by the vertical glass of Milton's studio. He was visible in the picture window, like a mannequin on display, doing the dance of art in front of his easel, stopping to frown with a hand on his hip; noticing them coming up the cracking cement walk, smiling down with a little wave.

Weesie thought he must be the handsomest father she'd ever seen. Or if not the handsomest, the sexiest. The most romantic.

What Maude had said was true, she saw: the pink front door opened into a black kitchen with the black living room beyond. A cramped black kitchen, in which a tiny, timorous mother hovered behind the strict blond table and strict, square, bright-red chairs. The mother quavered greetings and offerings while trying to peer to see the fancy car her daughter had warned her would be coming.

Milton boomed down the stairs into the living room. Maude dutifully advanced to introduce her friend, passing the white brick chimney that stood like a column, containing the modernistic fireplace that was the centerpiece of all these houses; the rooms were otherwise open space, defined only by where the gray carpeting ended. Milton was silhouetted against the other glass wall, of the living room at the back of the house, which faced an undeveloped field, and into which redwinged blackbirds regularly pitched themselves and died.

Weesie didn't know if she was more dazzled by the artist, so tall, so stalky, with his leonine white mane and prominent Adam's apple, or by the small, square canvases pulsating off walls whose darkness made their distance or even palpability strangely hard to gauge. Even the furniture seemed to float in this space—an amoeba-shaped armchair in chartreuse, square pillows in yellow, electric blue, purple, magenta; and big glass ashtrays, one in clear, thick slabs, another that looked like hard candies pressed together, into which the artist dripped ash.

Milton was responding to Weesie's stammering compliments. The house was like being inside a picture, she said. "Nah. I'd like to junk it all, build everything in. Not a stick of movable furniture, not an inch of waste. All built-ins. And you'd have storage." He put his hands on his belt, looking around with a satisfaction that suggested his vision had already been accomplished, as if the acts of imagining and creating were one and the same.

Though her father's plan appealed to her in its utopian efficiency and cleanness, Maude said, "Sounds cozy, doesn't it?" Because wouldn't he, if he could, obliterate any aspect of her inconvenient to him? All that was about *her*; all but the straight lines.

Milton smiled. A thin, angry smile. "Where does she get this? Not from her mother. She's so caustic! And she was such a sweet little girl." He squeezed Maude's cheeks between two flat, green-splotched palms. She deliberately let her lips go slack to look like a fish.

"Ach." He waved a hand in disgust. "You girls go off and share your secrets. Come up to the studio later if you have time for an old man." Milton was forty-five. He picked up a copy of *Life* from the coffee table, which was like a long shutter with rattley dowels where slats would be, and moodily leafed through pictures of mutilated Vietnamese civilians, ash dangling from the butt on his lip like the phantom of a cigarette.

"Ta-dah," said Maude at the end of the dark hall off the kitchen, throwing wide the door.

Her bedroom really was black—but, again, it reminded Weesie of Mr. Pugh's strict, bright paintings. There were two square little dressers, side by side, vivid yellow. Curtains of thick orange cotton, though the windows were squinty things high up in a corner, as if trying to huddle out of sight. The bedcover was turquoise corduroy. The floor was black linoleum tile, seafoam patterned, as in the rest of the house. Cheap looking, but she had to admire the discipline of the whole thing, the Josef Albers-ishness of it. Weesie had heard of Josef Albers. She had seen his endless reworkings of color-within-color like square targets.

"Do you really hate it so much? Living inside a painting."

"That's really funny." Maude told her about posing for her father. "I'm inside the painting, but I'm the one thing that isn't there. Where do I fit inside this painting? Look." Maude dramatically swept open the gray louvered sliding door of the closet that covered one wall. Inside was a different world. A miniature world. Clearly, Maude had saved every toy and doll she'd ever had, and there they all were, on gray shelves that reached the bar meant for clothes. Eyeless teddy bears with the fuzz worn off, a dented tin train, its curved segments of track in a neat pile; dozens of Golden Books, along with *Madeline*, *Eloise*, and dilapidated editions of Pooh books that turned out to have been

Mrs. Pugh's in the twenties. Not only were there a repellently cheerful hard-bodied rubber baby doll, with outstretched arms and molded hair, and a kind of older sister, like Chatty Cathy, adapted from a bride doll, but they had both been dressed in clothes that must have been homemade for them: genteel pinafores and long skirts and satin bows, as if they were Victorian porcelain dolls in the Museum of the City of New York. Even the Barbies wore long calico dresses, like extras on *Wagon Train*, or the latest thing in mod that could also be seen in the current *Life*. For the Barbies there was a carved canopy bed and teensy cast-iron woodstove. Weesie opened its oven door: twigs had been broken up to simulate firewood. Maude had piled a handful of gravel into a tiny coal bucket.

"There's this line in Emily Dickinson," said Maude. " 'Life is over there—Behind the Shelf.' " She shook her head. Her face looked the same, but something disappeared inside it, as though she felt she must retract what she had revealed; as if she could slide a door over herself the way she could close the closet.

Almost too impressed, and too enviously impressed, with this new acquaintance's casually rich cultivation and precocity, precisely because it was like her own, Weesie nevertheless felt a wave of depression that she recognized as being not hers. She felt it like a contagion. She knew this kind of private desolation, though her circumstances were so different. They were sitting on the chilly black seafoam floor, leaning on two baby-size stools knocked together out of boards by Maude's father and painted shiny red, long since scratched and chipped.

"You'll have to come over to my house. You'd love it."

"Maybe we can trade."

They could hear the afternoon students arriving and thumping up to the studio, and Nina, Maude's mother, in the kitchen, telling Ernie where the bathroom was and offering him tea.

The livery car driver was black. The bathroom wasn't. It was flame orange. Even the ceiling.

3.

NINA LOOKED LIKE a washed-out version of her daughter. Everything about Maude was more: More color, more height, more curve, more electricity. Nina's straight bangs and ponytail were pale with early gray, and her twittery, fragile-looking form was outfitted in the flattering bohemian uniform of thin black sweater, dirndl, and ballet slippers.

Dropping Maude off at school one morning, as sometimes happened, she got out of the car and stood inside the wing of its open door, looking around. The school grounds too were *more*: More and bigger trees, sweeping lawns, the mansion that formed the school's main building; the mansarded barn that was like a mansion, which housed the dance and art studios; and, at the moment, more color, as the maples sprouted the first fingerbursts of autumn vermilion amid the still summery lush green. Students trod winding paths in workboots, jeans, flannel shirts, and turtlenecks, all with long floppy hair, or springy hair that suggested egrets, angora cats, passion flowers. In a few years the look would be legion, but at the time it was hardly to be seen outside rock groups, and even they wore repressive little matched jackets.

"I'm glad you're going here."

Maude was collecting her books, piling them against her recently budded chest. "Daddy isn't."

Mrs. Pugh dodged this. "Well, I am. I think you're lucky. I wish I could have gone here myself."

Maude squinted, not wanting to start up the fight again by reminding her mother of how hard she'd made it for her to accept the scholarship she'd won after secretly applying and getting in. They weren't a private school sort of family, she had been loftily informed. Now, it seemed, they were. Half of them. (Her brother's vote wasn't in because, actually, they didn't know where to reach him to ask his opinion.)

The bearded, proudly potbellied art teacher came sauntering over, hands in pockets, as if recognizing a landsman by Nina's art uniform. (On top of this, the car was that emblem of nonconformity, a Volkswagen.) "Mrs. Pugh!" he said heartily, extrapolating from Maude's presence. "You've got a talented daughter." Irritation prickled like scalding bites along Maude's back. She could draw, it was perfectly true, and she liked people to notice. But she hated this kind of oozy worship, and she wouldn't tolerate flattery or praise as a come-on. It seemed to patronize the very seriousness of her intention to be an artist.

"I'm gonna be late for lit, Mom. Thanks for the lift." She wanted to blow her mother a kiss but didn't want Mr. Patrick to be its incidental recipient.

The mother watched her daughter blend into the stream of students. It seemed a miracle that this girl, *her daughter*, knew what to do, like an animal that has an instinct about where to fly in winter, how to perform a mating dance. Everything she did, no one had taught her. It was eerie, almost scary, her apartness and self-possession. Even her drawing abilities. Milt had steadfastly refused to teach her, even when she asked: "Daddy, will you show me how to draw a tree?" "Go out and look at one," he had answered. She hadn't done as he'd said, though; she just figured it out somehow. And in that same mysterious way she knew how to be part of this crowd, these children of millionaires and famous people, a Senator's niece, a movie star's son. She acted as if it were nothing, in her cheap deep-blue jeans from Penny's in the Roosevelt Field shopping center—which, however, she had embroidered with paisley shapes on one thigh and a peace sign on the back pocket. But how had she learned to embroider? Nina Resnikov Pugh, daughter of a garment worker, hadn't in her whole life mastered so much as how to hem a dress.

Nina felt the pang that always meant *Seth*, Maude's brother—sick, helpless guilt, as if she had wronged him by producing Maude. Nina couldn't help hating Maude, a little—as if Maude had wronged Seth by being born. Shown her older brother up. Everyone had always oohed and ahhed over little Maude, precious Maude. With each word of praise for Maude, you could see Seth flinch. She and Milt had been so careful, as a result, not to praise Maude.

She wondered at her daughter's boldness and ingenuity in applying to the school, and at its having occurred to her in the first place. She herself had wanted it for Seth, if anything. They had always known about the school, of course, in that vague way that you knew about things in your area; the way they knew that pioneer aviators had used Roosevelt Field before it got paved over as vast parking lots, though there were still cracked landing strips in the last grass of the flat field; the way they knew that the antiaircraft plants had come because of the flyers, and the farms started to go because of the highways coming out, serving the plants; and they knew the names of the families, which seemed like families out of Greek drama and British heraldry, by the beautiful lands behind brick fences where the few hills of Long Island rose—the Phipps estate, the Whitney estate, Coe, Woolworth, Pratt, Morgan—and saw the starry denizens in gauzy dresses and sequins on the society pages. They seemed hardly human and utterly inaccessible, a different order altogether, for all that Nina passed their gates when she drove to certain shops and always when she drove Maude to her school. And this new friend of hers—Weesie—Louise, who seemed like a polite, lively girl, apparently she lived on one of the estates. Not in the main house but some house on the grounds, so that it sounded not so intimidating, as if they might be gatekeepers or caretakers. Which they certainly weren't. Though, in any case, to be a caretaker to such grand people was in itself pretty intimidating.

Nina would never have admitted she thought they were better than she was, would not have admitted it to herself. Justice demanded that they be, if anything, worse.

But it was impossible not to be drawn to the green silent enclaves, to want to follow the narrow lanes that snaked from wrought-iron gates posted PRIVATE and TRESPASSERS WILL BE PROSECUTED, marked with reflectors so that a forgetful inhabitant coming home drunk at four a.m. wouldn't crash his own barriers, controlled by electric eyes and other devices triggered out of sight, beyond the fieldstone pillars to which the gates were hinged. It was impossible for Nina not to feel connected to places to which her senses were so attracted, or rubbed that much more raw by the rudeness of the inescapable larger culture to which she was consigned.

And that was why, two summers before, they had pulled onto the winding road that led to Bay Farm: anyone might look at a school, anyone might be a prospective student or student's parent, however fraudulent or out of place they felt. They had walked the lovely rolling grounds, the gardens no longer elegantly kept but planted with botany projects and provender for cooking classes and preserves sold at the school fair. That was one way they knew about the school: the fair was open to the public and advertised by fliers in store windows or piled on the counter at the cleaners and the stationery store. They always meant to go and always forgot.

They walked into the barn and saw student carvings in wood and stone left half finished on stands, and oil paintings piled against walls, and etchings and woodcuts pinned to the ubiquitous pocked beaverboard. Peering into windows in the main buildings, they saw classrooms. Instead of the usual thirty unconversational desks in grim rows, there were two long tables pressed together, surrounded by chairs—fewer than thirty chairs, for sure. You could see from how things were set up that the students were treated as something precious, not just noisy bothers to be processed and gotten rid of.

No wonder the upper classes had such a sense of their own consequence.

"Maybe Seth—" Nina had begun. Milt silenced her with a look.

But Maude caught it. They thought this place could salvage Seth. The crude way he laughed with his friends; the way he wrenched her arm behind her back until sweat beaded her face; the way he snapped the back of her bra and said "Littlest Angel," as if she would wear a training bra. There was his music—but, even so, she couldn't imagine him here.

From the hill on the far side of the old mansion they saw that they were only steps from the glittering bay.

A blunt-bodied fellow in tennis shorts, swinging his racket pendulum-style, had appeared from greenery that must have concealed courts and came up to the interlopers. "How can I help you?" he had unsuspiciously asked. When they said they were just looking around, he had assumed the then-twelve-year-old Maude was the prospective student and took her hand in his big, sweaty paw. Nina hadn't taught Maude to shake hands and hoped the girl wouldn't shame her. Maude, in a dark headband, pre-bangs, had shown her front teeth and returned a firm grip. The man had said he hoped he'd be seeing her there in a year or two. He was a history teacher, but Maude had evidently taken his words as prophecy.

"Isn't that funny?" Nina had said. "He thought you were applying."

Only she did. Without telling anyone, except to ask selected teachers at her two-thousand-student junior high for recommendations to the two-hundred-student high school. Not high school: the private-school people called it secondary school, suggesting that there was something gauche or intrinsically low about high schools. The fact that they were free. The fact that anyone could go to them. No one could be turned away.

The Pughs didn't know anyone who sent their kids to private school except the unfortunate couple down their street, who had finally put their ten-year-old, a boy like a screaming pre–Annie Sullivan Helen Keller, into a school for the deaf.

※

It came to Nina that Mr. Patrick—"Call me Rod"—was flirting with her. Feeling vulnerable, Nina reminded herself that a high school art teacher was unlikely to be as successful an artist as Milt. She made a point of mentioning her husband. "Have him come over," Mr. Patrick, Rod, said. "Maybe he'd like to address Friday Meeting."

Many students had dinner at the school and stayed for evening programs in crafts or for discussion groups, but on Fridays, staying late was mandatory. The whole school would sing a short work in four-part harmony from Bach or Orlando di Lasso and then listen to some uplifting lecture or presentation. The Senator was scheduled, as was someone's uncle who was head of the World Bank. Nina always found it painful when Milt spoke to a public audience and felt a familiar dread.

"Maybe."

4.

WEESIE WAS RIGHT that she would want to trade. Maude gazed around at the splendor that was Weesie's bedroom—her *bedroom*: Maude's whole ugly box of a house could fit in Weesie's bedroom.

Instead, however, what was in it was a canopy bed. Not some white-painted reproduction such as Maude had once envied a neighbor, and not even the spindle-tip beauties of historic houses she had been taken through on car trips, but a massive fantasy structure from the Indian Raj, with elephant heads carved into the posts and designs in orange, blue, and gilt: a paean to decoration.

What her parents would call, in Yiddish onomatopoeia, *ungapotchkeh*.

But it wasn't overdecorated. With all that space around it, it certainly wasn't too much, except as the boys at her school brayed the words: "Too much!" Crowing as if, by admiring, they appropriated what they approved.

French windows with a Juliet terrace and printed red curtains that reminded Maude of the richly colored frontispiece in her old edition of Grimm, with shaded roses and leaves so realistic they had holes bitten into them and, especially, glossy beetles with a green sheen that made her not want to get close to the polished cotton.

"My mother used to have to open and close these for me. I wouldn't touch them," Weesie said. "They like really creeped me out." Both girls shivered with the easily resurgent childhood belief in the aliveness of things, enjoying their fear. This was a room full of aliveness, from the tall windows that let in a welcome outdoors—a thick willow as reassuring as a farm horse, lawn, a white stone bench, artfully naturalized shrubs, a glint of bay—to the elephant trunks that undulated over a sleeper's head.

Softly shining wood floor, oriental carpet in tender, fading colors, a loveseat. Maude had never seen living room furniture in a bedroom before and wondered at the redundancy of upholstered furniture in a room that had a bed. But she didn't say anything. She wouldn't expose herself that way. An Empire dresser with mahogany curves like a woman. A pierglass: you could make the room into a hundred different oval-framed pictures, tilting it. Wallpaper that looked like flowers made with cream of tomato soup. Maude recognized it from one of her father's artbooks—William Morris. Milton approved of Morris, or rather the Arts and Crafts movement, as a precursor to the later, more rigorous German approach to better living through design. It wasn't that Maude didn't warm to the idea of better living through design. It was just that she had her own preferences as to design and as to what constituted better living.

"Oh! It's so beautiful!" she said about everything.

Weesie smiled her crooked smile, flattered, embarrassed—ashamed of her plenty, as she always was—pleased, but a little sarcastic and not wanting credit.

Maude turned to some framed photographs standing in front of books on the shelf. "Oh, my God, is that Mary Jane?" It was a girl in a strapless white evening gown and tiara, from the rather recent days when teenagers already looked older than grown-ups did now.

"Her coming-out," said Weesie in a voice that seemed to curl her mouth like lemon juice.

A terribly English-looking young man in tennis whites was the young Jock Herrick, now a distant, intimidating power with gray hair, a big American. "Who's this?" Maude asked about a chubby girl, around nine or ten, with a forthright expression, not quite smiling but looking straight at the viewer as if she could see ahead to Maude.

"The real me," said Weesie. She laughed. "The fat me. I wore glasses too, but I took them off for the picture."

It was hard to believe.

It wasn't the little bit of fat that was so different, though that was different; it was a lack of tension, a frankness instead of the wild tenseness that added a frisson to Weesie's confident gesticulations, plunging, headlong narrations, and laugh that popped like a cork. She was so keyed-up, every exchange with her was many notches more exciting than with other people. But you never felt you were quite altogether enough to occupy Weesie's attention. The girl in the picture wasn't like that.

They were lost for a while in Weesie's children's books, which Maude began plucking from the arched bookcase, and then her artbooks, agreeing that Renoir was a pornographer, whereas Modigliani was erotic. They loved saying the word; it was erotic to say *erotic*. It was almost erotic making these kinds of distinctions, being able to articulate them, and having someone to share them with.

Weesie had the tiny paperback Edward Gorey books, of which Maude had only ever seen one and felt it to be her own private discovery. They immediately made themselves a cult of two, the only initiates, they felt, into the poetry of poverty, yearning, loss, and death made wistful in spidery lines. Like Maude, Weesie had a crumbling paperback called *The Beat Generation*, with its cheerfully appalling account of insulin therapy (you got fat!), and she had the square, black-banded stapled volume, as doll-like as the Goreys, of *Howl*. It was cool to have it, but they both felt abashed by the poem's grandiloquence. They had not gone looking for an angry fix and did not, really, intend to. Weesie had a book of lyrics to the songs of the folk-gone-rock musician that everybody worshipped. Maude, who was just learning to love the electrified version of the singer, found the lyrics, bald without their music, not so great as poetry.

"You're wrong," said Weesie, folding the oversize paperback to her chest and closing her eyes in a way that was just short of wincing, her silence, as much as the aristocratic ridge of her nose, suggesting she was too fine to comment but that Maude was damned by limitation of understanding and bad taste. Maude was afraid it was all over. But really, *reality resists its curlew wing, it rides against fur-pawed silent woods* was kind of . . . *ungapotchkeh*.

Rather than never speak to her again, Weesie opened her eyes and asked if Maude wanted to go with her to the city on Saturday.

On Long Island, "the city" only meant one thing. It was New York, but it was not Brooklyn, the Bronx, or nearby Queens; it was never New Haven or Newark; it was only Manhattan— museums, ballet, Greenwich Village, and restaurants that had meaning beyond food.

They ran down the back stairs, a thing it was amazing to have, to find Weesie's mother. In her studio.

Mary Jane Herrick looked like a dowager in a cartoon. Not only because of her solid bosom and full waist, giving that ship-in-full-sail effect, but her hair was an iron gray flip streaked with rust, as stiff and disguising as a nun's coif. And even though, as Maude was breathlessly to tell her parents later, "she was working in oils, for Christ's sake," she wore, above a neat, blue, Peter Pan-collared smock, at her pinkly powdered throat, pearls.

Maude felt sorry for her. She was the consummate version of what her father called "lady painters." And Weesie clearly saw that too. That was why she was so impressed with Maude's father: he was a real artist.

That was why, to Weesie, his whole house was a work of art, while her mother had only this one room in their conventionally furnished dwelling, and even that was really for plants, a conservatory, glass on three sides, its herringboned brick floor protected by a canvas tarpaulin. This canvas looked to Weesie more like "real" art than her mother's over-careful, too neat pictures. It was blotched and spattered in random colors underfoot. Gorgeous.

"Louisie-lou," said Mrs. Herrick, leaving a lipstick kiss on Weesie's forehead. Louise: Weesie. Maude hadn't gotten it till that moment. She would never have looked for a resemblance between this mother and daughter, unless that streak of deep rust suggested Weesie's wavy-to-curly caramel and butterscotch hair. Until they smiled. They had thin-lipped but wide, warm smiles, as if their faces cracked open in a great happy wedge, Weesie's mouth pale and freckled, her mother's a bright, conservative, no longer fashionable red.

Mrs. Herrick was working on a still life: a piece of Imari china, so that you would have to render not just the light and shadow but the pattern and shaded colors. This was next to an old pink doll, maybe once Weesie's, with macabre holes where its arms had been and one eye crazily half closed, the other staring open. The doll rested on a garishly embroidered shawl; and behind the doll, a box of detergent, the kind of ugly thing one instinctively looked away from, so that it looked like *What is wrong with this picture?* But in Mrs. Herrick's rendering, with its frankly evident, confident brushwork and naturalistic tones, the box was shadowy, and then you saw the joke: the way each object had some of the same colors. It was unclear why this should have the effect of a joke, but you looked at the picture and felt yourself smiling; then felt as if you had grinned at a skeleton or corpse.

But it was a studenty thing, a naturalistic still life. It wasn't part of the dialogue of contemporary art. Anybody knew that.

Maude looked at fuzzy-leafed, profusely blooming African violets, gloxinias, the downturned kisses of cyclamen faces pushing through jungley fronds. Down among the pots and pot stands were paintings leaning on the low wall, in danger of water damage. "Can I look?"

"Certainly." Mrs. Herrick had turned back to her little picture.

There was a whole stack of portraits of Weesie. So many it would have been like stop-action photography of the growth of a child except that each was so psychological a study too, the moods and angles too different for continuity. The chubbo, relaxed Weesie around ten, not posing, sprawled out reading, tumbled with a patchwork quilt whose floral colors had the synesthetic effect, as pattern and color often do, of melody. Though splashy and loose, the picture was detailed enough to capture the morsel of flesh that fascinated Maude in class, or catching Weesie's face in repose, the bud at the center of her upper lip, at the end of the deep groove, which could give Weesie the baby innocence of a prattler but could also look beaklike and predatory in ways Maude thought the person behind the face would not feel.

There was even a picture of baby Weesie, no more than a little bunched ham, an uncooked veal roast—fists, open mouth, closed eyes. A portrait, if such a thing were possible, of love.

"My father painted me once. It looks like a bunch of sticks. I mean, you can't tell at all! He calls it 'Study.'"

"You know, it's never *occurred* to me to name my pictures," fluted Mrs. Herrick, as if Maude's father were a wonder.

Maude could not express the immediate and secretly formed wish that Mary Jane Herrick should paint her. *Because* she wanted it she couldn't say it.

Weesie proposed their outing, and Mrs. Herrick's face cracked into its wedge to say, "We'd be delighted, Maude Pugh."

"I—but—the thing is, I was going to go to the Whitney. With my father."

"Oh, the artist himself. Well, we could join you. Would that be all right—do you think?"

The way she said this, with a clear display of consideration but also certainty that it would be all right, made Maude believe that there was something to the term "good breeding." It made her wary of making a misstep, and oddly mistrustful. Parents always liked well-behaved Maude, but Weesie's mother was too emolliently warm. She treated Maude as an equal. It couldn't be real.

They agreed they would meet at the museum, unless Mr. Pugh objected, and then the girls could go off and take the train home when they wanted to. The parents would fend for themselves.

5.

I T W A S A giggly business for the girls, meeting under the
auspices of one of each set of parents, in the city, and had
necessitated dozens of preliminary phone calls as to clothing and such pressing transient states as "I'm depressed," which
both considered an enticing opening gambit, leading away to
happy hours of expressed longing or character analysis.

Maude wore a high-necked ochre jumper seamed from bust
to hip so that it emphasized her fairly emphatic waistline, under-
stated and expensive-looking, though it was from Ohrbach's,
a store Weesie would be unlikely ever to have entered. Weesie,
in what Maude would come to understand as a certain high-
WASP carelessness, was the one in something cheap-looking, a
pastel-flowered miniskirt with a low-riding white patent leather
belt, which went all too well with her pearlescent white lipstick.
Maude had circled her dark eyes like a raccoon's. Despite the
infantine, mod, modish white tights both wore, Maude, with
her dark, straight hair, looked like an expensive French hooker,
and angel-haired Weesie like a runaway on Forty-Second Street
compelled to turn tricks.

Both parents felt misgivings about the plan to let the girls go
off afterward on their own.

The girls meanwhile were preoccupied with ecstasies over each other's shoes, dancerly and medium-heeled, Maude's T-straps with the pleasing detail of a triangle that seemed to have been cut off the pointy toe and outlined as a cutout on the instep like modernist eyelet, and Weesie's glove-soft mauve (which seemed an echo of Maude's name) laced with olive-green grosgrain ribbon. Like almost everything for them at that age, the shoes had meaning beyond their exquisite prettiness, a meaning like a flag or a club insignia. It said they were citizens of the country of opulent femininity and desirability, of sophistication, of everything they hoped to be. The triangle seemed to mean something jagged and raffish, freer than other people, and the olive bootlike lacings made you someone in a Toulouse-Lautrec poster, pensive and magnified. Even the brand, Capezio, signaled knowledgeability coupled with lyricism.

For the adults, dress was more prosaic. Men did not go without ties or suits, except laborers, and a woman in the city wore stockings. Except bohemians, other artists. Milt was in a turtleneck and a belted Norfolk jacket of a different corduroy from his soft trousers, and his hair, while not as long as a Beatle's, was not as brutally short as a businessman's. Unwritten rules are the most powerful, and the girls felt that power. It was exciting to see someone push the rules, nudge them. It wasn't just a fashion choice, on a par with other consumer choices. It announced your own power and said, *I do not recognize the world's right to judge me. I do not recognize this court.*

It was what Mary Jane Herrick, in Maude's view—and in her own daughter's—seemed to lack.

Yet it seemed to them relatively just that artists had to live by the world's judgment in the form of the presence or absence of worldly rewards. They were quite sure that the good art would be recognized.

Mrs. Herrick wore a gray side-buttoned skirt with a black leather belt that must have cost as much as the rest of them put together. In heels, she looked thinner and almost sexy, for someone so essentially over the hill.

Though the new Whitney had been open for a month, none of them had yet been to it. They hung around a few minutes outside, where they had linked up. "It's horrible," said Maude, standing in the gloom under the bulging upper stories.

"I kind of like this, you know, like a drawbridge over a moat," said Weesie, skipping along the entry that bridged the dark troughlike courtyards below.

"Maybe modern art needs a fortress," said Milt.

"I don't think so," said Mary Jane. "It's won."

Inside, there was immediately the feeling of expensive flooring, echoey high-ceilinged space, and, above all, wealth. The entry fee was shocking.

Upstairs, the girls were attracted to the trapezoidal windows deeply set into prismlike embrasures, which they tried to sit in, sliding off. "They're much better than the art," said Weesie when her mother attempted to call the girls to order, seeing a guard coming their way.

"What art?" said Maude.

And this was something they all felt, with varying degrees of glumness, as they made their way around the grandiose halls sparsely set about with creations that themselves were spare in their aesthetic. "Sometimes," said Milt, "less really is less." Not in the case of his own purist paintings, of course.

Lined up in front of what looked like a blanket rack hung with satin ribbons, they stared, wondering what they were not "getting." Then Maude cried out—she had so long borne the brunt of Milt's critical nature that she didn't know how her swift criticisms could cut—"This just isn't art. It's the emperor's new clothes."

"But these ribbons are so pretty," said Weesie, as if it were her duty to defend the establishment, of which her parents were so much a part. She had picked up, God knew where, some of the official formalist line, the line to which Milt's work seemed to conform and of which Mary Jane's seemed oblivious. Weirdly, it was Mary Jane who seemed to believe in it, sharing in its denigration of her own mode of work. "It's all about color and, uh, composition. Line."

Maude snorted. "I expect one of the guards to come over and tell me how much a yard," she said, fingering a satin strand just to get a guard to move that way. Quickly she removed her hand, though she was tempted: she would have liked the ribbons to tie her hair.

Mary Jane fought a desire to tell them that she had contributed money to the building of this museum and collection. Quite a lot. She blinked at the offending artwork, feeling mauled.

Milton put a hand on Maude's shoulder, quelling her but possibly also protecting her from retaliation.

Mary Jane looked sharply at his self-assured, attractively worn face. You would think they were under attack, she thought, these Pughs. But humbly she told herself that, after all, she couldn't know what it was to be an artist. Maude's snort recurred to Mary Jane. What a Tartar that girl was! "No one would ever guess you were fourteen," she said to her conciliatingly. "You sound like a professional critic."

"Is that a compliment or an insult?" said Milt, his mouth twisted into an S that was a smile on one side and wryly downturned on the other. This was meant to be a joke, and the well-bred Mary Jane accepted it as such. But it had the element of challenge and contempt that made Maude always fear her father.

They moved on to a lifesize plastic rendering of a young woman rinsing her hair under a shower, realistic in every detail. "Well, Maudie," said Milt, "you like things to look 'realistic.' Any more real than this and it would be asking us for a towel."

The figure was meticulously explicit. There was pubic hair, there were bumpy nipples, there were red painted toenails. Maude was particularly fascinated, much as she might be in a locker room, by the depiction of tan lines on the plastic skin, so that the figure looked both naked and clothed. She had never seen tan lines on a nude. This was not a nude. It was a naked. "It just—it just doesn't seem like art."

The inarticulacy of this made Maude feel feeble and open to attack. The shiny, oleaginous figure seemed to mock the very condition of being female, as if what you saw were really all there was to get.

"It's too literal," said Weesie.

"That's it! That's *it*." Maude clutched her friend's forearms. She had seen in Weesie's edition of *Long Day's Journey into Night*, which they were reading for lit, her scribble in the margin, where the mother goes back on morphine: "The mother is going into the fog. The fog is a metaphor." How brilliant! She felt again that same laser that both sliced and illuminated. The fog had just been the fog till she saw this. And that was what was wrong with all these objects at the Whitney. They were just fog, just objects. "It *is* literal. There's no—no—"

"Transformation," said Milt. "No intelligent agency has intervened. It's just a mechanical translation into different materials."

They all looked at Milt with respect, Maude with the addition of the helpless love that felt to her like slavery. She wanted to please him. She needed to. It was just that it was never possible.

A wall near the stairs was covered by a canvas that was simply painted red. No brushstrokes, no variation, just red canvas on stretchers on a wall.

"Color-field painting," murmured Mrs. Herrick.

"Minimalism," said Milt, whose own paintings could look minimal to the uninformed eye.

"Yup," said Weesie with droll dryness, "pretty damn minimal."

She could see Maude struggling to go along with this attempt to lighten things, but Maude looked near tears. "Don't they see? Don't they see how they're wrecking—? There isn't any room for—" She wanted to say "us" but finished, "anything that matters." There was no point in being a painter if she had to grow up to do plain red walls. She would never feel moved to do that. She might as well be a house painter. Or live in a cave in the woods and not have to know about any of it. It was hard not to imagine being dazzlingly successful, but in the unlikely event that she wasn't, that seemed not a bad alternative, being purely at one with nature, in a cave.

Milton brought up a heavy sigh, a puff of the unhappiness and isolation that made Maude his partisan despite herself, protecting him from the shame of his failure. "Aah, well," he exhaled. "What can you do?"

It took only as long to go through the museum as it took to cover its physical space, and it seemed that the building, for all its jarring architectural distinctness, conveyed nothing so much as the message of costliness. That, as much as the fortresslike air, said Do Not Enter Here.

"An hour later, you're hungry," said Milt, lighting a cigarette on the drawbridge. "Let's hit the Modern. What do you say? Sink our teeth into Matisse." He had the manner, teacherish, of one used to addressing and leading groups.

Waved in on Milt's member's card, cheered by the uncontroversial Matisse, they went up the steps, where that Joseph Stella of the Brooklyn Bridge that Maude never could like, and the it's-a-tree-no-it's-children "Hide and Seek" that she used to admire always were, to the members' lounge.

It may have seemed like her own private club to Maude, but Weesie had never been in. If they had lunch in midtown, it was always that boring French restaurant where she always had boring things like celeriac salad and escargots. Here she could take her own tray, and everything looked bright and exotic. It was a cafeteria, but a Bauhausian cafeteria, full of foods that were cheap and possibly avant-garde, with white-white walls, not antique white or oyster white, industrial carpeting like the Pughs', and everything fitting, stacking, slender, streamlined, steely, white or black, as if color took up room or wasted visual energy. And the people—Weesie was sure they were all artists, unless they were folksingers. A blonde woman in a tunic made from a Mexican rebozo looked like Mary from Peter, Paul, and Mary, and half the men had beards. Many wore black turtlenecks.

They all looked as though a secret message passed among them. Milt recognized someone and went over to greet him. The three females watched as the men bared their teeth but stood with wary stiffness, like dogs who may at any moment snarl. Milt came back and named a name they all recognized.

"You know him?" Weesie squeaked.

Milt waved this away. "Aagh, we were in art school together."

"What's he like?" Weesie leaned forward over her arms.

Milt looked at her a moment. "He still thinks his shit don't smell."

Parents never said shit, at least not to mean, actually, turds. To Weesie's relief, her mother laughed.

Maintaining his aplomb, Milt cut into a pear, approved its ripeness with a little "mm," divided it into four sections with the pits cut out, and handed one to each of them. They picked chunks of cheese—cerulean; pock-marked cadmium extra light; and creamy Naples yellow: Roquefort, Bel Paese, Swiss—from a white Arabiaware plate. For the rest of her life, Weesie would consider thick, stackable Arabiaware superior to hand-painted, gilt-edged porcelain from Tiffany's, whose existence, in any case, shamed her as a mark of privilege.

She sympathized with Maude's dissatisfactions, out of friendship, but congratulated herself on the luck Maude refused to acknowledge: there would be room for her in the place Maude wanted to vacate. How could Maude not understand that her family knew the true way to live?

The girls were allowed to have coffee.

6.

THERE WERE BOYS at Bay Farm School. Cute boys. Boys with shaggy hair and a lovely way of tossing it. Inscrutable creatures, louder, bigger, more careless than the girls, they inspected the girls across the tables in class while teachers talked, and looked away if Maude or Weesie caught them gazing, or sometimes smiled back if what the teacher was saying seemed ridiculous enough to justify it.

In a town where Maude was regarded as stuck-up, there was no way for her not to be an oddball: she used arcane words from the nineteenth-century novels she devoured; she was regarded as hoity-toity for going to the library every week to take them out. In this town, it was outlandish to go into the city for entertainment, much less to art museums. But she had grown up wondering, for her part, why her household did not offer such amenities as soft-crusted white bread, grape jelly, a subscription to *TV Guide*, or a new brother or sister every year or so. She had cried when she couldn't wear a communion dress, like her best friend—"a bride's dress," she had sobbed. She only experienced the cultural divide between them when they got to the age of rock 'n' roll. It was never heard in her own house, and she didn't like it.

She so didn't like it that she didn't believe anyone she liked could. Her pickup friendships tended to shred away upon the other girl's first attempt to recruit her to something she recoiled at as alien. She soon learned to recognize its attendant earmarks: teased hair, ankle bracelets, training bras, add-a-pearl necklaces, and partisanship on such issues as whether you were on Liz Taylor's or Debbie Reynolds' side. It would have surprised Maude to discover that Milt or Nina knew who Liz Taylor or Debbie Reynolds was. In the other type of household, they were as passionate about a movie star's divorce as they were about Republicans versus Democrats.

And they were Republicans. That was another mistake Maude had made. She assumed everyone shared her family's view that Nixon was a variety of slime mold; instead, there were girls who showed up with pink eyes the day after the election. The only time her parents didn't vote Democratic was when some of these other parents did, for handsome Jack Kennedy. It was remarkable, she was later to think, that at the flag-sprouting brick firehouse, it was possible in 1960 to pull the lever for Norman Thomas, the Socialist candidate. Milt said Kennedy's father was a crook. And these people went to church every Sunday! The Pugh view was unrepeatable, publicly.

So Maude had gone around in a cramp of semidisguise, trying not to make herself the object of a social football tackle. Equally she feared being pathetic. There was a girl in her seventh-grade class, Rosette, whose offense was her painful thinness and the way she smiled at everyone without distinction, a sweet, shy smile that showed no consciousness of social degree. She looked like a concentration camp victim forgiving the Nazis. Maude used to watch Rosette, wondering how she could stand it, how she continued to smile with such forgiveness, how she could be so dreamy and placid under the scourge of rejection. One tenderhearted girl once said something nice about Rosette. "Yeah, well, it doesn't help to have a name like a Kotex ad, does it?" Maude had said, raising a laugh she cringed to remember.

At Bay Farm Maude expected to find her soul's affine group. Among them would be the best friend she had always looked for. Having found Weesie, she looked for the boy who would become her magically frictionless match. The Boy. Weesie and Maude spent a fair amount of time discussing The Boy. A huge amount of time. They might as well have been teasing their hair and adding a pearl.

Early on, there was the epoch of sharing a crush. It was wonderful having a crush together, almost better than having a boyfriend. They settled on the same soft-spoken, bookish but popular (athletic) boy, taking fire from a casual remark one or the other of them made: "John Bates is kind of nice, don't you think?" "John Bates is *incredibly* nice"—he had spoken to one of them. Their mutuality gave them courage. He accepted little offerings from them and, once, they went together in the middle of the night to his house, not far from Weesie's, and had a disappointingly chaste visit through his window. Not long thereafter, he could be seen with the school vamp, her long fingernails digging into his upright back during assemblies.

Maude made a list of the Bay Farm boys she would welcome into her embraces. It was not short. Weesie looked stunned when she saw this list in Maude's stilted printing that looked like a hand-written manuscript Weesie had once seen at the Morgan Library, handwriting that was like printing. The a's were like someone kneeling under a palmetto leaf and the g's looked like goggles. That was how Maude's were. Spelling out the list of boys.

"All of them?"

"Not all at *once*," Maude said.

"Adam *Exner*?"

"Don't you love the way he stands? It's so—" Maude stood, twitching to one side to imitate this short, slim-hipped boy's cocky grace.

Weesie just shook her head. Maude wasn't sure if she had over-stepped some personal boundary of Weesie's or if she had violated some norm of good taste. She felt she had revealed something gross about herself.

But this was forgotten as Weesie began numbering her own choices on the list, in order of preference. "You think the tall guys, I mean the skinny ones, you think their, you know, penises are like long and skinny?" Maude could barely choke out an answer between gasps. "Do you think, like, fat guys, I mean they probably can't even see it anymore."

"Oh, God, what if you were sitting on a guy's lap and he got a boner?" They shrieked, beside themselves.

Weesie pointed out that at least half the boys on the list had girlfriends.

Maude hoped she wasn't making another avid gaffe: "They could break up."

❦

But the great mystery was, how did you get a boyfriend, or was it something you didn't get but just allowed to happen? What could you do to make it happen?

They disdained to believe in the efficacy of the hair-teasing, specialty-bra-wearing version of femininity—though they might have noted that the vamp, who had the loyalty of the best boy in the school, only pretended to such disdain. All but the newest inch of her hair was still blonde from a summer experiment with peroxide; she was dazzlingly slender and didn't hesitate to show it in tight suede pants that invited touch; she mascaraed her lashes and was rumored to have tried falsies. One day she came to school in a belted raincoat and made sure everyone knew she had nothing on underneath. But even when she wore the same workboots and jeans and turtlenecks as everyone else, she still had a way of smiling complicitously at boys, always speaking with a Minnie Mouse cheerfulness that was implausible to any girl but apparently a token of an unthreatening, forgiving nature to every boy, even as they were excited by a manner that suggested cruelty: a terse way of moving and possessive high-handedness.

Not that Weesie or Maude could have made themselves like that. Not that they could have stood being like that. They couldn't even bear Lainie, who was unremittingly friendly to them, in her Minnie Mouse voice—"*Hi,* you two." They wondered what The Boy, now the ex-Boy, had told her about their shameless, shameful pursuit of him. Lainie caught them staring as she combed her hair in the girl's dayroom in the basement under the dining hall, where they had lockers and could change clothes. "I only tease it just a little. If I had hair like either of you guys, I wouldn't have to."

Swann's Way is the Guermantes Way. Even at Bay Farm, apparently, the Pugh view was a bit finer. But, because it was Bay Farm, Maude felt the urgency of crossing to the non-Pugh side.

One of the reassuring facets of life at Bay Farm, as the catalogue told it, was that rock music, pop music of any kind, was outlawed. Three things could get you expelled without appeal: sex on campus, an illegal substance, or using the cubicles in the music wing to listen to rock, pop, or jazz. People had been caught just sitting there wearing the earphones that were like boxing gloves: they'd given themselves away by the rhythm of their bouncing.

But—as if teenagers could not be expected to go the entire day, much less into the evening, without the vivifying sounds of their patriotic anthems—a ramshackle outbuilding had been set aside in acknowledgement of this need, at a distance from the civilizing business of school. It was equipped with electricity but no heat and only one primitive window, as if to say they shouldn't be too comfortable. Because, if adolescence was a country with its own anthems, the allegiance the listeners pledged was to their bodies and the separateness of their culture. That, however, supplied enough heat and light. As other freshman girls paired off with boys, Maude began to understand from them that this hovel was as much about sex as music. The music was as much about sex as music. This was the hot spot for pickups.

Maude came to school with two albums from her brother's untouched if not exactly forbidden room. Naturally, these were not the Beatles or the Rolling Stones: one was a sickly sweet folk duo favored by his old girlfriend, and also Maude; the other was a singer obscure even to folkies, so pure that the addition of anything more than a dulcimer to his guitar constituted sellout capitulation to the pop forces of slick commercialism, or so it seemed. That summer Maude had fallen in love with certain lines he sang in a plaintive, rough voice,

> *Thought I heard somebody call my name*
> *Painting a picture across the amber sky*
> *Of love and lonely days gone by.*

They had a power for her, sitting on the black seafoam floor, she didn't even try to formulate, and she had played them over and over.

The other song she wanted to hear, or by which she intended to display herself, was fairly popular: the pretty couple depicted on the cover begged each other to pack up their sorrows and "give them all to me." Maude saw herself as offering this service to her unknown someone—a selling point (and she knew how good her help could be)—but underneath, she felt the longing, as if her sorrows really were a heavy sack she dragged along behind her, for an offer of the same from someone else, or just for help in dragging the sack, which seemed to contain her entire family, especially the missing member.

In the tiny pop hovel, you had to wait your turn, and this was partly its advantage, that you were pressed close together in the pulse of driving songs about love and lust. The one bulb, over the turntable, was blue. Five boys eyed her. There were no other girls. None of the boys was on her list, but you never knew. She didn't meet their eyes, waiting for the look of recognition that would come when she played her music.

She stood through a twenty-minute solo by Ginger Baker, whose percussiveness she was beginning to appreciate, when two of the boys began a catalogue of past musical alliances among members of the Cream and an analysis of how this solo related to the backup on another album. When the cut ended, it was the next boy's chance. You were allowed two cuts apiece. He played the "Blues Project." Maude's brother had a wall covered with big reels of taped blues singers, ancient and dead Mississippi Negroes, austere and faintly suicide-inducing sounds between hymn, work song, and dirge, sometimes with guitar or a shaky horn or harmonica but often austerely unaccompanied.

This was electric instruments and the kind of voice, white, that goes with self-display. You could imagine the young man's soft, easily lived-in face and almost the precise bulge of his pants, which seemed to be the voice's message. Yet she found the songs almost irresistibly pretty amidst her discomfort, about violets of dawn and the sounds of a winter's love at nighttime.

Pop music was never *about* anything; it was just *love* songs, she thought, as if her brother had witnessed her betrayal of him.

As she went toward the turntable, a boy, seeing the album cover, crowed in tones of the purest adolescent derision, "Mimi and Richard Fariña!" By the time the one cut was over—the lyrics begging a lover to unburden himself of troubles—only two boys remained. Another boy stuck his head in and left as soon as he heard what was on. As she put on her second cut, "Somebody's Gonna Miss Me," boy one said to boy two, "Let's go for a smoke." She had cleared the pop hovel.

> *The train leaves at ten.*
> *Only I'll be back again.*
> *Somebody's gonna miss me when I'm gone.*

Or was it *Honey, I'll be back again*? She never was sure.

She realized that when she heard this song, she heard her brother. She had adored him when she was little—that brother. The brother who listened to this music and could be funny, her once rebel-hero.

A boy came in as she tried to wipe her eyes without ruining her eyeliner. He was a thin, juvenile-looking sophomore whose name she didn't know. Despite looking eleven years old, he had the beauties of olive skin like a child in a U.N. flier, long eyelashes like a llama, and straight black hair like Maude's own. He tilted his head and smiled in a welcoming manner. She brushed past him, eyes downcast, feeling she was bruising an innocent bystander.

If she had played those records a few years earlier, in 1962, say, the more esoteric phase of what would only after the fact be "the sixties"—her brother was four years older than she was—the music would have struck the right, so to speak, chord. Her brother could not be wrong. It was as if she had expected to catch up with him here, but the new, disappointing classmates were out of tune.

At the same time, she felt she had revealed herself as a Rosette—drippy, sentimental, *girly*. It was mysterious why being *girly* if you were a girl was so awful, but it was. That's not who I am, she wanted to say, but of course it was; what was wrong with who she was? She had disastrously revealed herself. But her soul's affine group had to be somewhere, and she still believed that *somewhere* to be Bay Farm, if she could suss out exactly the right way to be.

7.

M R. PATRICK CAVORTED in the backyard with Mrs. Pugh. Rod and Nina. Maude watched with narrow eyes from where she had planted herself on the black couch. Milt couldn't see what was going on. His big north window faced the street. She looked up from the book again—and there they unbelievably were—and back down at Margaret Meade, for history class. They were doing prehistory and anthropology. The teacher said history was anthropology. He said every era constituted a different culture. How would you mark them off, Maude wondered in an instant of fleeting concentration. Culture must be changing every minute. At this very minute, she could be living in a different culture from the last time she looked up. "Culture is no more nor less than the aggregate of customs, practices, and artifacts of a group."

Mr. Patrick, that dopey art teacher, was definitely out there in her backyard. In the dual tracking at Bay Farm, he ran the farm program, which produced salad greens in spring term, up through the first peas, and more solid vegetables for autumn lunches. It was part of the student program to work the farm, their cultivation and harvesting chores an element of the utopian program intended to make the school a self-sufficient community. Before Mr. Patrick had taken over the year before, the gardening had declined to mere fields of potatoes. Upperclassmen talked about how awful the potato harvesting used to be, with machines and a conveyor belt. Though "Rod" had expanded the farm to include the full spectrum, Maude thought he must be too fond of potatoes, because what other vegetable could have made him such a tub? Somehow in sharing his gardening enthusiasm with her mother, he had elicited her offhand agreement that organic vegetables were better. Nina would have had to show off that she had read Rachel Carson; she hated for people to think she knew less than they did. As if her defensive display were the expression of desire, he had offered to help her start her own vegetable patch. And there he was.

Maude could imagine it: Nina not wanting to have this bear of a man over but not wanting him to think that as artists they were high-hatting him. What Maude wouldn't have imagined was her mother bent over and jerking with laughter and clutching his hairy bowling pin of an arm to keep her balance. It was a silent movie from where Maude watched, and she couldn't see that his arm was hairy. But she had noticed it when he showed the class how to soak etching plates in the acid bath. His workshirt had been rolled up—the hair was reddish and also gray; one side of the arm was freckled and brown from all his work in the sun, but the bottom was troutlike and pale, with blue traces. Bubbles of acid gathered in the lines of the zinc plates, digging in.

Their backyard was just a little patch of shaven weeds. Beyond it, the weeds were allowed to grow into wheatlike heads and wildflowers where the developer had left a square of unbuilt-on land onto which four streets backed. It was Maude's favorite place in Levittown. You could half-close your eyes, to block out the backyards on the far side, and pretend you were in the country. Once every summer it got mowed, and she ran out to collect the fallen black-eyed susans and pinks from the cool, bouncy, mounded lines of grass.

Off on one side of the field was a desolate concrete court with a wall in the middle. It was intended for handball but always seemed eerie, a piece of city somehow broken off, alone in a wild field. As children, they had enjoyed scaring themselves with it. Maude remembered her brother hurling a hardball at it as if it were someone he wanted to kill. Well, as if it were Milt, probably.

There was plenty of sun for the vegetables Mr. Patrick was foisting on them, Maude thought, embarrassed for the one tree, which her parents had planted. Couldn't they have found out first that weeping willows need tons of water? It had barely grown, a moping, twiglike sapling with its tongue out for the garden hose.

Aside from the dark square Mr. Patrick was creating with his pitchfork, the shaven weeds came right up to the cracked cement terrace at the back of the house, dandelions and crabgrass alike. Next door, the Lyonses pulled crabgrass, put down bulbs in rows every fall and took them up after they bloomed and wrapped them in newspaper. "Where do they have *room* for them?" Nina had asked, pulling at the skin on her hands. God knew where they found the room in those tiny houses, which didn't even have basements, but that wasn't Nina's real concern; she was just hoping to fend off the expectation that she engage in such housewifery.

Even cooking scared her. She was happy to serve scrambled eggs for dinner, letting Maude add ketchup to her portion, a dish to which they had given the name "blushing bunny." More often she left it to Milt to broil hamburgers and lower frozen vegetables into boiling water. They came out of their boxes in the shape of the boxes, pebbly rectangles of peas or criss-crossed nests of stringbeans beneath the opacity of ice in which they were embedded. When Maude saw her first Louise Nevelson sculpture, a mèlange of found objects glommed together in a rectangle coated overall in a unifying color, and also John Chamberlain's briefly chic works, chrome car fenders compressed into cubes, they reminded her of that 1950s contact with nature, these industrial foods. The jolly chrome giant.

Here the rectangle gradually taking shape, sod by ripping sod, under Rod Patrick's orange work boot, suggested nature might have more to offer. Nina picked up each square of sod and shook it like a mop. Despite her air of limp helplessness, a spray of earth was released from the grass roots. Unable finally not to be curious, Maude left her book facedown on the woven black of the couch and pushed open the back door. Aluminum, it offered a small symphony—a squealing upward note followed by whispery rattles, a wheeze, and then a whack as it pulled itself shut.

"Whoa, Maudie," yelled Rod. All the boys at school yelled *whoa*. It was part of their big, excluding pleasure in themselves. From this, Maude had the sense that Rod too thought of himself as seventeen.

"Grab that and take it over to the corner by the fence." He gestured to the wheelbarrow he'd brought along with the other garden tools. The barrow was piled with the discarded sods, on which the plants still surreally sprouted, heedless of their fates.

She squinted at him a long moment before complying. Hot in the October sun, he had removed his flannel shirt and glistened hairily, his belly looking Vaselined and pregnant over his low-slung jeans.

Nina beamed and excitedly began saying where everything would go in the spring, when the mulch was turned over. She explained mulch: "Hay, that is. It decomposes into the earth and feeds the plants. It's this cycle—"

"I know, Ma. We learned it at school." Her mother's face puckered, looking for what she'd done wrong, like a toddler's, mystified but distressed at a cross word. Maude took the worn wooden handles of the wheelbarrow. "You making a compost heap?"

Nina looked hopeful again, loved again. "Yes!"

Maude loved her gardening job at school—liked her job

assignments better than the required sports, even though she'd chosen the least gymlike sport, bicycling. The boys always managed to find hills to race up on their ten-speeds while she plodded behind with her ancient Schwinn, walking the second-hand three-speed as if it were a balky burro. By contrast, forking up potatoes was like finding treasure, like uncovering clutches of eggs hidden in the earth, offering themselves amid the rich smell of fecundity itself. Even stacking tomato frames or rubbing trowels with steel wool and oil had the appeal of establishing order. A raccoon preyed on the compost heap, waddling down its paw-wide track to pick at cabbage cores and squash pulp with polyplike black fingers. If Maude came too close, it looked testy, pausing like a teacher in black spectacles who's been interrupted while pondering lecture notes.

"Where are you getting hay?"

Rod straightened his back and rubbed his beard. The school grew and baled its own. He looked at Nina, who shrugged and giggled. Maude had to look away from her. She offered to gather the long dried grasses from the field.

"Oh, could you?" said Nina.

"I just offered, Mom."

"What would I do without you?" she cried. It was her catchphrase.

None of them realized what weeds the wild grasses would introduce into the virgin soil.

PART II

1.

B Y MID-MAY, THE garden was beautiful, with its
florettes of exotic lettuces—reddish, icy green, frilly,
tender as tongues; filigrees of pea vines with curlicues
like harpsichord music; and clumps of chives like exuberant
brushes, bursting into purple pompoms. The garden would
have formed a new center for the family if, as Nina complained,
Maude were not always at school and Milton in his studio or
out giving lessons. He was giving lessons to Mary Jane Herrick,
at her studio, and she had recommended a friend who had
recommended another friend and so on. He was making house
calls. And sometimes the ladies came over—in their toggled
car coats, in Pucci, in perfumes that smelled like sitting in the
good seats at the opera, in silk scarves as intricately patterned
as illuminated manuscripts. Sometimes they looked at his work
and actually bought a picture.

They complained and exclaimed that his prices were too low.
When he'd heard this enough, he browsed a few galleries in
the city and realized it had been a while since he'd examined a
price list. His eyebrows shot up as he flipped over the onionskin
with the lists' little red dots for the stupendous prices. He went
home and quadrupled his asking, sure that no one would ever
pay it, and one of his holdouts promptly snapped up a quartet

of his smaller squares as if, by raising their prices, he'd raised their value.

And he didn't even have to hand fifty percent of it over to a gallery.

His teaching Mrs. Herrick changed the painting style that had been as easy to like as patchwork quilts, and it made Maude feel exposed as well as proud, but it pleased the girls in practical ways. It was easier for Maude to visit, because Milt always seemed to be putt-putting over in the little VW. Whenever they hit a bump and were bounced, sometimes as high as the car's sloping roof, "Never lose the feel of the road!" Milt would mock. That was what it had said in the owner's manual. Nevertheless, when Nina complained that she had no way to get around, with his new practice of house calls, he went out and used his recent earnings to buy another one, this time the VW "bus," a van with even harder seats and more awkward handling, but in which he could transport paintings and field trips, and the girls could stand with their heads through the sun roof, waving like princesses.

It was odd that a car whose advertising boast was its unchanging sameness was the very marker of automotive nonconformity. Owning this cheap car, you could feel superior to all the slobs paying extra for bad mileage and an illusion of power. It was such a phenomenon in their subdivision that even after weeks, children still hung around to see it and ask for rides with the sun roof open. The local teenagers had always called the VW owners communists or (much more rarely) Nazis, depending. It was almost a happy day for Maude when this changed to, "Yah, what are ya? Flower children! Hippies!"

(Milt, on the other hand, in addition to intoning "Never lose the feel of the road," also liked to say of the skinlike cover over the sun roof that "the numbers only show when it rains." They all knew Germans and Austrians with numbers on their arms and relatives whose fillings had been melted down for God knew what.)

They jounced along the private lane that led through the estate—always looking for a glimpse over the high rhododendrons of the former ambassador and cabinet member who never seemed to be home in the main house, a grand brown-shingled cottage—up to the white-and-stone Herrick residence, with its pleasing confusion of porches and additions, surrounded by hydrangeas not yet ready to bloom. The air was Long Island steamy but not yet sticky hot.

The girls did homework together up in Weesie's room. They were working on papers that had different subjects but, sprawling on the rug, they liked to read sentences out to each other. Maude kept being so excited by what she was coming up with, or worried that a sentence didn't make sense, that she had read half her paper out loud. Eventually she read something out and Weesie didn't look up.

"I'm trying to think, Maude."

Maude jumped up and strode to the bedroom door. She intended to storm out, but the egg-shaped porcelain knob turned from the other side as she touched it.

"I just thought you girls would be wantin' yer snack." A good-looking middle-aged woman from Ireland oversaw the household. She was always offering Weesie things she didn't want or, rather, wanted but didn't want someone *serving* her.

"Mrs. O'Donnell, please, really, don't bother. If we want something, we'll come down to the kitchen. Please, you're too good." Weesie, in her excessively keyed-up way, looked so pained, Maude couldn't imagine someone persisting in the face of it.

"I couldn't cut you a wee sandwich? There's some lovely ham. A bit a chicken, then? Just a few biscuits on a plate, let me bring you up, and a jug of milk. No?"

Her accent seemed to slip sideways through familiar syllables, making them watery or brisk in surprising spots. Maude thought a ham sandwich magically appearing on a plate in the upholstered bedroom sounded pretty good, but Mrs. O'Donnell wasn't hers to refuse or accept, in her plain apronless uniform and a molded-looking hairdo that could have been the ambassador's wife's.

Mrs. O'Donnell kept offering, with her sad, beseeching look, and Weesie smiled back hard, such a back-tooth-to-back-tooth smile, you might almost have been fooled that she was delighted to see the housekeeper. Finally, Mrs. O'Donnell accepted her defeat, with one last "Yer sure, now?" and softly closed the door.

"That is so creepy," Weesie said. This was her peace offering to Maude, who stood at the just-closed door. "That woman doesn't have enough to do."

"She looks so sad, Weesie. She's dying for you to let her do something for you."

"I can't go into the kitchen—you know how it is. I'm not allowed to open the refrigerator by myself."

Mrs. O'Donnell came with the house. She was part of the rent. She had an apartment on the third floor.

"I wish we were poor Jews," Weesie continued, "living in the West Thirties. You know—I *am* kind of hungry," she finished. She pushed papers, books, an embroidered cotton jacket and other bits of clothing she'd abstractedly discarded to the side in a colorful pile. Maude admired this—beautiful scarves trailing over a jumbled hairbrush and perfumes on a dresser, an open drawer with something pretty hanging out, a spangle of glittering Indian earrings on the bedside table, a red leather belt over the back of a chair—a casual, decorative carelessness that, she was sure, came precisely from having Mrs. O'Donnell around. Maude knew she could never achieve this effect—at once royal and welcoming, since there is an openness in such display, as if it opens its arms to you as a novel does, capturing ongoing action *in medias res*—could never achieve it because if it were done by her, it would be on purpose, which was antithetical to the effect. Sometimes it seemed to her that the very beauty-marked whiteness and length of Weesie's snaky arms, so thin that she had slipped a bangle well above the elbow, came from money rather than genes.

They crept down to the kitchen as quietly as possible; Mrs. O'Donnell's apartment connected to it by the back stairs, so they used the big open front ones, suppressing giggles. Trying not to clink plates, opening the closetlike stainless-steel refrigerator with its double doors as gently as they could, they removed the remaining ham, still on its bone, and a bunch of green grapes, feeling it too risky to carve or search out condiments in the echoey lifeless white profusion, under racks of tub-size hanging pots or on the marble-topped table for making pastry. Thinking it safest, they went directly out of the kitchen door to the garden, where suddenly all constraints were off.

"It's so beautiful!" Weesie cried in her uncontainable, popping, wildly exuberant way—meaning the spring, meaning being outside, being fifteen and at the end of an arduous year; arduous just in the way it demanded the assimilation of new ways of seeing and doing things. Maude's paper, in fact, was on Bay Farm as its own culture. Maude had shown a wild rush of freedom in interviewing seniors with questions like "Under what conditions can it be cool to sit in the dining hall with a freshman?" Addressing the implicit values so brutally made her feel she had lost whatever status she had left to lose, and she had been astonished to uncover an essential dynamic: that this was, precisely, what cool was—utter carelessness as to what others will think. Combined, of course, with social knowingness.

In any case, she continued to care and, for the most part, to be inhibited by caring. And not caring could be feigned no more than carelessness in scattering beautiful clothes and bibelots.

"Mm," said Maude in her inhibited but, as it happened, equally heartfelt way. Something sweet and vegetal hung in the air, linden or honey locust. They came around a corner of the house, heading toward a gazebo, when they saw movement in the conservatory. It was not unlikely that there would be movement there, where teacher taught pupil, where two painters conferred. But it looked—through the fronds inside and the ivy trailing across the glass—like a couple pulling apart from an embrace.

Weesie made a little sound like the languageless wild child of Aveyron, about whom they'd learned in lit. As freshman history started with human evolution, lit had begun with an examination of language and how or whether it affected worldview: could you, for instance, express something, or even think it, if, like the wild child, you had no word for it?

The ham tipped onto the grass.

They did not find a word for it. They retrieved the ham and continued on to the gazebo, where they sat on the bench that bent its way around the octagon. Weesie brushed blunt slices of green from the pink meat. "It's probably pretty clean." The garden, a mostly green place of grass and shrubs more than flowers, was so clipped and trimmed, its furnishings so white and neat, it looked clean.

"Probably," said Maude, nevertheless discarding the first, exposed, slice to get to the piece underneath. Weesie watched her cut, chew, and swallow the entire piece before saying, "How can you eat?"

"I'm hungry!" said Maude. She felt like a peasant.

Weesie hugged her elbows. She glared, but not at Maude.

"You have a crush on him!" Maude cried.

Weesie turned away, squinting into green.

"Do you think they're really . . . ?"

"They'd better not be," said Weesie.

"He's only here in the afternoons. They're always in the conservatory. It has glass walls, for God's sake."

"So I noticed."

"Did you ever see *On the Beach*?"

"Why?"

"That's how I feel now."

"You mean when everybody knows they're going to die and they're the last people alive anyway and that the world was ending and there was no way to stop it?"

"Yeah."

Weesie considered. "You're right. It is the end of the world."

Infidelity. Adultery. Divorce. Adulteration. They didn't say the words.

"Would be. If."

Weesie reached her pale arm, turquoise-veined, the tiny beauty marks that dotted it liked flocked netting heightening its whiteness and elegance, to pluck a green grape. They both sat hunched over, feeling hollow and sick.

"Has your mother ever—?" "Has your father ever—?" They spoke at the same time and answered together: "Of *course* not." They had to look away from each other again.

"You know—I wouldn't mind if my father had an affair with you. It would make us kind of sisters."

Though what she would have liked more than anything was for motherly Mary Jane to be her mother. It would be perfect, in a way, for Milton to annex Mary Jane. Maude would have everything. Still, "I'd a lot rather he had one with you than, you know," she said loyally, only disloyal to her own wish.

Weesie's thin, sharp lips curled at the corners in her pale, palely and attractively freckled face. In the sun, her hair was fire colors. She herself looked as delicate as an apricot. She pushed a sparkling curl behind her ear, past the spot where the freckles grew denser next to a narrow band of shell pink. Maude couldn't imagine how someone could fail to fall in love with Weesie. She had thought this before, in relation to the idiot boys at school, who didn't. You would love, she thought, her pale-blue gingham boat-necked sleeveless top, unlike anyone else's, and her collarbones, and her unself-consciously new jeans, stiff and rolled at the hem. You would love her prehensile-looking rosy feet, with their big knuckles. You would love the wrought-silver ring that always ended up twisted to one side.

As they walked back through the house to resume work on their papers, the textures of carpet, cool stone tile, and polished wood rich under their bare feet, they passed within earshot of the conservatory.

"Hey, girls—Louise, come see what your mother has done. Maudie."

"Your mother"—this was just the way Milt always referred to his wife if he was talking to Maude.

They were doing a crit, Milt said. Mary Jane had been working on still lifes. They were not like the still lifes Maude had seen in September. It was as if, to begin with, color had been leached away. Maude knew her father's rap on this; Milton was always telling students they were "using color irresponsibly," though he only bothered to attempt the issue with the few he found less than hopeless in terms of understanding or aptitude. What he'd been telling Weesie's mother—if it was about art—Maude could imagine. Maude had liked the old pictures, the unembarrassed sweetness of their colors, but she could see in these new ones something more serious, or serious in a different way. She thought of this quality as "museumy."

On a broad white sheet of heavy, ragged-edged paper, bigger than most of her actual paintings, Mary Jane had rendered with great meticulousness a tumbled pile of garbage. You couldn't take in quite what it was at once, the jumble of crumpled papers and springs, empty cans, God knew what, so that the immediate effect was of an abstraction in black ink, gouache, and delicate grayish pink—mauve. And then you realized what it was, how exactly realistic it must be, so that you almost felt tired looking at all the detail. But you didn't get lost in the detail. The rhythm was what stood out, a pattern of light and dark. Maude could see it was a better picture in some way than the unstudied ones had been—better or just more "museumy"—but she felt a sadness that its subject had been made not to matter, as if it were her, Maude's, responsibility to uphold subject matter, to make a claim for the subject's integrity. She had posed. She knew what it was to be a subject. She felt the weight of that on her chest. In a second of nonthought, the kind that comes at moments between sleep and waking, as full of compressed meaning as the *Oxford English Dictionary* that you read with a magnifying glass, this seemed like a worse betrayal than whatever else Milton might be doing with Mary Jane Herrick. Or the same betrayal.

Weesie looked listless, inspecting the pictures. Her mother had installed a fluorescent light, which, unnecessarily on, imparted a harshness to the pictures and gave the people who looked at them sad black crags in their faces as if they'd been painted by Roualt. Weesie was leaning over a drawing, her Botticelli hair hiding her face. Maude leaned next to her and hissed a direction into her ear: "*Flirt.*" Weesie's profile, when it emerged from the curtain of hair, was pink. She looked right into Milt's eyes, smiled, and twitched her hair back between two fingers, swaying her skinny shoulders.

Milt grinned, amused; and pleased, registering knowledge received.

Though her clear blue eyes went from Weesie to Milt, and her chin went up a notch, Mary Jane had that all-too-fine-to-take-notice look, like those matrons on *New Yorker* covers. "Mrs. O'Donnell is going to be serving tea in the pouch," she announced. The pouch was what the Herricks called a certain small sitting room or lesser living room that they found cozy. Mary Jane lifted her hands to signify helplessness. "We'll hurt her feelings if we just ignore it. What can I do? We're just her creatures."

Weesie hated for her mother to be "charming." "Oh, come on, Mums. She'd listen to you if you put your foot down."

Mary Jane emitted a "charming" laugh and fluttered her hands in ushering motions that made it impossible not to go. The girls caught her sharing a pals-y, parental look with Milt.

"Anyway," said Weesie, "she already tried to make us sandwiches. For a snack."

"I think she thinks American girls are too thin, dear," said Mary Jane, draping her smock over an umbrella tree, emerging into skirt and blouse. "And I agree! You're both so thin, you'd go right through a crack between the floorboards." She always said this. Weesie finished the sentence along with her, and the girls shrieked with laughter, leaning on each other and setting each other off again each time one stopped. It was so normal! They couldn't have seen what they'd seen.

❧

The party of four obediently settled onto the comfortable chairs and two-seater couch of the pouch. The furniture wore its summer slipcovers of white painter's canvas or linen, and the carpeting had been replaced with sisal matting. Even a week earlier, a fire might have been lit, but instead the French windows were open to the melting late afternoon. Just as they arrived, one of the ubiquitous tawny Long Island bunnies hopped along the brick veranda and perched on hind legs at the room's threshold, ears like a two-fingered salute. Then it registered their presence and shot into the shrubbery.

"We should feed it," Maude moaned in a stricken, possessive tone.

Mary Jane laughed.

"But really. I mean, we've taken over so much of where it might have lived or found food."

"I never thought of that," said Mary Jane. "You know, with your sense of justice, you could be a lawyer."

"Mother!"

"What's wrong with that? No, really."

Maude struggled against showing disgust. "Oh, I don't think so."

"Maude's going to be an *artist*, Mummy. You know that."

Mrs. O'Donnell came in, weighted down by a huge silver tea tray. The females all tensed, fighting the desire to jump up and help her with it as they had tried to do in the past.

"Great stuff!" said Milt, reaching for the bread and butter before the tray was settled on the low table.

Maude knew that bread and butter: rounds of firm, fine-grained white bread spread with sweet butter and, where crusts might have been, butter also had been spread and the edges rolled in parsley. The parsley reminded her of Passover—and then, this past April, at Grandma Resnikov's, as she placed on her tongue the sprig of parsley dipped in salt tears at the seder, it was as if tea at the Herricks had materialized, not just in her mouth but as a presence, as if she'd lost consciousness a moment and in that moment dreamed. Looking up, she was startled to see balding and pudgy Uncle Lou instead of Mary Jane. She would never again be altogether in one place, or even just a Pugh. She might never after this year, she thought, in a strange mingling of comfort and tension, be altogether at home. She loved this bread and butter. But in its delicate flavors, its green crunch and rich mildness, it had also developed for her a taste of homesickness and nostalgia. She already missed it while she ate it.

"Are you sure I can't lay you a fire then?" Mrs. O'Donnell pleaded. "T'would be no trouble."

"Goodness, Mrs. O, it's almost iced-tea weather. Don't even think of it."

"Shall I get some ice, then, and squeeze a few lemons? Let me make up a wee jug of iced tea then."

"No, no, no, no, no." Mary Jane waved her hands in front of her face. You could see how sorry she was to have started that hare. "Don't even *think* of it, Mrs. O'Donnell. You've done far too much already."

"Oh, it shan't take the slightest effort. T'will be a pleasure—though I don't know about mint leaves; you'll be wantin' yer mint, I'm thinking, and it's only just coming in."

"No, really, please, *please*, Mrs. O'Donnell. This is quite enough, much more than enough, far too much—please."

Mrs. O'Donnell sighed. "Well, ma'am, if that's all yer wantin' . . ."

"That's *all*, Mrs. O'Donnell. Thank you *so* much. Really."

Squeezing her hands together, Mrs. O'Donnell reluctantly left. Mary Jane turned her exasperation on Weesie. "I can just put my foot down?"

"I think she's insane," said Weesie, eating her way around the bread, biting off just the nonfattening parsley and mouse morsels of what it was fastened to.

"Persecuted by kindness," said Maude and put her hand over her mouth, turning the color of the winey dogwood blossoms outside the window, sure she'd been rude. She often felt this at the Herricks', as if she were feeling her way through a marsh, sinking into chilly water where she'd expected a firm tussock underfoot.

"Exactly," said Mary Jane, but Maude didn't feel any better. Once she felt she'd misstepped, it couldn't be undone.

Milton had polished off about ten of the little rounds. "She's welcome to come to our place any time."

"Oh, Daddy."

He popped another in his mouth. "You're right, Maude. I take that back, you're absitively right. You can't live this way and be an artist."

"That's—tosh," said Mary Jane.

"Well, now that you say that, I feel as if you're right. But then I look at this—" he gave a little push to the silver hot-water kettle, which was in a kind of silver sling over a filigreed burner—"and I know it's true."

"You think if you're comfortable you can't have an artist's vision?"

Maude had never heard Mary Jane sarcastic. It was intimidating. But Milton was unperturbed.

"Comfort is great! I'm all for it. But what's comfortable about dealing with Mrs. O'Donalds?"

"O'Donnell."

"O'Donnell, O'Shmonnell. When you're making art, nothing else matters. Nothing can get in your way. You can't go around worrying, is that just so, is this just so, my clothes, my lipstick—sorry, Mary Jane, but if you're serious about your work, you should—your *life* has to be serious, dammit. That's what it is. It's high seriousness. And to hell with the rest. There's none of this—asking permission. Keeping it neatly in place. You go ahead and do what you need to do and that's it."

"Oh, very romantic." Mary Jane spoke with gathered dignity and such scorn you expected the ends of her hair to emit sparks. "And I suppose your family just happens to feel that way."

"Of course we do," said Maude hotly, not adding: we have to. She felt mortified by her father's rudeness, but furious at Weesie's mother for attacking him. The clash inside her almost seemed proof that there were two systems at work.

"So if I go around in paint-stained dungarees with my hair unwashed, this will make me a genius."

"Well, I don't think it's necessary not to wash."

" 'Scuse me, 'scuse me, beggin yer pardon." Mrs. O'Donnell dashed in holding sugar tongs aloft like a torch. She clanged them onto the tray and backed out.

"I've seen dogs dragging their ass after a beating that look happier." Milton chugged cooled orangey tea from the translucent cup, which was curved like a bell.

"You're saying propriety and—conventions are incompatible with . . . Are you saying you need absolute *social* freedom to make art? No, not freedom—license. Just pure untethered fancy. Whim," said Mary Jane. No one could have accused her of looking whimsical.

"It would be nice. It's probably not possible in this world." Milton looked thoughtful.

"Oh, you're just as conventional as you could be; it's just a different set of conventions. The conventions of bohemia instead of whatever you think these are."

"If I lived by those conventions—which only look like conventions from the outside, anyway, but maybe that's the nature of such things—I'd still be in our old place on Minetta Lane."

Maude looked at Weesie. They had discussed the mystery and tragedy of the Pughs' leaving Greenwich Village, like any bourgeois couple, for the suburbs when Seth was born.

"Anyway, the convention of bohemia is to be free," Milton said.

"Oh, yes—and dress a certain way, be 'hep' to certain things, go to certain places. It's all just fashion, being 'free' in such prescribed ways. It's a wonder that—"

"There are always lesser lights. There are always people who imitate prevalent forms. That's just fashion. It has nothing to do with values, or not enough. And none of it is the work of *art*. Of making art. The point is, you can't go by what comes to you. You can't be obedient. It's a disaster, you can't just take what's ready-made, what comes before you. You can take it, that is, but you have to make it your own.

"Just look at Gertrude Whitney. She lived a slightly bohemian life; she had some talent—I don't know why she couldn't become an artist. But she couldn't. If you can be free in this house, in this life—" the skinny man with the magnificent white hair and bobbing Adam's apple, who came from a cramped tract house to deliver this message, spread his arms—"more power to you."

"Having money should make you freer," said Mary Jane.

"Yes. It should. Money itself isn't an impediment unless you don't have it."

"You have to interrupt your work to teach. That seems worse than stopping for tea."

"It is. But I *have* to."

Maude wanted to say that the Herricks ate so late—eight, nine, even ten at night—they'd never make it to dinner if they didn't have a meal in between, but she was embarrassed to reveal their own plebeian six o'clock dining hour.

"Robert Motherwell came from money. And Frankenthaler— she's well fixed; I run into her at charity events," Mary Jane said.

"I'm sure having money has made their careers much easier."

"Mm. I wonder how much fashion does come into it, now that I think of it. Into art. I mean, the whole way *style* is everything these days . . ."

"Fashion! *Mum.*"

Mary Jane arched her eyebrows, clearly feeling she was on to something. "Maybe abstraction is just today's fashion. Maybe it's just chic. If that's true, I'm knocking myself out just to be 'cool,' like you kids, not to do something higher and more pure and fine. Pared-down art, girls who want to look like Twiggy—"

"*Mu*-um."

"All right, all right," said Milt, raising a hand like a cop halting traffic. "It was just a thought."

2.

MAUDE HAD THE impression that people went wild around graduation, that all the hierarchies and divisions that ruled the rest of the year dissolved and anything could happen.

For the last ten days of school, classes were suspended and students undertook self-assigned tasks that ranged from studying all available sources on Aztec culture to living in and off a local marsh with no resources but a poncho, matches, and an ax. (It was rumored that the boy who did this, though he may have boiled marsh grass and roasted frogs, was in fact hitchhiking into town and getting candy bars and beer—which was going to do little for the weight problem that, many suspected, had led him to design the project in the first place.)

The school still had Meeting every day, but the days of Selected Work Week were loose and unpredictable. The sculpture studio was full morning to night, theater students appeared at meals with lavender circles under their eyes from rehearsals that ended at dawn and spoke lines while they ate together, their real world the one of the play; the lawns were dotted with readers whose shoulders were growing pink in the sun, someone finishing off the ends of a piece of weaving, a trio of long-haired girls twining through the intricacies of creating and learning a piece of choreography; the library rustled as if with cockroaches, and classrooms were empty.

Maude was consolidating her study of Bay Farm culture, which she was illustrating with line drawings of cultural artifacts as if it were a real ethnological monograph. She was copying it, in her maniacally neat Edgar Allan Poe typefacelike printing, into a black-bound artist's notebook that looked like a book. She used an old-fashioned pen that had to be dipped, but the professional effect was undercut by the fact that she dipped into India ink of psychedelic purple. Luckily the pictures to be pasted in were more conventional black and white, except a drawing of shirts colored in purple, one a carefully rendered fine European crinkle cotton, the other a tie-dyed T-shirt, together labeled "cool." Next to a wigglily outlined pair of harlequin glasses, the maniacal printing read: "Also known as 'cat's-eye' glasses, uncool in any color." A freshman who'd been so uncool as to enter the school wearing a pair—plaid, admittedly—had been unable to recover any social standing even, after returning in acceptable oval tortoiseshell frames.

She was copying out the summation, with which she was pleased. She loved it when her thoughts seemed to bite into something and actually raise her, as if she were striking into rock and inching up an otherwise inaccessible peak. First she demolished the possibility the school's charter held out, of utopia, saying there were more cultural variables (as Malinowski called it, in the text she had taken in only in its broadest outlines) than anyone could isolate or account for and that no planned society could possibly coordinate them all, much less in a smoothly ideal way. Among the variables beyond Bay Farm's realm, to start with, were students' families, the culture at large, and the school's nonexistence as an economic unit except for faculty and staff. But while it failed as a realization of a promised or implied utopia, it had evolved its own culture. Subculture.

A shadow fell over her half-empurpled page. She was sitting

in the orchard, where when she looked up she could half convince herself that the trees were covered in snow, while the scented air felt like bathwater, and bees buzzed like fuzzy little machines. For whole seconds she had achieved this deliciously paradoxical winter-spring effect, fooling herself. But this time when she looked up, Danny Stern's head was silhouetted against the blushing blossoms. He was smiling at her, but his face was upside-down, so this too had a paradoxical effect: if she let go of what she knew and just let herself look, then he was frowning or, going a perceptual step further, a weird flopping lesion had developed in his forehead.

"Hey. How's it going?"

Danny Stern was the olive-skinned juvenile boy from the pop hovel. She squinted up at the flopping lesion.

"What?"

He dropped onto the grass beside her, his smile righting itself. It seemed that there should be a boy beside her in such a place. It always seemed as if there should be a boy beside her, sharing her feelings, offering meaningful looks, holding her hand or putting a protecting arm around her shoulders. But not Danny Stern, who, though he had grown over the year, just looked like a longer, more stretched-out eleven-year-old. Even his head was long and thin, oblong from crown to chin so that the genial way he had of angling it as he smiled at a person was exaggerated.

"The skewering of Bay Farm pretensions and social iniquity," he said.

"Skewering? Is that what people think?" She held a hand in a visor as though it would stop the treacherous prick of tears she could feel inside her sinuses. She hadn't meant to be judgmental, just realistic.

"Hey." He almost touched her raised hand with his own but stopped just short. "People feel like you're doing a service."

"Which people? Not the coolies."

At Bay Farm School, coolies were not Chinese peasants in

conical straw hats but the most sought-after students. It was in her glossary with the sentence, "He thinks he's such a ~," the way the dictionary did it.

"Of course coolies, are you kidding? Nobody wants to think they're the, you know, hypocrites or snobs."

Maude remembered why she wanted to be accepted by them. They were admirable. They were better at being people. She remembered seeing the circle of them the first day of school, laughing together, regal.

Danny asked if he could see. Instead of handing him the neatly copied artist's book, Maude rifled through her sheaf of unlined notebook paper mixed with torn-off corners on which she'd scribbled phrases. She held up one of these. "This is what they're going to find when I die. Thousands of scraps of paper with these—cryptic messages." She had just learned *cryptic*. It was a test. But he evidently passed, since there was that smile and the exaggerated, easy, oblong tilt.

Instead of making a comment on the page she handed him, he made a mark on it. He was the kind of boy who used a cartridge pen and carried it in his breast pocket. Neat, as she was, but in a squarer style. She looked at what he'd written. Even though it was on a messy page, she felt encroached upon, slightly violated, but her face lit when she took in the meaning. He'd written just "m."

"Girls can be coolies," she nevertheless objected.

"Name a girl who's a coolie."

She pictured the coolie table in the refectory, where the queen of the coolies reigned with her crinkle-cotton shirt, leather vest, and big guffaws like a boy. She pictured the other faces at the table under their scrolls of hair. They were almost all boys.

"Dale Handler."

He shook his head. "Not really."

"Linda Haverstyk."

"Maybe. *Maybe* Linda Haverstyk." Then he wrote, in graceful, easy script that was as far from her maniacal print as you could get and still be in the neat spectrum, "No female variety known. The closest an f. can come is to be a ~ girlfriend. For f.'s, such transferred status may in some cases outlast the relationship."

"Linda Haverstyk," said Maude. Linda Haverstyk was known even to freshmen as having been the girlfriend of a legendary graduate of the year before, and it was as if his coolness, never glimpsed, lingered like a purple aura around her Mexican embroidered muslin smock-dresses and center-parted hair. She'd had boyfriends this past year, but they were like the emasculated second and third husbands of a professional widow. *They* derived status from *her*, mere consorts.

Danny's head tilted to read the rest of the glossary. *Newie.* That was any new student, freshman or sophomore or the rare new junior, though new juniors were so rare and unpacklike that no one bothered putting them in their place but accorded them the dignity of upperclassmen. *Daisy chain . . .*

"You can't put *daisy chain* in here!" said Danny.

The definition was only "Something that supposedly goes on in the boys' day room that no one will tell me about."

"Does it really happen?"

"We-ell . . ."

"What is it, homos? Are they all—like one behind the other behind the—? Yech. Ugh." Maude shook her hands as if she were trying to get peanut butter off.

"All teenage boys are homosexual. I mean, they'll stick it in anything."

"All? *All*?" She looked at him pointedly.

"Okay, not *all*. But—let's put it this way. Your daisy-chain participants are pretty much your same subset as your coolies."

He had that ability Weesie had of making fun of the very thing he was saying, disowning it, putting it in quotes, as if only repeating the words of some fool, that was partly the choice of words (*your*), partly inflection (an unnecessary, nasal emphasis on *set*, on *coolies*)—and of course the "your" was just the opposite of the case: he knew they weren't her coolies, and she wasn't theirs. Maude could have entered *irony* on her list of what made people cool. Yet Danny seemed to be able to exercise irony—as Weesie did—while inviting you in. It was warm irony. He made it a private joke that included you. If coolies thought you were getting too friendly, they *excluded* by making allusive jokes that you had to be one of them to get. *Exclusion* should be on her list. Danny's kind of irony, and Weesie's, was really too appealing.

But Maude couldn't afford to admit that anything was more appealing. She felt it was necessary to be accepted by the group that was accepted. Everybody, more or less, wanted to be, but she felt damned by her exclusion, as if it specially branded her, as though the exclusion weren't shared by people all around her, people she liked. She had intended to crack the code by her study, as though by observation and deduction she could argue her way into inclusion or acquire what was needed.

At the same time, the study was an argument against hierarchy, a protest against status, and she took pleasure in this with a spiteful sense of strength.

Far from this spite, Danny's interested, intelligent questions, the concentrated way he listened to the answers, the astonishing perceptiveness of his responses were like a forbidden pleasure. Forbidden because it would not further the project of being in with the in crowd. So even though Maude left the orchard with Danny when they heard the bell that was tugged by a long rope from the barn every hour, and even though they walked up to the refectory together, she managed to wander off vaguely, as if to look in her message box, so as not to be seen with someone uncool.

He sat at one of the nondescript tables of miscellaneous too-young-looking boys. Maude always sat with Weesie. The arrangement approached the security and protection of having a boyfriend. But Weesie was already seated at a table where every place was taken—and was in animated conversation. Maude looked desperately around. The tables were mostly full. Still remaining were places at an outer post where the absolute greasy-haired rejects sat. She spied an empty seat between two very cool boys not sitting at the coolie table. She took it and was punished with an uncomfortable lunch period of being ignored and talked across.

"You anine," said one boy, leaning in front of her to punch the other boy's shoulder.

The other boy dripped milk through his nostrils, laughing, and found that so funny he gave up his mouthful of chewed cake to his plate. "You douchebag," he replied.

Maude made a note to include these in the glossary. "Noun form of *asinine*." It was small recompense for the reminder of her nonentity and presumption.

❦

The night before graduation, everyone was staying at school late to finish their projects, and a special van was scheduled for midnight to take the last stragglers home. Maude had finished her Bay Farm ethnography well before time but pretended not to have. For a while she sat in the barn studio, doodling, in purple, pictures of dreamy longhaired boys. Around her, less dreamy-looking creatures rubbed at woodcuts and sanded carvings and cursed at slashes and thumped thumbs from impatiently wielded razors and hammers.

Outside, the sky was indigo, with a last band of paleness at the edge of the western horizon. The outlines of bushes were visible in spilled light from windows, and trees were solid and rustling against the dark sky. The pale, pompom-like blossoms of a bush outside the library smelled intensely of cinnamon. Maude felt that love must be very near, just waiting for her to fall into it.

From the pop hut she could hear "Eleanor Rigby," which had reconciled her to the Beatles. It was *about* something. She strolled toward the muted tune, which died suddenly, leaving the sound of crickets. It had been hot earlier, and the night air moved at exactly the temperature of another body against her. She felt her naked breasts inside the thin cotton of the little dress she had made, the coolness of grass along her sandaled feet. Two cigarette ends glowed illicitly. Why isn't it me, she wondered.

※

Inside the scruffy shack, boys were passing a pint bottle that could get them expelled on the spot. Maude pretended not to see, turning toward the propped-open window, where she met her reflection in the angled glass. She had taken to parting her hair along the center. I'm beautiful, she thought, amazed. Her arms rested on the declivity above her hips, and she imagined a man's hands there, discovering that sharp inward curve that no one else had touched, recognizing her in her most private self.

This was what she'd always wanted: recognition of who she was.

A tall senior with deep sideburns and twinkly John Lennon-ish wire-rims shambled in. Seeing Maude, the only female, he went to her corner and stood an inch from her.

"Wanna go for a smoke?"

She could smell the sour, suggestive scent of liquor in his breathy undertone, and pungent, almost tasty marijuana. They walked in silence a long way into a rustling field, far enough so that when they stopped and turned, the yellow lights and the silhouetted school buildings looked like a postcard, Maxfield Parrish, innocently unaware of them. She accepted the illicit cigarette, grounds for expulsion, struggling to appear to inhale, putting up with the acridness on her palate. Looking at the boy, looking away when he looked back. Under their feet the crushed grasses released a flowery essence.

Nothing had prepared her. For all the fantasizing, observing, and imagining, nothing had prepared her. Not for the wet slipperiness of kissing or, even less, for the current it generated in unrelated spots, leaping in her womb and licking at her crotch and burning there like honey, making her want to push against the knob offered behind the cloth of his pants. His hands on her breasts intensified the surge. When he met no resistance, he inserted his warm hands up through her dress and she felt the softness of her own breasts as fire between her legs, and when he sucked her nipples, felt she would do anything to satisfy the surge of yearning that erupted and made her have to suppress something in her throat. She didn't know what satisfaction could be, so surprising, so flabbergasting was each subterranean tug on her parts.

To lie down he had to let go a moment, and she felt a chill where his hands had been, where his mouth had been. The disappointment, momentary, was nevertheless so sharp she could have hit him. When his hand wandered into her underwear she felt, first, the astounding shock of being naked to someone. Like being in one of those dreams where you are in public and realize you have no clothes on. Only, in this dream, the next realization was that the public approved. It was all right.

That was before something of keening sweetness—but, yet, with a tang of salt akin to tears coming or the urgency of a full bladder—led to her inner vision's being engulfed in spattering sparks and sparkles. Some part of her knew this was his fingers on her, but that wasn't where her mind was. She let it go dark, absent, a backdrop for the sparkles the touch of him on her generated.

She didn't think of touching him except to clasp him to her. He was just the opacity between her and the sky, the wandering warmness between her ass and the cool, silky grass. He was the fur of his sideburns, and horse breaths. She didn't think of his penis or its state inside his jeans, where he kept it; she did not consider his satisfaction, which he may or may not have had. It was sheerly the new wonder of touching skin, of her skin being touched, of its being allowed, of its being exciting to someone else.

Surprise gradually yielded to a softer stroking and bumping pleasure and then amazement all over again, on the surface of her skin, in tingling, in a sticky pressure her tongue demanded. Time disappeared.

In later life, when satisfaction is available and availed of, nothing would be as exciting as this mere touching, this limited exposure that feels more naked than literal nakedness, more dangerous, even, than the far more intimate embrace of wet inner flesh.

They heard the muted bell like a distant cry, like their own complaint at stopping. They stood up, leaning together, brushing themselves down, flicking off strands of scattered hay, and walked toward the lights. At the edge of the field they glued themselves together a last time.

With startling swiftness, like a safety curtain shooting down at a cry of fire, Maude was suddenly bored. She would never see him again after tomorrow. She let him hold her waist, the very spot she'd longed to have known, as they walked into the light. She felt companionable—grateful. She let him kiss her lightly on the lips in front of everyone. He was driving home, but she told him it was better for her to take the van. "See you tomorrow, babe," he said hotly into her ear.

※

Maude had been correct in feeling she was about to fall in love. But it wasn't with Mr. Sideburns. It wasn't with a person. It was with the place. She had wanted the place, welcomed it, had a kind of crush on it, but it was only in the lush, teary, piercingly lovely scenes that were its final embrace for those departing that she encountered the rich solidity of this feeling that left its possessor more vulnerable.

The girls fluttered over the green lawns in long dresses. The daughter of a diplomat who'd served in India appeared in a shocking-pink sari that looked at home with her straight blonde hair and pink cheeks. Weesie wore a gown in wild purple and turquoise. "Is that a real Pucci?" girls kept asking, giving her the opportunity to reply, "Yes. A real Pucci *nightgown*." Her hilarity was self-mocking. But no one joined in the mockery—they admired her cleverness and her thinness swathed in curlicues. Maude wished she had been so clever—and yet she didn't like Pucci and loved what she herself was wearing, wasp-waisted gauze from an antique shop a bunch of them had gone to together.

It was such a drag not having mainstream tastes—not even elite mainstream tastes! It wasn't a matter of feeling different, inappropriate, left out—or of feeling jealous. It wasn't so simple as approval or its absence. The bunch of girls had insisted on her buying this dress, because it so suited her. But she could see how *at home* they felt with Weesie's choice, as if it better expressed themselves than their own choices did, while Maude they built a fence around, like an exhibit, exhaling as if she were holy.

But this was only a moment in a day that, for once, tended to obliterate the tensions of being separate people, people with skewed visions and disparate destinies. The sheer prettiness of everything, of themselves, made them each feel a movie-starrish sense of being adored through every eye. They all felt daring. They dared show themselves as desirable young women. Maude's peach slip was visible through the lace-trimmed web; another girl wore a yellow empire nightgown she had also decided could pass for a dress; a couple glittered or shone in old evening gowns of their mothers'. The very atmosphere seemed to be of that naked-in-public dream where it was strangely all right, as if the school really were a lover.

"Like butterflies," said Mr. Patrick, passing a group of them. "You've come out of your winter cocoons and you're butterflies."

They waited for him to pass before they rolled their eyes at one another. Feeling beautiful but as if they needed to brush something off.

Weesie flew away for the a cappella performance by the madrigal group she'd joined, a chiffon shawl trailing from her thin arms. The chorus assembled in two rows before the flock of parents on folding chairs and underclassmen cross-legged or leaning back on their elbows on the grass. All attention was on the two rows of singers, who might have been chosen for their Pre-Raphaelite beauties: hair wafting in the soft breeze off the plashing Sound, an armload of golden frizz next to Weesie's sparkling pale orange next to swirling black and a satin curtain of chestnut; the fluttering Easter-egg-colored dresses, the boys' earnest, concentrating faces under swept-aside bangs, the sheet music like bird wings—all were a decorative display whose only purpose was pleasure.

But a pleasure so transitory, as ephemeral as the girls' dresses were ethereal, that it was a melancholy pleasure, melting like the harmonies that went swiftly from major to minor, lingering in inexplicably tragic tones over phrases like "Rejoice in our happy, happy loves" and dying on the moist air.

Maude was crying as one by one the graduating seniors stood up, tall and jerky, swift and confident, dimpling, diffident, to accept their diplomas and a hug in their ribbons or flounces or, among the boys, in the first dashikis any of the audience had seen or wearing the occasional muslin peasant shirt with their jeans instead of the standard oxford. As she furtively ran her finger under her eyes, she saw Weesie doing the same—yet grinning.

Weesie shrieked as the ceremony ended, "Here it is! The rehearsal for the Big One. The first of the long goodbyes!"

"It's not a funeral," said Maude, scandalized. She wanted things to be the way they were supposed to be. She wanted to believe. She was not the same person as the author of her scathing study. "It's called *commencement*, for God's sake."

"*They* get to commence: fucking, LSD—"

Weesie's welcoming mockery was irresistible. "Living away from home," Maude joined in.

"But we alone survive." Weesie's lit class had done *Moby Dick* a year early. "It *is* a funeral. It's the first harbinger."

This felt as piercing as the day's beauty and as undeniable. "How can you know that?" She looked sidelong at Weesie's comical expression—eyebrows lifted, freckled lips smacking as if it were satisfying to know all life's losses in advance. This was what she was keyed up for. And Maude, who hated the holy fence other people built around her, couldn't help adding a rail to the one she had set up around Weesie's specialness, which seemed to her greater.

※

The rest of the day and evening passed in a jumble of tears and hugs, of coq au vin eaten while parents made polite conversation in the refectory and their children tried to pretend not to know these living embarrassments, of shrieks and kisses as people who would never get in touch with one another exchanged addresses, and a general breaking up into groups as parents were urged to go home, go away. But the students were being made to go away too as the campus was closed up, so that the groups gravitated to different houses, cramming in with whomever had a car to take them there. As faces streamed by in the dark, Danny Stern's, smiling garishly, cried, "C'mon. Come over. A bunch of us are going." He grabbed Maude's mesh-covered arm.

His father drove them, in a stoic or apathetic silence, in his Cadillac, and vanished upon arrival.

Danny, like the largest proportion of the students, lived not on a socialites' estate but in a rich suburb, where one large, land-scaped house followed another down muted, tree-lined streets. Each house was like a Hollywood set for a costume drama. There was mock tudor, "colonial," Spanish-inflected stucco with wrought iron, a front porch from Tara. They presented history in a manner so tamed it was the same as being forgotten. It obliterated the real history that was there, the thirty years over which the houses had been built in incarnation of families' American Dreams. Danny's was brick, with white shutters.

The students shuffled up a graveled driveway where a lawnboy (black) held a lantern (electric), past azalea bushes rounded by pruning. The last blossoms, stickily fallen onto the gravel, adhered to the visitors' sandaled soles. The Bay Farmers trooped into an entrance hall too small for its grandiose double staircase and chandelier, which was endangered by the head of one of the taller boys.

They proceeded on, sinking into the dense wall-to-wall carpeting that exactly matched an excess of squarish upholstered couches, chairs, ottomans, loveseats, and an immense TV. Someone flicked it on. "Turn the sound off," said someone else. Unnatural colors blared and were replaced by the black and white of an old movie, though with magenta and acid green vibrating at the edges, as if the technology could not help showing off, being expensive and new. Someone switched the channel to a show Maude had not known was in color. There was a chorus of no's, and it was switched back.

As people goofed on the old movie, providing lines for the silenced action, Maude found a bathroom. The sink's faucet was a giant swan, wings spread, the water gushing from its brass beak. The walls were covered in metallic patterned paper. A brass bowl made to look like a shell held soaps also neatly molded into shells, the same aqua and peach as the rank of terrycloth "guest towels" monogrammed in metallic thread. Poor Danny! She cringed inwardly, embarrassed for him, as if Milt were over her shoulder, viewing it all with contempt.

But she might have saved the humiliation for herself. As she crossed the thick carpeting, she heard, "He made out with

Maude *Pugh*? You're kidding. How'd he have the nerve? Weesie
Herrick I could see. She's funny. But Maude Pugh is *scary*."

She didn't want to be scary. She didn't think of herself as
scary. She didn't recognize the voice, but it seemed to be saying
she should keep to herself.

3.

THE GARDEN WAS the best part of that summer. However, as Maude learned to love its sun-warmed earth sinking under her naked feet and the discovery of swelling zucchini in green light under umbrellalike leaves where, the day before, there had been only a nub, it became her main point of contact with Nina and then, as such, the unbearable embodiment of the summer's events.

"Daddy? Where's Mommy? She's never *around* these days. What's she *doing*?"

Milton looked at his fierce, wandlike daughter and had the fleeting thought that it was kind of too bad he didn't do naturalistic work. She stood inside the screen door like a representation of bounty, but Ceres crossed pleasingly, if confusingly, with virginal Athena and, uncompromisingly, herself, her long hair scrolled at the back of her head and trapped with a barrette so that the ends of it flared upward, her skin brown, her cheeks pink from heat, her arms overflowing with silky lettuces of pale green tinged red at the edges and a pile of pea pods whose threadlike ends and stems coiled like the curls nature hadn't given Maude, as if they wanted to decorate and soften her. Clutched against her radishy chest were also a handful of leafy radishes, the dirt turning pale and tan on their hard, white-streaked, rosy curves.

"I thought I'd make a salad for dinner." She was doing most of the cooking.

"Yes," he said as if he were answering a different question from the one she'd asked, "you look like a salon painting."

"A salad painting?" Exasperated, she stepped around him where he stood at the foot of the stairs. "It's not to look at, it's to eat," she said, as if to deny the vegetable beauty of which she herself had said to Weesie, "It's so gorgeous, I want to roll in it. I want to, you know, fuck it." They giggled, *fuck* still a forbidden mystery. "I go out there in the morning and I could practically *cry*. They're like *babies* growing in there." That was what she had said. But that couldn't be shared with Milt.

Nina came in as Milt and Maude were at the blond wood table enjoying the salad—they did enjoy the salad. She was wearing a denim wraparound skirt and a dreamy smile. She seemed not to see them even as she said hello and wafted past, stopped, came back, sat and folded her arms on the table and laid her cheek on them.

"Mommy? Are you—are you *stoned*?"

Nina popped up from her ragdoll lassitude as if transformed into a jack-in-the-box, laughing, laughing. "I'm just, I'm just naturally high," she gasped, wiping tears away. Milt joined in the laughter.

"I don't see what's so goddamned funny," said Maude. That brought up new gusts. "You—shitheads," she said, standing up.

"Oh." Nina gulped. "You're like a stern mo-mo-mo-mother."

Pretending to ignore her mother, tossing the black satin curtain of her hair back with one hand as if she were flipping the bird, Maude flounced down the black hallway and slammed her unsatisfactory door: hollow-core, it barely made a thud. She opened it again to call, "And I'm painting my room. *White*," and thudded it again, kicking it for good measure. She threw herself into her pillow. No one would come in to comfort her. She felt she'd already lost her parents, that her family had dissolved. She alone survived. I didn't do anything, she thought, flipping over and staring at the ceiling, the only light surface, where she could sometimes picture faces and odd mutating tableaux. They don't care about me. They only care about themselves.

"They don't care about me" pricked a gush of tears, salty and slightly relieving the pressure that felt as if her chest and head were filled with saltwater. "They don't love me" released a better torrent. It was strange how comforting the thought was, a relief.

In the past, if Maude was upset, Nina had made helpless mewing sounds and looked distressed, her hands dangling like rabbit paws. But Maude had often comforted her mother, cuddled to her as Milton cut into Seth with sarcasm or railed at the unfairness of life. And now Nina was running around at all hours and laughing at her and saying Maude was like a stern mother.

In the tiny box of a house, Maude could hear the kitchen sink running and the clank of the dishes being washed. She heard Nina's giddy, oblivious laugh and felt a flash of hatred. She thought of something cruel she could say, about Seth. None of them ever said his name, as if they had agreed to the injunction without need for discussion. She clicked open her door: silence from the kitchen. It was easy to be noiseless as she padded over the linoleum tiles; underneath, the floor was a cement slab. In the kitchen, Milt had Nina clenched to him as she dangled dreamily, her new vague smile, less anxious but as evasive as ever, melting over her lips as his hand cupped one breast.

Maude dashed back to her room.

If anyone had been watching, it would have looked parodic, the way she grabbed brushes and hurled herself at the easel she had set up in the tiny black room. She was glad no one could see. She jabbed violent colors onto the canvas she had brought from school, impastoed strokes molded into expressive, expressionistic figures. As she slowed down, pausing, late in the night, long after her parents had gone to sleep—they at one point called good-night down from their room like obedient if mischievous children—she became aware that the picture was startlingly better than those she'd made with more care. It seemed a betrayal of her own sense of being betrayed to notice this, a mere aesthetic consequence. Once she'd had the thought, she couldn't go on. She watched the bright, lurid picture a while as though it would tell her, now that she'd given it life, what she felt, who she was, what it all meant, stirring the stiff-bristled brushes against the bottom of the can, which still advertised Pomadori Pelati though filled with turpentine, in which color rose like mud.

Unwilling to go to bed, as if she wanted someone to tell her to, and uninterested, for once, in reading, she slid open her closet and sat on the floor in front of her improvised dollhouse, setting up the doll family in scenes of serene domesticity until the first piercing cheep promised dawn.

4.

"**D**OES YOUR MOTHER—? Has she ever—? I mean, it's like, it's as if Nina isn't here even when she's here."

"God—I wish. My mother, it doesn't matter what she's doing; it's, like, she's on me."

"Really? She seems so—polite."

"Yeah. She does it in a polite way."

"I always think you have all this, like, great privacy."

"Mm."

"I don't know." Maude exhaled from deep within. "I mean, who cares; it's, like, my mother, right? I should be glad."

"No. I know what you mean. I think. I mean, my father. I mean, he's Mr. Absent While Present."

Maude was too polite, herself, to agree.

"Not that he's present all that often."

"Your father scares me," said Maude, thinking of the gray-suited figure she had seldom seen. Once, when looking for Mary Jane, she had peered into the wing that contained the master-bedroom suite, and Mr. Herrick had been standing there, silvery and forbidding, and had asked her what she wanted with an air that told her she had no right to be there.

"Yeah, well."

"Also." Maude had dragged the heavy black phone from

the kitchen counter as far as it would stretch into the hall and pulled the curly cord of the receiver taut to get it into her room. She checked to make sure the door was really closed over the obstruction of the vinyl wire. "There have been these hangups. Like, I pick up the phone and I can hear, like—"

"Breathing?"

"No, it's not like that. I mean, someone's there but not, you know, panting and—gross, or anything. Just someone there, and then he hangs up. There's a click and, like, I'm saying 'Hello? Hello?' Like a fool."

"He?"

"That's the thing. Once he said my mother's name. Like 'Neen?' You know, hopeful but not really sure."

"Jesus. And we were worried about—" Milt and Mary Jane.

"Please. I feel awful enough."

"I'm sorry. Jesus, Maude, I'm really sorry. Oh, God. That's really—well, can you—?"

They offered a moment of silence to the potential gravity of the situation.

"You didn't recognize the voice or anything, did you?" Weesie went on.

Long silence. "It did sound familiar. But I can't, you know, figure out why."

"You really could use a vacation. It's a good thing you're coming with us to Deer Isle."

But as the time approached, it didn't feel like a good thing. It felt like a bad thing, full of disquiet and apprehension, as if, if Maude let go of anything she was doing, everything would fall apart. She told Weesie, "I'm like obsessed with, you know, weeding the garden. Nina hasn't been around and there are like new weeds every time I go out there." She was hoping Weesie would say she couldn't possibly abandon so important, so critical, a responsibility, as if it were a magical task in one of the fairy tales they both cooed over and were as precious about as if they were babysitting their own infant selves.

But Weesie could not imagine Maude pulling the sprouts as a girl in a fairy tale—the one with the girl who has to collect nettles and spin them into thread to weave into cloth to sew into shirts to throw over the wings of her brothers to turn them back from swans into men, keeping silent the whole time or the magic won't work. That was the way it was with magic, you couldn't speak of it. So Weesie did not say in awed tones that of *course* Maude mustn't let the weeds grow in the face of Nina's dereliction—which would have been to say, really, that of *course* Maude had to keep her family together, bring back Seth, hold it all in herself for her own sanity and that this could, *obviously*, be accomplished by pulling weeds, by keeping up with them, keeping the black earth immaculate. She said, "So what?" And Maude could only, helplessly, agree; fighting down that physical sensation that yanked at her stomach and twisted her diaphragm, shameful fear.

"And there's, you know, my job." Maude was working at a sub-minimum wage part-time at the local library, which was in a shopping center, between a cobbler's and the five-and-dime.

There was nothing Weesie could say to that. Maude was poor. Her income for the weeks away would be less than what other girls got for a month's clothing allowance, and she would use it for textbooks and the school studio fee. Theoretically, Weesie was in love with such real-world constraints. But when it came down to it, she didn't believe them: Maude couldn't really have to work. It was a sort of game that made you more romantic, like walking around carrying a hardbound black notebook of unlined pages or outlining your eyes in kohl. Both of which, after all, Maude also did.

"You don't want to come."

"Of course I want to come."

"You'd rather pull weeds and shelve library books."

And Maude could feel it. The satisfying instant of release when you tugged a cluster of green to get at the thin pale roots gripping the soil beneath, which cling as the feet of mice will grip and cling if you try to lift them by the tail, the moment the whole plant top and bottom came free. She felt her fingers in the soil, warm for an inch or two, cool and secret beneath, delicious to the touch like anything warm and yielding, but also gritty, irritating beneath the nails and yet, again, satisfying to scrape away. The earth, at first cluttered with spikes and dots and bead-like clusters, cleared to yield a backdrop as color-enhancing as a black wall, highlighting the pattern of tomato plant or lettuce, the growing pile of intruders limp and then shriveling on the grass next to the garden bed. The pop and caress of the smells. You were goodness, doing this. You were the queen of creation. You were taken care of; you were mother. Early in the morning, sun on your arms, not too warm, a fearless nearby robin pulling up worms. Twilight, a cool current like water, fireflies. It seemed far too much to give up.

And the library, so quiet, the only sounds for long stretches the standing fan's throat-clearing and creak as it lurched to the far side of its half-rotation and started back the other way, lifting the same page, with the same barely audible rustle, on each pass. Maude felt the abstraction of pushing the wooden cart, scanning the soothingly orderly shelves, plunking a volume into its home slot, with a pleasure that was like sinking under water and discovering that you could still breathe. Yes, there too, you were taking care of things, you were putting the universe in order, and all would be the way it was supposed to be. It was a good magic.

At the end of the story, the last shirt wasn't finished, and one brother was left with a swan's wing.

"No, I don't. I want to go to Maine."

"Just a minute. My mother wants to say something."

Maude heard some shuffling on the other end of the line. "Now, you're coming with us," said Mary Jane's cool, plummy tones, "or you've got me to answer to. And that's that."

Maude knew she was sunk then; there was no retreat. Mary Jane thought that she was a poor person being too embarrassed to accept bounty—and that was there too.

"I'm looking *forward* to it, Mary Jane."

Sometimes Maude sounded like Mary Jane when she talked to her.

The day before she was to leave, Maude complained to Nina that she didn't know what to pack, that nothing she had was right. She never appealed to her mother in this way. Nina lit with delight, so that Maude felt almost ashamed of her ruse, guilty of not seeing her mother as a source of help.

"It *is* dark in here," said Nina as they stood leaning over Maude's narrow bed, where clothes folded into smooth, flat squares were stacked by type, everything she would need.

Nina made her rabbit paws of helplessness and distress and then chewed on a finger, looking harried and scared. Maude, lifting her hair off the back of her neck in the heat, thought: I shouldn't have taken care of everything; I should have left something for Mommy to do.

"Where's your bathing suit?" said Nina, peering as though she might have overlooked it on the flat surface.

"Oh, I'll swim in cutoffs and a tank top."

"You have to have a *bathing* suit. What did you do to your old one?"

"I outgrew it, Ma. I haven't had one for a year."

Nina sank to the bed and put her face in her hands. At that moment, Milt came to the open door. In the second before his face changed he had a familiar look that expressed his satisfaction at having arranged his life so intelligently: a worshipful, eternally young wife; a clever, talented daughter; a house and land of their own; means to do his own work . . . Then he took in Nina's abject posture. "What are you doing to her?" he growled at Maude and shoved her as if her proximity to Nina represented threat.

"No—oh," said Nina. "She doesn't have anything decent. She'll look like a ragamuffin. They'll think we don't take care of her."

Milton plucked up Maude's tattered jeans and tossed them across the bed, toppling the piles. "Why didn't you tell your mother you needed clothes? Hm? Why did you wait till the last minute?"

Maude was crying. "I don't need them. We can't afford them. I just wanted—"

"Don't you treat your mother this way! Don't you do this to her!" He shook his finger in Maude's face. "Always think you're smarter than everybody else! You're not so smart. You don't know what you do or don't need."

They heard students arriving at the front door. Milt shot Maude a threatening look and went out.

※

Maude let herself be taken shopping, not at Roosevelt Field, festival of bad taste and cheapness that was familiar and safe, but at the Fifth Avenue department stores and boutiques of the North Shore's Miracle Mile, where she finally had to choose something just to forestall purchases of the inappropriate things her mother seemed to want to see her in. Nina held up one crisp, perky matching outfit after another, urging her horrified daughter to try them on. Yet even as Maude reluctantly accepted the hanger from which dangled a lime green piqué shorts set, Nina moaned about the price. The forbidding prices let Maude off the hook of her mother's desires, but she didn't dare look at the things she really wanted, which cost just as much. She just hoped that

Nina would somehow insist on those very things. They did come away with a rather opulently sexy bikini fashioned out of purple velveteen. What she most needed was socks, but she couldn't bring herself to ask. She would wear Weesie's clothes.

"Forgive me?" said Nina, pulling up in front of their mass-produced house and stopping the little car with a jerk.

"*Ma.*"

Nina's face puckered, hurt and uncomprehending. "Kiss and make up," she whimpered.

Maude leaned across the seat and brushed her mother's cheek. It was soft, with a new slackness. Maude immediately got out of the car.

"Don't forget your *suit,*" Nina moaned, brandishing the bag with its arched handles, restrained logo, susurrus of tissue.

There was another fight over the suitcase. There was no suitcase. Then Milt got out a heavy, boxy thing with his father's initials on it. Maude liked its ruched satin pockets inside, the leather stitched around the awkward handle, and the fact that it looked like a prop from a 1930s movie. "Exactly," Nina said. But they let her take it. They had nothing better to offer.

"Thank you, Mommy," Maude said, clinging a little too hard and too long, so that Nina pulled away with a girlish laugh, holding her hands free.

"Have a nice time, dear," she said coldly, as if to lower the emotional temperature.

Maude looked hard into her mother's face, trying to fix her evasive eyes. "Don't forget to weed the garden. Okay, Ma? Don't forget."

Nina laughed unhappily.

5.

WHILE SHE WAS in Maine, Maude admitted what she had been afraid to hope and therefore to say: that the calls were from Seth.

"You think your mother is, like, seeing him secretly?"

They were hunched on the frayed oriental rug in front of the fire, which they had been feeding with pine cones for the crackle and burst of flame. Mary Jane and all the others in a shifting cast of guests had gone to bed. Maude wore a cashmere sweater left behind by some male visitor which, with her knees against her chest, she could pull down to the tops of her sneakers.

"Why would he call her and not you guys? And why wouldn't she tell you?"

"Not if he doesn't want her to. He would *never* call my father, never. And, I don't know. He hates me."

"Maude."

"No, he really does. It's weird. He was nice to me when I was little, and I used to try to stop Milton from, you know—doing mean things to him—"

"Milton *mean*?"

"Oh—he probably doesn't mean to be. He just doesn't notice anything for incredibly long times and then, whomp, you get in his way and he's ready to, like, kill."

"Oh, come on."

"I guess he seems like someone who would never get angry. He seems so floating above it all. But he has this—you can't believe his temper. I mean, short fuse does not describe it. He even killed my cat."

"He killed your *cat*?"

"It was an accident. It was me he was angry at."

"What was he angry at you for?"

"He was pounding Seth, and I called him a bastard. Milt, that is."

"And he killed the *cat*?"

"He was chasing me, and the cat was like sitting there, and he kicked her. She hit the brick wall, you know, the chimney. It was really awful. She just lay there with her eyes open and blood coming out her mouth."

"I can't believe this."

"He said, 'Oh, for God's sake,' like really disgusted, and left us to clean it up. Seth helped me bury her anyway. Oh, poor Ghostly. That was her name. She was white."

A log, burnt through, shifted with a spray of sparks and settled once again to a steady crackling.

"I can't believe I'm telling you. I never talk about this stuff."

"It's pretty, I don't know, incredible. Your parents always seem really sweet with you."

"Well, it's not as if I'm making this up. Why do you think Seth left?"

"So, what did you mean he hates you?"

"Oh, it's just—like when I used to come home from school, I'd try to get into my room without him seeing me. Not that he wouldn't come into my room. I used to *beg* my parents to let me have a lock on my door, beg them."

"What'd he do?"

"He just really, really hurt me. Like he'd grab me and twist my arms so that—I can't describe it, I guess. I always thought something was about to break. I even heard cracks; I'm not kidding.

Sometimes I blacked out. That scared him. Once, he got my head between the wall and my dresser and pressed, and I guess I stopped breathing or something. I really thought that was it. And it was so weird: one minute he's trying to kill me and the next, we're sitting there; I'm holding my throat—it's so awful when you just can't get air. He said I was blue. He's like staring at me. And that's the thing: it felt as if we were in this conspiracy together. He's trying to kill me, but in this weird way, I'm *still* on his side. I can't explain it. I don't think I even told my parents. Not that it would have made any difference."

"I wish I could meet him."

This made perfect sense to Maude. Weesie had seen the impressive tape collection and heard of Seth's participation in Freedom Summer, his summer jobs as a migrant worker picking cherries, then peaches, and working his way north to apples just before he had to go back to school. It was easy to imagine him in some gorgeous wreck of an apartment in a broken-down neigh-borhood in Brooklyn or Hoboken, or in some tough waterfront hotel maybe, letting his mother know that he was still alive, was all right, but swearing her to secrecy or she would never hear from him again. Apprenticing himself to a bookbinder or working on the docks or something.

※

Maude was only away a few weeks, and nothing in Milt's letters hinted at anything amiss. It was always Milt who had written the rare times she had been away. The one summer she was at camp, when she was so young she couldn't read, he had sent let-ters that were mostly pictures—him climbing up a ladder with a nestling he'd found in the grass; the nest with the other baby birds, beaks gaping; a toad with which he'd been rewarded for making one of his coerced attempts on the lawn; a picture of his brother, Maude's uncle, who had come by with his loud wife, Marjory; a picture of Maude's teddy bear, Rusty, who missed her, he said, so much that the thread holding his chest together was coming undone.

His two letters to Maine were more grown-up but showed a similar consideration for her concerns, something that didn't happen when she was around. He told her they finally had tomatoes from the garden and that if, when she got back, she wanted to paint her room, he'd pay for the paint. It was Milt the good father who wrote, as if letters made love safer.

He'd always offered this kind of care to Seth. Seth's interests had prestige. Milt built them up, if anything. Then he hated Seth for losing interest and disappointing him.

Standing in the comfortably blowsy old-fashioned Maine kitchen that looked out at an overturned boat being repaired, Maude was so moved that her guard fell and she forgot to worry. It was like being cradled in comfort. This momentary lack of vigilance so frightened her by what might have happened—she was like a nervous passenger who believes that she must pay attention every second to keep the plane in the air—that her anxiety surged back with full force. She could feel the sensation—like squirrels chasing each other through her chest—of her heart missing beats, and the fear inflating her belly.

Yet she swam in the freezing water; took sweaty, apparently pointless hikes; fell in love with meadows of wildflowers; was baffled at why waiting for clams to roast on a damp chilly beach with sand getting into your shorts was supposed to be fun, and was equally baffled at why, afterward, it seemed to have been fun; could at no time be coaxed into a sailboat; and loved lying in the dark in the spool bed, in a room that smelled of old wood, talking to Weesie in the four-poster.

No one wore perky matching outfits except the tourists they saw when they went into town. Maude's instinct for what was acceptable had not been far off—a preference for the worn and the casual prevailed, as at Bay Farm—but she was not practically equipped: her cheap acrylic sweater was as useless for keeping warm as it was nasty to touch; her grayed, delightfully hole-ridden sneakers wobbled and slid on steep trails; and her paint-stained sweatshirt was a bit much, looking either grubby or ostentatiously arty. Everyone had suede hiking boots that laced over hooks and peculiar shoes whose lower halves were ribbed rubber—so ugly that Maude felt, when she saw them, they surely couldn't mean it. Then she wanted a pair. In one of her tiny sundresses, with the rebozo she had saved to buy in Greenwich Village, she had looked, at an outdoor chamber music concert, unself-consciously to the manor born.

Then she came back to the manor she was born to.

As she was dropped off, the usual children were drooling and pummeling each other in the crabgrassless lawns of the houses all around, while teenage girls on towels glazed like rotisserie meats basted with Coppertone. At the verge of their own dandelion-studded lawn, only her father's van rested like an obedient elephant by the curb in front of the pricker bush and green-apple-filled tree.

A class was letting out as she walked in. Departing housewives turned their teased heads to look back at the master counseling a woman who was explaining that she just couldn't make charcoal *work*: "It doesn't *do* anything fa me." She had the kind of New York accent that was starting to be called a g'Island accent, after people who glued together the *g* and *I* of Long Island, Long-*gy*lind. Matching the bright shirt she wore was a perky hemmed triangle of cotton, tied over her ears at the back of her neck.

As soon as he got the last of them out and closed the pink front door, Milt's face, affable and wise, crumpled. It was like the stock shot of demolition where an apartment building folds in upon itself and silently bursts into clouds of dust. He fell on Maude's shoulders, gasping and weeping.

"Daddy?"

She didn't have to be told. She knew what she'd really known for weeks, and somehow he hadn't—that Nina was leaving them, slipping away. It wasn't Seth coming back; it was Nina leaving. Bearing the unbearable weight of her father, her shoulder wet, Maude could see the vegetable plot, which once again looked like an extention of the uncut field beyond. He hadn't weeded the garden. She'd *said* to keep it weeded. Her hands rested uneasily on his thin, shaking back. His bottomless need for sympathy and reassurance and his equally bottomless contempt would, now, fall all on her.

PART III

1.

I T WAS A geodesic dome, its many faces made of old car doors welded together, their original colors intact, some shiny, some dull: orangey, turquoise, pale green, flat gray—colors no one was making cars in anymore. The welds looked like bluish, shiny, badly healed scars. Maude ran her finger along one as she hesitated in a yard messy with pottery wind chimes, a picnic table improvised from an electric-company spool, planters made from the giant cans army-surplus peanut butter came in, and a large vegetable garden that bore little relation to the one from which Maude was taking the final orderly harvest. This one had no rows; it was sprawled with zinnias and other random flowers, and guarded by several inventive scarecrows that tended to be taken as lurking people at first glance. One wore, or was, a suit, with Clark Kentish black glasses—a sarcastic scarecrow. Her mother, who thought that to be around rich people your clothes had to match, was living here? Maude knocked on the metal, which, by itself, already ticked in the October sun. Cornstalks grew to either side of the ugly scrap-wood door.

Annoyingly, the song that had been a hit that summer, which Weesie and Maude had sung along to in the car, collapsing in giggles, would not stop going through Maude's head: it said to put flowers in your hair, to be a part of the Summer of Love, in a voice so syrupy it had to be cynical. Maude had loved maidenish flowers in long hair before they were a hippie cliché or, anyway, before hippies were a cliché.

It had certainly been a summer of love, for some people.

Nina burst through the door. "Oh, Maudie, Maudie. Thank you for coming."

Inside, the dome was oddly dark—odd because plexiglass hexagons appeared at intervals among the metal ones, overhead and at every height, one so low it showed scrubby grass and insects, next to which a cat sat poised, twitching. The effect of the curving walls and small, unpredictable windows was unsettling and unhomelike, outerspacy yet claustrophobic, no doubt a perfect illustration of the *unheimlisch*—unhomey because reminiscent of the original home, the womb. It was as hot as an attic.

Nina, her hair in two gray-streaked braids, shyly indicated a shadowy corner—if anything could be called a corner—near the mattress on the floor. "Rod built it all himself, just this year."

Rod Patrick came forward, aggressive belly first, his face red above the beard, though only from heat. "Hi, Maudie."

"Only my father calls me Maudie."

Nina swiveled away. She got something out of another dark niche and placed it on a tray she had ready to take outside. "I make my own yogurt," she announced. So pleased to have made something herself.

"That's great, Mom. Did someone give you a culture or you just start with Dannon?"

"Oh," she said sadly, "you know all about it."

"Well," Maude said, helplessly apologetic, "some kids in evening rec were making it. They're even trying cheese. They had to get rennet. Did you know there was stuff in cheese from a cow's stomach?"

"Your mother was thinking of trying cheese," said Rod Patrick.

Maude ignored this, taking the tray from her mother's hands

and stepping into the breathable air outside. "You want it here?" she said, setting it on the electrical spool. It had been spread with an old tablecloth Maude recognized. That cloth had always been folded in a trunk in her parents' closet, full of stuff no one used. The pattern showed a trellis covered with nasturtium, like a message about a neat, decorative world.

The yogurt, just made, was in a big mayonnaise jar, still warm, with little bubbles that had jelled at the top. Fresh pickling cucumbers were sliced into a bowl of the kind that was becoming an icon of the nation of hippiedom, hand-thrown in a less than perfect round, with an external surface like a day-old beard, its thick sides glazed in unshiny earth tones. A similar bowl held applesauce. "I made it," said Nina, seeing Maude's gaze.

"What's come over you, Mommy?" She narrowed the range of her query: "I thought you hated cooking."

"Maybe your mother just needed someone to believe she could do something," said Rod, swaggering out and planting himself near the table. "Maybe she needed to know something was worth doing besides trying to be an artist in terms *The New York Times* can understand."

"Don't you mention my father. Don't *allude* to him. If you want Nina to have the—. I won't see her. Do you understand?"

She muttered to the side, but audibly, "Anine."

Nina twisted on her seat, knuckles against her cheek, Bernini updated. Rod touched her averted shoulder and left his big hand there as though to protect her from Maude. "It's all right," Nina choked out. She swallowed ostentatiously, demonstratively. Then she pulled herself together. All dignity, a little stern, the braids over the front of her blue scoop-necked leotard giving her the look of a member of a Plains tribe in a painting by Remington, Nina held a bowl toward Maude, who sat and took it. Despite Nina's display in rising above hurt, rising above the hurt was about the most grown-up thing Maude had seen her mother ever do.

"I see," said Rod, sitting heavily. "Business as usual."

Maude raked him up and down with her black-olive eyes. It was exhilarating to be able to hate someone without reservation, without obligations. She enjoyed hating Rod Patrick.

"The applesauce is great, Ma."

Nina told her about the apples, too lumpy and bug-bitten to eat uncooked but more delicious than any that could be bought once made into a sauce, from an ancient tree, an artifact of a defunct farm, discovered in some scrubby eastern Long Island woods.

2.

ILT MIGHT OR might not have been an artist in terms *The New York Times* could understand, but the sales to the Herrick connections were having their effect. His pictures hung among Mondrians and Rineharts, Alberses and Klees, in the houses of people who bought serious art and where other buyers of these rarefied objects saw them and where, it was seen, the Pughs looked at home with the Mondrians, Alberses, Rineharts, and Klees. They fit right in—though Milt much preferred them in the museum of his house, emerging spacelessly from black walls. But he could not demand that his customers paint their houses black and hang nothing but Pughs.

It was no surprise that a show emerged out of this, a one-man Fifty-seventh Street gallery show. It was the kind of thing that just "happened"—people talked at a party, and the artist's name was heard at another party; then people wondered why they didn't know about this much-talked-about artist and why they hadn't heard of him before; and this was connected to a sense of uneasiness about whether they were, at that moment, part of the in crowd or had been deluded all along about being part of it; and then the artist was no longer an obscurity but rather a mystery, which they believed it in their power to solve.

They could be among the discoverers. They could be one of the people who knew him first, who bought a Pugh way back when, when *no* one had heard of him. Except them and their friends, people who bought art.

Milt was introduced to a famous gallery owner. It was at a party. She was a woman who'd had a little money and lots of luck, and who, in exchange for the money and renown her artists brought her, was generous to them, and so her fame grew as artists flocked to her. She leveled on Milt's saleable looks her assessing gaze. That distinguished white mane, she thought, that height, that skinniness like Giacometti without being so tubercular-looking or unhealthily intense.

Her assessment rapidly kindled to warmth. In its glow, her artists tended to forget business was involved at all; so grateful, they would forgive anything: they were collecting tens of thousands: what did they care that it was only fifty percent of what their creations brought?

Milton, introduced to the gracious, polished lady with the short, expensive haircut, was not so self-destructive as to remind her that for years he had sent her his dearly purchased, unreturned slides, or that he had been introduced to her before by an art-school classmate of his who had done well but not quite well enough. He bowed slightly—maybe the bow was a little sarcastic, just a little, but who was to say?—and said he was so pleased to meet the legendary———. He behaved like gentlefolk. Because in a way he was. And he was pleased to meet her. Again. Though it could truthfully be said that it was the first time she met *him*.

It would be a small show, just the back room. The gallery was really booked for the next two years; she was shoehorning him in. Because she was so *excited* about his work. His work was so *exciting*. It was hard-edgy without that tapey, machined look; it had a little op without, thank God, being op, which had become passé almost as quickly as it was snapped up to copy for dress fabrics: Pughs were oppy without being, so to speak, go-go-esque. They were minimalist, maybe even color-fieldy (despite the tiny size—had he done any *larger* work?) without being, she didn't like to use that word, but, *barren*. There was something reassuringly old in feeling about them, as if she had discovered an unknown early modernist, and yet it was so—modern. Making no gesture toward gesture, it yet had the feel of hands' having touched it. Devoid of imagery, with only incidental, accidental signs of brushwork, it was yet unmistakably human. It felt believed in. It was solid.

Most of all, she could sell it.

Though the show was months off, it was in many ways as if it had already happened. People somehow knew. Milt got calls from people he hadn't heard from in years. "It's Lou Jacoby," Maude would say, handing Milt the receiver of the clunky black telephone with an ironic look; "It's Jake Rosenfeld"; "It's Anton Slack"; "It's Harry Sigmeister." And they congratulated him. They'd always already heard, and they congratulated him. It had been believed that some of these old classmates and colleagues had become successful enough to feel uncomfortable with those who weren't. It had been received truth in the Pugh household that they were afraid you would ask for a handout or had become too grand for people in tract houses without New York galleries.

Maude, in the last years before this crowd had dropped away, observed her parents with it and had seen, over tinkling cocktails, her mother's awe, which translated into an awkward, giggly eagerness to attack. How could they remain friends with someone whose wife asked, "So how'd *you* end up with Kennedy?" (a grand gallery), her shoulders stiff as a cat's with a dog in sight. Despite Milt's assured equanimity, Nina's defensive responses had made friendship impossible.

Maude did not like to think that these people now regarded Milt as restored to them, free of Nina's jealousy. Maude would have to prefer the explanation her absent mother would offer. "They only like him because he's riding high," she'd snort.

"Jake! How goes it?" Milton picked up where they'd left off, as if they'd never been out of touch. "It's marvelous," he'd gasp to Maude afterward. "You never really lose the connection!" And he'd look happy. Until he looked sad.

They didn't seem to have any more money than before. That was mysterious.

Other old colleagues had also disappeared, but these into abjectness, into an angry obscurity that was as comfortable as a smelly old favorite blanket. One day in November, Milton asked Maude to come with him to visit one of these, who had also renewed contact, Saul Partridge. Saul had a friend who had died, leaving him to deal with his large body of work. "I thought maybe, with you so big these days, one of your fancy connections could help out," Saul reiterated when father and daughter had arrived at his walk-up in Little Italy.

Maude could hardly believe a person could address another with such direct yet seemingly undetected, and certainly unacknowledged, hostility. But it was also oddly familiar to her, and her father took no offense.

"Whatever I can do." Milt spread his hands, palms out.

The apartment was on a narrow street built for carriages and never widened, across which squat tenements netted with fire escapes eyed each other and where, on lines across airshafts, archaic laundry flapped. Heavy women, purple under the eyes, sat on garbage cans in front, looking censoriously at the length of Maude's legs exposed between boot top and skirt hem, clamorous in yellow tights. But they nodded gravely in response to Milt's not at all sarcastic bow. He sighed as he and Maude started up the stairs and said the ladies reminded him of the old neighborhood, stories of which had always been like legends of Greek gods and heroes for Maude and Seth, the ur time before they were born.

The building's hallways were sour and dark, the black-and-cream ceramic tile in mosaic patterns browned and missing sections, which had been filled in with inappropriate greens. It took a very long time for Saul to answer their knock—the doorbell was rendered static by layers of shiny brown paint—but he finally opened the door. Maude thought of a dog's mouth opening, releasing bad breath.

The apartment was three tiny rooms all in a hodgepodge, as if one squareish room had been divided unequally into a rectangle and two tiny squares, but most remarkable was what was in them. Racks to hold paintings had been built into the kitchen, wedged between the bathtub and a chugging yellowed refrigerator, up which a brown stain crept from the chipped linoleum floor, its own color lost beneath ageless films of dirt. But the racks, from which stiff tufts of dust and grease grew, had long since overflowed, and the kitchen cabinets were equally crowded with fungoid wooden stretchers, the wood darkened and brittle-looking, frayed canvas edges furred with dust, poking the flimsy metal doors permanently open and askew.

There was not a bare surface anywhere, or a clean one. The kitchen was the biggest room but no longer had a place to sit, so they sat in the living room, which had the artist's pathetic bed in it because the bedroom, which had the two windows not on the airshaft, was the studio. Adding to the sensation of crowding were the paintings on every inch of brownish, peeling wall, not just the Kandinsky-like garish swirls of this artist but the many gifts of pals and lovers collected over the decades. A charcoal nude showed a long-departed wife, its outlines just a little too thick, too insistent, for art.

Saul offered them coffee, which Maude refused, and which he made with instant plus hot water from the faucet. "This freeze-drying, this is wonderful technology, no?" Saul had been a teacher at the art school Milt went to, one of many short-term jobs. He insisted Maude have something and thumped a glass

of orange juice before her. She got as far as finding a place on
the rim without lipmarks, but when she brought it close a reek
of something foul overwhelmed the orange scent, and she set
it down.

"Whatsa matter, you don't like o.j.?"

"No, no, it's fine. I'm just not thirsty."

"How about milk? I've got Carnation's right here, for the coffee. It's sweet, mm—try it."

"No, really—"

"A girl like you, such a skinnymarink! You gotta get some
flesh." He pinched her cheek and turned to Milt. "A beauty. A
little beauty. Well, no wonder." He sighed deeply. "It's all luck.
Everything in life, it's just luck."

Before sitting, Maude had spread her coat on the bed, over the
brown blanket. As the men talked—argued, as if contradiction
and one-upmanship were an expression of affection—she took
in her surroundings in more detail. The blanket wasn't brown.
Or at least it had once been blue. When she took her coat as
they at last were to make their way to the dead man's apartment,
she saw that it would have to go to the cleaners, just from lying
on the bed. She hoped Saul would not once again notice the
undrunk orange juice, separating into liquid and solids, and
wished she were capable of noticing less.

The dead man, Immerman, was a few blocks away, where
Little Italy gave way to Chinatown and the lower east side,
where the streets were soft with wadded garbage underfoot and
no one sat on cans guarding them. Terrifying men looked at
the outsiders with calculating, predatory keenness and whistled
through their teeth at Maude's legs and whipping hair. She kept
her eyes down.

Immerman's place was worse than Saul's. As he went through
the heaps of crumbling, dusty junk, Saul came upon a little
volume, its cloth cover cracking, that turned out to be a book of
poems he'd written. "Oh, yes, I write poetry too," he said as if

everyone surely knew this, and began declaiming from memory, stumbled, and stopped to turn pages forward and backward to find the line and speak it correctly. Saul held the wafer of dusty poems toward Maude. "Take it. I have enough copies, God knows. Here. It should go to someone new and young." Maude reluctantly accepted the volume.

"Here, here, look at this one," he said, not taking it back but turning pages, knowing from upside-down the spot he was looking for. Maude felt that she herself could be devoured by this hunger to have her see, to hear, to understand, and above all to receive this unappeasable egotism of art, grown monstrous from starvation.

Immerman's work was as depressing as his former surroundings. It was meant to be depressing, or at least the subjects were inarguably sad—dead children, mourners at coffins, a grieving mother, or, in a mode that declared the artist's virtuous condemnation of lynching, a man hanging from a tree, with red paint at his crotch and another grieving woman. (The title, written in harsh brushstrokes on the back, was "*Golgotha*.") Compared to the aesthetic in which, at school at least, T.S. Eliot was a god, *Nausée* was required reading, and the first movie shown in Bay Farm's film series was *Last Year at Marienbad*, these paintings were wriggling with irrepressible, unfashionable life. Sorrow suggested a livelier connection to the world than did existential despair and the elegantly presented assurance of the pointlessness of it all. Like the popularly grim works, however, these claimed seriousness by tackling death.

But there was something about the way it was shown that was too lively, that said "Look at me" and said it with the same neediness as Saul's declamations, inducing the same cringing. The children, the mourners, the mother, the widow—even though they had nominally different features, all had the same face, and somehow it was Immerman's face: Immerman's inner face, the face he was dying for the world to see. To mourn for him. As if, by depicting sorrow, he enacted sympathetic magic that would make the viewer feel how noble he was, how tragic his deeper understanding, and make them beat their own breasts for having misunderstood him.

But apparently he himself didn't know that inner face, because what the faces shared above all was generality. They were the generic face of sorrow, not Immerman's, not anyone's. He probably thought this made them universal, but it didn't. They did point at him, but they didn't express the tragic. What they showed was the artist's weltschmerz. Self-pity, actually. And that was what he had to give the world; pity was what the world had withheld from him, long before he recognized it as his *donnée*.

Even the artist's bewilderment that others could work in this mode, on these themes, and be blessed for it, but that he was left out, was visible in the paintings' imitative and calculated grays and reds. His desire for success might have been their real subject.

"Forget it, Saul. You can't do anything here."

"This one—it just needs a little cleaning. A little patching." The cheap or badly mixed paints were deteriorating, and the pictures had been treated by the artist with such inconsideration that canvases had been pierced by other pictures jammed in next to and on top of them.

"Saul. Saul. Forget it."

"But—" If Immerman could be legitimized, then Saul too could look forward to redemption.

"I'm telling you, there isn't anyone to buy these paintings."

Saul's fingers covered his mouth. "Maybe I'll make some donations. The Modern. The Whitney."

"Sure, Saul. Sure. You do that."

3.

A T THIS TIME of year the accordion sunroof of the van was sealed against a cold, colorless sky. Once they got past the attached pastel houses and litter of stores that was Queens, driving between the cement walls of the sunken roadway, the white sky began to be fretted with bare limbs of trees. Shallow hillsides and fields were torn open for new housing developments, a row of cement foundations appearing in formation, a scaffolding of two-by-fours on one of them, a few filled in with raw plywood, and, on a finished model, sod rolled out but stopping geometrically short to expose the gashed earth. These days the speculating builders varied the houses, so that every third had a gable or picture window or "traditional features," though their asbestos-brick or asbestos-wood family resemblance couldn't be disguised. The eye flicked away, seeking relief, again and again deflected by the same ugliness.

They passed into the more glaring clamor of the commercial strip that heralded the approach to their own manufactured town, one-story buildings you weren't supposed to register as part of a landscape—to do so was as rude as looking up a girl's dress when she was trying to smile into your face. Their smiles were in blinking, swooping letters made of ribbons of light, window displays. Or maybe the analogy was of looking at the whole girl when in fact she was flapping her crotch in your face—"3 for $5" or "all you can eat" or the painted statue of a grinning imbecilic boy in chef's whites on a roof. The Big Boy. Sometimes Maude was exhilarated by the exuberant commercialism, as if it were a welcome and she were one with the people who disdained her and whose tastes she found oppressive; but under the opaque sky, where the streaking reflections along the sides of cars and store windows were the highest lights, and after burrowing into two lives of apparent futility and desperation, she felt nothing but dread at returning to that house from which the other half of her family was so stubbornly missing.

As if her own inattention were her father's, the car lurched. A pain spread up Maude's arm. It was her wrist bracing against the dashboard as the car pulled up short. Their snub-nosed van loomed over the car below. Maude looked for a bloody body. But the car in front was untouched. There was about an inch between them.

"We're okay. We're okay," said Milt with a belying froggy catch in the middle.

Maude's heart wouldn't stop beating double-time. "Oh, Daddy." She put her hands over her eyes. Her wrist throbbed.

"It's all right. Nothing happened."

※

At home, outside the glass wall of their living room, another redwinged blackbird had fallen onto the cracked patio. Maude went out the back door still feeling the sick dread that wouldn't go away. As she went toward the bird, she thought of a picture she had loved and been moved by, unlike Immerman's, though it too was of mournfulness and death. It was an etching, square, mostly blank. It hung on the wall of a friend of her parents who was paralyzed, and that might have been part of its pathos. Down on the lower right corner, as if forgotten and overlooked, was a small black bird, finely rendered—very black—its eyes curled tight, likewise its feet. It could be asleep, but you looked and knew it was a dead bird. And what happened was, you loved the bird. Some small part of your heart curled up. That felt painful—a small pain, like a sting—and the sting was pleasurable. You could look at the picture again and have it all over again. Unlike a real dead thing, the loved object had not gone away or changed, and nothing in your life had changed either. Unless it had deepened a little, or been clarified, a little.

Maude bent in her high suede boots and lifted the glossy creature. Its head dropped and one exquisite, scarlet-marked wing fell open like a fan. A bird's eye, closed, has a look of illness and struggle, of inadequate defense. The body still had warmth, like a table on which a cup of tea has been sitting. She should bury it, she thought, surveying the matted grass that surrounded the garden. Her parents always just dropped the corpses in the garbage, which was collected from beneath a hinged metal lid set into the front lawn. But the dead bird was so beautiful. Maybe she would paint it. Not in the corner of the canvas, but whatever way it filled it, in its ringing scarlet and shiny black.

As she came back into the house, she could hear her father already at work upstairs, in his white, overlit studio, tapping and clanking with his brushes to opera oleaginously broadcast on QXR. How could he be so happy and unaffected? Did he not feel in danger? It might be that failure and desperation could rub off. (She had quietly left the cracked volume of dusty poems behind.) In the lifeless kitchen, she set the limp animal on the table, lurid against the light wood, and sat in one of the chairs as though, if she waited, her mother might come in and wonder what she should do for dinner.

When the music stopped and Milton Cross came on indistinctly, Maude, as if excusing herself from the table, got up and went into Seth's light-blue room. She sat on the bed with her knees bunched up and the olive army blanket pulled up around her. The same pictures cut from magazines covered the walls—

Bob Dylan looking surly and about fifteen, demonstrators being firehosed, an Indian miniature with a blue elephant head on a dancing man, a torn reproduction of a painting of Judith holding Holofernes' head. (She hoped Seth didn't think of Judith as date material, though she was beautiful; it was more likely that some Judy had turned him down and he thought of her that way, as a killer. He had not been a forgiving boy.) There was a picture of Georgia O'Keefe's breasts from the Museum of Modern Art, and a picture of Lyndon Johnson wearing ass's ears.

Seth had a piano in his room, an old upright someone had been giving away, on which he used to pound out blues progressions. She wondered if he got to play piano where he was now.

She'd gone through his papers for some clue as to why or where, but they were just old math assignments and things like his satin-stitched Cub Scout merit badges in the drawers. Because Nina couldn't sew (and Milt, who could, wasn't asked), Seth used to pin them to his uniform with safety pins. The pins were still stuck through the badges' cloth, browning and spotted by corrosion. Maude ritually went through the embroidered circlets before huddling again on the bed, feeling, as always, that if she'd known how to sew then, she could have kept him from leaving, though he had left so many years later. He had grown raspberry-colored, screaming at Nina, screaming, when she admitted she couldn't help him attach the badges, Maude looking on, an astonished four-year-old.

Sitting on the bed, she remembered lying on the black couch later that day, when she had started feeling there was a veil between her and everything. She had never been able to throw this feeling off, and she thought of it just that way, as an endless net of filmy dark chiffon over her face and body, transparent but interfering, that caught and clung when she tried to pull it away.

She was startled from these dreamy reflections and mysteries by a loud squawk from her father, come downstairs. Not, she hoped, where he would see that she emerged from Seth's room rather than her own across the hall.

"What?"

Milt stood with a broom raised overhead, thrashing at the ceiling. There was a frenzied sound like towels being snapped. Then it stopped. Milt was breathing heavily. He pointed.

The redwinged blackbird, with a somehow baleful expression, huddled against the glass back wall, flatfooted, looking back over his shoulder at the giant and giantess.

"Oh, Daddy—I thought he was dead. The heat must have revived him!"

"Ugh! It's disgusting, a bird in the house."

Maude looked at her father in wonder that he felt disgust where she saw a miracle. The bird began fluttering along the window again, scratching against the glass with its spiny, futile feet, trapped within the modernistic square of the lowest pane. Milt came over, paddling with his broom. Maude cried, "Daddy, stop, no, you're terrifying it." She achieved a second time-out, and the bird once again settled, visibly palpitating, a picture of rumpled misery.

"Here—give me the broom. *Give* it to me, Daddy. Dammit. Now leave the room. Or at least stand *back*. Jesus. The poor thing could die of fright."

"I could die. I thought the goddamn thing was a bat."

Maude let her lids fall to slits over dead eyes. "Just stay still. All right? Promise?"

The bird flew to the highest corner and fluttered frantically along the join between window and ceiling. Maude took one step forward, then another. As she got near the left end of the window, farthest from the door (which Milt had propped open), the bird threw itself to the right. Slowly she took a small step to the right and stood still. The bird flapped rightward. She took another, and, again, the small creature moved on.

By slow steps and with some retreats, as if they were playing Mother May I, the bird made its unwitting way toward freedom, all the while thinking freedom was just where it was. The window looked like sky.

Then it found the place where it could get through. Bursting at last into a piece of this obdurate sky that gave way, it was gone.

Milt found the joy in his daughter's face as she turned to him unbearable. He'd be the Partridge, the Immerman, whose book she would leave disdainfully in the dust. She would leave and be successful and have a better life. Because of that school. She would leave too.

4.

"YOU NEVER HEARD Beethoven?"

Danny Stern grinned, smooth, olive-skinned, his eyes lustrous, soft, and amused. "Nope. Was just a name to me."

"How could you never hear Beethoven? It's on the radio."

"Not the station my parents play."

"What does it have?"

"Cocktail music. I don't know. Perry Como."

"I used to like Perry Como. On *TV.* I can't believe I'm admitting that. Well, except for his singing."

"You liked him *except* for his singing?"

When they stopped laughing, she said, "So when did you finally hear Beethoven? I mean, I'm assuming that you have *now.*"

He looked as if he had something delicious in his mouth. "It's the first week of school, right? Heck does his song and dance about the music library, all those shelves of, you know, boxed sets. Not just Beethoven, but you can compare Von Karajan with Kondrashin or whatever. I mean, I'd heard all these names, but it was like the names in the Bible. You don't expect to get to meet Moses or Gabriel. So, I take out this set of Beethoven symphonies—"

"Von Karajan or Kondrashin?"

"Are you kidding? Von Karajan, of course. And I go into a listening room and start with Symphony Number One, and I just go on. I think it was like five, six hours. I just listen until the Ninth is done. And I'm like—I can't tell you. It was—it was amazing." He closed his eyes in a way that, instead of shutting her out, seemed to include her in the most intimate privacy.

She turned her head away, as nervous as if he had touched her. His shelves—looking improvised and, so, as out of place as possible amid the oppressive décor, which really was décor, as if ordered all at once from Bloomingdale's—were neatly ranged with Beethoven, at the end near the Bach cantatas, and running through a record of songs by Hugo Wolf. He had his own record player, with speakers that folded out like the panels of a tryptich. "High Fidelity" said embossed squares in the corners of the tweedy boxes. He put on the Wolf. Really sad songs, not that she could understand the German.

"So, do you listen to Beethoven all the time now?"

"Never." He looked both pleased and rueful.

"That's awful!"

"It was too much. I listened too much. I used it up or something."

"But it was only a year ago." Maude was shocked. Her aesthetic pieties were outraged. "You can't ever use up Beethoven."

Danny shrugged. "There's a lot of other great stuff."

"But the greatest stuff—the whole point of it is that you can't use it up. I mean—" But she encountered within herself an unwelcome little plug or blockage, and she knew exactly what it was, her unwillingness to admit that she no longer felt for Botticelli the pious fervor she had felt only the year before, in which even the least bit qualified or tempered assessment of his work felt to her like a personal attack. She had discovered herself in these pictures and secretly embraced them as *the* way to paint—color without paint texture, all flowing line and limber, limpid decoration. If only someone would teach her how to use egg tempera.

Because of the coincidence that, at home, the cover of the Pughs' album of Beethoven's Seventh was a reproduction of *La Primavera* (one of the cheapie albums Milt was always picking up at Roosevelt Field), Maude heard that music as a ballet of the Three Graces, of Flora presiding in a flowery dress of the kind Maude espoused, of getting handsome Mercury's attention and rolling on the carpet of spicy crushed flowers . . . She felt herself to be the melancholy lovelies in the picture. They themselves seemed to be representations of the artist's yearning and, so, embodiments not only of all that was lovable in women but of the very consummation that art represented, consummation as intensely rich and desired as the other kind and doomed to disappoint. The women looked like objects of desire, but their hurt, puzzled, yet detached expressions were the portraits of the artist's need to create them and his own sadness at, having done so, still lacking satisfaction.

She had felt, in short, in the picture (and so in the music) a way to be an artist and herself, Maude, a girl. And before she even got there, already it was failing her. It had already begun to feel wan, distant, faintly immature, like the poet-faced doodles that covered all of her last year's textbooks in purple ink. Nobody else's work, however much you loved or identified with it, could show you your own work. Maude knew that any artist's vision was as individual and differentiated as an individual face and as little to be meddled with; that your duty as an artist was to make your sense of things manifest in the world, and that if you did this faithfully and fully enough, the world would feel its meaning and take it into its own heart.

She ventured articulating this to Danny Stern.

"You mean like fucking?"

She could only imagine what that might be like, as she could only imagine what realization as an artist would be like, though she had spent an enormous part of her life so far fantasizing about one or the other. "Well—or love," she answered, feeling her ears hot. "Both sides have to go out of themselves toward the other." The blush only got worse. She looked at him, daring him to let on that it all meant too much to her.

He considered what she said in his prudent, doctorish, fair-minded way. "It's funny. These things, I mean, the books you love and all that stuff, they give you so much, you kind of worship the beings who make them. But it makes them, the artists, you know, seem kind of inhuman."

"You mean, 'cause you couldn't write *War and Peace* or a Beethoven sonata?"

"Yeah."

"But you could write a Danny Stern."

"Nah. I couldn't." He grinned his good-natured grin.

"And that's what you love the art for. It's *so* human—it's where you meet the parts of yourself—you feel *more* understood, in a weird way, in a work of art that you can love. You feel as if you're in it; you feel as if it's *about* you."

"That's true."

"You feel it *is* you. Or that you made it."

"That," he said, "I never feel."

She snorted in annoyance. He must be lying. How could you not feel that?

Before she could voice her skepticism, she felt something soft and warm touch her eyelids. Kisses. She had not even taken in his face coming at hers so that she had closed her eyes in automatic self-protection. He kissed each closed eye and then somehow they were kissing each other's mouths. The feeling of the other time, with the sideburned senior, poured back, only more keenly. It was a surprise to feel it, but she had felt it once before, so after the surprise of its presence, she could greet it, in a sense, welcome it back. After the first bout of kissing, they pulled back and looked at each other, side by side on the soft, thick carpeting. She looked into his face and the feeling increased. That hadn't happened before. It became too strong and they had to lock their mouths together. As if through the mouth came the rest of the body and all the feelings within it.

᯽

They spent hours and weeks of the winter and spring semesters in Danny's room or sneaking into Seth's entombed chamber, making out. They themselves used the ugly term, heedless of the way it deprecated the sweetness and intimacy of what passed between them. Or not wanting to share it with the rest of the world.

Though there was also the immense comfort of being seen by the world as linked. After the first inadvertent, gasping tussle on Danny's floor, however, Maude felt she would be ruined by being seen with him. She confided in Weesie, or tried to. "Don't you think he looks kind of goony and *young*?"

"Kind of young maybe. I don't know. He has those beautiful eyes."

Maude didn't know if she liked Weesie noticing Danny's beautiful eyes. "But I mean, he's kind of not romantic. I mean, I didn't exactly put him on, you know, that list." The list of desirable boyfriends already seemed childish, and a long time ago.

"He's the smartest boy in school," said Weesie factually, and Maude felt a fool. She hadn't noticed. He was so modest and uncompetitive, the thought did not occur. He didn't need to compete. He didn't chase success. He didn't seem to fear failure. Maybe he didn't need to.

She was more aware of his easy grasp after that. She felt his modesty as a law she had unconsciously observed, as if praise were insult and it would offend him for appreciation to be lavished. But her appreciation was in an odd way a new appreciation for herself. She had to explain herself to almost everyone.

She didn't have to explain herself to Danny Stern. Or not quite
so much.

Maude's clamorous social anxieties and the steeliest competi-
tive edge of her ambitions were softened, tempered, or muffled
from within this nest of safety and understanding. She felt
strong enough with Danny to dare to go on her way and be
happy. For a while.

5.

"I can't believe you'd go away for months, just like that, without me."

"You knew I was applying, Maudlin."

"I didn't think you'd *go*. Don't call me that."

At the end of his junior year, Danny was beginning to look no longer just boyishly pretty but manly and so, even to Maude, handsome. They were in a bucolic park she had asked to go to, where people offered stale bread to swans and geese along a calm, narrow river flowing between bands of velvet grass, blooming shrubs and trees, and artful groves. She had just used up her last bread—the last of a loaf Nina had made, that collapsed back to what seemed a state of raw grain in Maude's fingers—gulped by the greedy geese who looked astonished by what they had taken in, their heads popping up like burps at the ends of their long necks almost in Maude's face, they were so tall. She had been laughing, talking to them like overgrown children. Then the couple came to the giant beech that was like a cathedral inside the dark embrasure of its branches, and he had said casually that he'd been accepted for the two months in Africa that summer. Maude had her hand on the grainless bark, over the scar of a heart cut into it with two names inside. HOLLY+DAVE 4EVER.

"You'd never carve my name on a tree," she went on, low Maria Callas tremolo.

Danny dug into his jeans pocket and came up with the red enamel of a Swiss Army knife.

"No. Don't hurt the tree."

He threw it up in the air, casting his gorgeous, lustrous eyes to heaven.

"Don't make fun of me!"

"Maude. Maude." He took her wrists. "Stop giving me orders a second."

She let him hug her and in fact clung to his neck, pressing into him. Then pushed him away:

"I hate you. You don't give a shit about me. Just about some people you never met, because they're poor and black and—chic." She knew this wasn't true: he was the kind of person who would refrain from something like joining the Peace Corps if he thought it was too easy a way of looking good. Not that he was old enough for the Peace Corps; his program was a sort of pre-premed clinic in tropical diseases. "The cost of your plane fare could probably keep a whole village healthy for a genera- tion." She flung herself out of the beech cathedral through a wall of leaves.

Danny bent to retrieve his penknife from the cool grassless ground before following her out. It was a shock to come back to sunlight on the broad lawn. Maude was standing in the middle, surrounded by acres of perfect grass, clearly lost in her own dark- ness. She let him walk up to her without running away.

"How do you know you'll come back? You might get some horrible disease. The plane might—. Or maybe some nice medical student—some girl who actually likes science, someone sensible, someone *literal*." By this time she looked as tragic as if she'd already lost him.

"Maude—I'm *here*, for God's sake. Look up! I'm not going anywhere."

"You're not?"

"I mean, I *am* going, but I'm *with* you. Don't you get that?"

"No," she moaned. "No. I don't see how—"

"It's *two months*."

"When my brother—I remember exactly when it was two months. I kept like expecting every day, today he'll come back—if I just believe, if I just have faith—and I'd trick myself into seeing him. You know how you can see someone disppearing around a corner, you're sure it's them—I'd go unlock the door at night after Milt checked that it was locked, so he could get in. My father *patrols* the house every night to make sure we're safely locked in. In this really *angry* way. Anyway, it was when I realized it was exactly two months that it occurred to me I might never see him again. He might be—"

"I'm not your brother, for God's sake. Don't map your family onto me. I mean, really. Here I am. How can you talk about your *brother*?"

"But how can you want to leave?"

His eyes, normally so soft and lustrous, sparked, and his lower lip stiffened with anger.

"Please don't be angry at me."

He made a helpless sound and let her burrow into his arms.

"Please don't leave," she said into his warm, delicious shoulder. "I wish you wouldn't." He would leave no matter what she said. "I don't understand why you want to go."

"It has nothing to do with you, Maude. Don't you see? It's just something I want, and being temporarily away from you is just an unfortunate side effect."

"I don't understand how you can want it if you can't be with me."

He let out a great compression of air but just patted her back. They both knew she'd lost.

Perhaps to give her something, almost by way of a promise, the next time they were alone together in his bedroom of a

future professional, he helped her slide on a condom and guide
him into her.

She had wanted to from the start—it had been he who was
cautious, even when he said he couldn't stand it. She hated his
self-control. Repeatedly, she couldn't stand it but had had to bear
it. By this point, they had been naked together, had touched each
other everywhere. To let the most intimate parts of themselves
go inside and embrace each other's seemed at once surreal and
unremarkable, not a big deal.

But it was. He was slow and careful and, still, it had been so
painful. She knew it had to get better or women wouldn't be
able to stand it. The thin, sensitive tissue seemed to strain and
pull less when he was all the way in, but each time he moved,
she was shocked at the intense jab she felt where she had never
before experienced sensation. She showed the pain by no more
than jagged intakes of breath. "Are you all right?" he'd say, halting, and she'd say yes, to encourage him to go on.

By the next day, the very soreness felt pleasurable, triumphant,
and at the same time like a seismic gulch gaping to be filled. At
the least she already doubted what she remembered and needed
to test the sensation again, like a second olive or a second sip of
a parent's martini. But he was flying that day. She had thought
consummation would give her a way of holding on to him while
he was away. But—much as adults had always warned—it made
it more painful.

They said goodbye on the phone. They had agreed it would
be better if she didn't have to go with his parents to the airport
she still thought of as Idlewild—his prosaic parents, the bald-
ish, matter-of-fact businessman father and stolid mother who
it seemed astonishing should have hatched him, these people
who couldn't even have imagined him.

6.

D ANNY HAD LEFT as soon as classes were over, not staying the rest of Bay Farm's unusually long (for a private school) year, for the beautiful ceremonies the last week of school, the graduation of those Danny's own class was about to replace. Maude remembered the year before, when it was like falling in love with the place. She had come into a sense of ownership. For this year's madrigals and lushness and frenzy of preparations, she was like an established matron, replete in her requited, sealed, and approved love. But in all of this she felt both the absence of her love and a connection to him: the school had brought them together, and everyone there saw them as representatives, in a sense, of each other.

Then the year ended. Maude, once again working at the public library, alone in the artificial town with her father, felt marooned, lifelines snapped. Weesie too was unavailable, busy in a museum intern program in the city that Mary Jane had arranged for her.

As a few sad irises struggled through the weeds of the back-yard, Maude was still waiting for Danny's first letter. Instead, through the slot in the pink front door came a letter from Bay Farm, addressed to Milton and Nina, saying that, due to the increase in the Pughs' income, Maude's scholarship had been reduced for the following year.

Milton handed it to Maude to read and dropped the bill that came with it into the trash.

"Daddy—what are you doing?"

"Well, at prices like that, we're certainly not sending you back."

"What do you mean?"

"I mean we can't afford it." With that, he turned and went up to his studio, where in moments the classical station and the happy scratching of brushes could be heard.

He had recently discontinued a number of his classes. Though he had more than enough canvases for several shows, he was painting, with the upcoming show in mind, a group of pictures to hang together. He didn't have to tell Maude that he was buying time with the painting sales, time for his own work. Still. There had to be more money. The *school* said so. They saw the tax returns.

As when someone close to you dies, it takes a while, sometimes a long while, for the fact of this disappearance and absence to be believed as death, so Maude at first did not absorb the news that she would not be returning to Bay Farm. There wasn't any something-else. Every once in a while she stopped herself, to make it real, to remind herself: she caught herself planning what she was going to do for her next Selected Work week and then remembered: right, I won't be doing that; that won't be happening. She fantasized what she would wear for graduation and then remembered. She thought of which teachers she had hoped to have for certain courses, which school jobs, evening programs, a certain person she had just begun a tentative friendship with—it was as if each element, large and small, had to be fondled and considered in detail for her to say goodbye—and she couldn't say goodbye.

One afternoon in the library, working the untrafficked checkout desk, she composed a letter on the library scratch paper (old notices Xeroxed on yellow paper, cut into eighths and stacked

blank side up) with the stubby eraserless pencils the library supplied for jotting down call numbers. It addressed her headmaster,
but it was a love letter to the school, or a eulogy. She wrote about
what Bay Farm meant to her—what she had learned there, how
great the people were, how she wished she were going back. She
used a whole stack of the little chrome-yellow slips. Later, when
she was typing out overdue notices, she typed the letter.

She imagined the decision as all in the hands of the headmaster, a genial, ineffectual fellow who, in truth, putting his hands
nervously in his pockets and looking away the few times he had
spoken to her, found Maude Pugh discomfitingly intense and
cosmopolitan. But she thought: a plea of love like that, surely
they would forgive the tuition, make some arrangement, let her
stay. Teachers—except the ones who couldn't stand her—valued
her, she knew it. She was practically a faculty stepchild! Faculty
children went to the school free . . .

Within hours of dropping it into the jaws of the blue metal
mailbox, she wished she could pull the letter back.

❧

When an envelope came through the door, she felt a pang of fear
and then a thumping, slightly nauseating relief that was almost
the same as disappointment. The flimsy overseas envelope with
its florid, exotic stamps was from Danny. She rushed into her
room and lay on the bed with it against her chest until her heart
slowed, as if she could absorb him through the paper. But she
couldn't wait to see what he had to say.

"Oh, Maude, I miss you and love you," it began. "I wish you
could be here so I could share this with you in a real way," his clear,
flowing, fountain pen-blue script read. What he then described
reminded Maude of films she had been shown in elementary
school UNICEF programs, of African children with yaws. The
surroundings had been dusty and squalid, the children crying or befuddled, their mothers impassive, the few men shown

who weren't doctors making sharp, angry gestures. She couldn't imagine feeling welcome there, but Danny said it was amazing how friendly everyone was.

Mostly the letter was about the other kids in the program and the leaders and—since it was written almost on arrival—about their twenty-hour trip on a cheap propellor-plane flight, followed by a ride in the back of an open truck with their frame knapsacks and duffel bags. "There's only one word for a bunch of rich kids singing 'I Ain't Gonna Work on Maggie's Farm No More' in the back of a truck on a barely existing track through an African jungle: surreal." There had been a rat in the back of the truck, enormous, and they had shooed it out, shrieking and making cracks.

> Dear Danny,
>
> I can't put enough into that "Dear." It sounds so pathetic. I imagine the feeling of your skin, touching your cheeks, and then I can't stop imagining, and so I've been in bed all afternoon, *not* sleeping. Sweaty. It's incredibly hot here, and I try to think what it's like there and if it's even worse, and right away I'm with you under that mosquito net (I hope there's a mosquito net and not with a hole in it—please don't get malaria). Being there with you in my mind, it is hours before I come back to this room or the reality of this letter. The only reality we have right now. The only us. I feel as if, while you're there, you're so far away. Of course you *are* far away, but I mean you are going away while you're there, changing, while I'm in the same place, not changing. I'll try not to whine. It's a sin to despair, I remember.

Maude sat with her pen over the tissuey air-mail paper she had bought with her library money for writing to Danny. How could she convey the *is*-ness of it all? What she wanted was to convey herself; transport herself. But should she even be writing? He thought she was a Bay Farmer, and she wasn't. Just a girl from Levittown.

The pen was slippery with sweat and humidity. At the library she had a fan, but in her room the wet, heavy air seemed part of the general oppression of the household. On a pad she added up the amount she would earn for the summer and subtracted it from the amount of tuition. It left over a thousand dollars. Two Milton Pugh paintings, she figured; one, maybe; but she couldn't think how *she* could make the money. Which was really the only solution.

She was embarrassed to tell Danny any of this. If he were there, she could tell him, and he would make up the difference by caring. But he seemed remote in more than miles. Maybe he didn't care. Maybe she'd made a fairy tale of him.

She had written pages of longing for him in a letter already sent, which he probably had not yet received. She pushed down the weightless page. The sheet of ruled lines that considerately came with the stationery showed through clearly. She lifted her hand off the stationery and watched the lines cloud and become diffuse. She felt that it would take just nothing, the merest slip, for her to end up like the hapless painters Saul Partridge and Immerman. She'd always thought art would save her, if nothing else did. Maybe they had too.

She had biked home from the library with groceries from the Grand Union in the shopping center and as usual made dinner for her father and herself. Planning meals and trying out new recipes offered the chief variation of her days, and she found herself focusing on it in the slow hours, looking at *The New York Times Cook Book* in the library, thinking about making a scallion soufflé with the onion grass that grew in the empty lot and wondering whether that would go well with the string beans dangling in the garden and looking up different ways to cook them. And then they ate the increasingly elaborate and accomplished meals in silence.

"My goodness, look at that," Milt said when she brought the soufflé to the table. She thought of soufflés as something fancy, upper-class and unknown. She hadn't realized it was considered a bit of a triumph to get one to rise, particularly in a dented aluminum pot. She couldn't understand why cooking had eluded her mother—all you had to do was follow the recipe. It was so much easier than art. It always turned out.

"Well, Maude, you could be a professional chef if you wanted."

Maude looked as if she smelled something bad instead of steamy egg and baked Gruyère. He would never have said something like that to Seth—Seth who would be *lucky* to be able to be a chef. He'd be glad for *Seth* to carry on and be an artist, he wouldn't regard *Seth* as competition . . . She didn't let her eyes rise to her father's gaze. Yes, he would like it if I were a *cook*. He wants me not even to try.

It seemed dangerous to let him know her thoughts or anything she might want: he was sure to keep her from having something, if he thought she wanted it. Seth always said what he wanted and he always wanted too much. With big fights, he got much of what he wanted in the end. But with her, she only got what she wanted if she kept it a secret.

Nevertheless, she let out, "I *don't* want. As you know."

Though it was even more perverse than that, what happened inside her. It suddenly seemed glamorous to be a professional chef, attractive; and at the same time an utter attack on her that he should suggest it; that he saw her that way.

That was the first time he called her the Ice Princess. As in, "Well. The Ice Princess speaks. Not good enough for you, is it? You think you're so high and mighty. Think you're better than where you come from. Just see how long that lasts, now that you're not at that cockamamie school." As if *she* had done something to hurt *him*.

Before July ended, Maude heard from the headmaster. He said he was so moved by her "lovely letter"; she described the specialness of Bay Farm so well; could he, he wondered, have her permission to reprint passages as part of the next alumni fundraising appeal?

PART IV

1.

DANNY WAS PICKING her up in his parents' giant Caddie. He'd been back a whole day before he called, a black mark against him already. She wanted just to be glad, but resentment dragged at her.

He got out of the car to watch her walk the path to him. He'd changed. The preparations of her imagination left too much out; they had changed or reduced him, so that the reality of him was a shock. It was as if everything she had thought or remembered was a little wrong, and everything about him was not only subtly different but a little contradictory, so that he looked at once thinner and broader, older and younger. His face wouldn't coalesce. It was both handsome and weirdly stretched and rubbery.

It seemed even stranger that he was unaware of this and responded to her just as always, his words spaced out by laughter. His arms opened to wrap around her in a huge clasp. Danny never made declarations, and his measured, gentle affection never suggested the kind of desperate passion that could give Maude the reassurance she craved—of being the unique entity that could satisfy a bottomless need. This hug delighted her with its enthusiasm.

She disengaged herself quickly, however. They were still at the curb, the studio window above them like Milton's jealous, baleful eye. She got herself into the big, heavy car, its hot seat not uncomfortable in the air-conditioning. Air-conditioning! As he drove, Danny took his hand off the wheel and put it on her thigh, where she covered it with both her own. She was letting out only the good feeling and hiding the resentment. Maybe the resentment would go away. On a shady street where the houses were set far back, he pulled over and kissed her until they were both gasping.

At his parents' tomblike house, they ran up the pretentious curved staircase and shut themselves into his room, giggling and shushing. "Wait, wait," he said. "I have to show you. I brought you something." He rummaged next to the head of his bed and whirled to unroll a rug over the beige carpeting.

"Oh, my God, Danny! It's beautiful."

"It's East African." He had traveled a little at the end of his medical stint.

The rug was mostly a deep orangey-yellow, with small squares of red and cobalt, stair-stepping to make a diamond and two triangles. Square-headed lions marched across a darker orange in the mosaic of the border. The rug was like panels of sun on the floor. It made her think of Greenwich Village apartments she had visited. She thought of a song she'd heard that summer, high-voiced, that evoked such a life—music with an acoustic guitar (Seth would approve). It suggested, as Maude had always wanted to believe, that if you had the material things right—sunshine, a bowl of oranges, a farmhouse—happiness followed. Better living through design.

They lay on the rug. It scratched their bare skin as they writhed, reasserting their claims on each other. They wouldn't feel able to talk until this was accomplished. "Oh, oh," came deeply out of Danny as he rolled them both to their sides. "Now I've really come home."

"Dann-nee?" They heard his mother's creaking footsteps approach down the hall.

"Just a minute, Ma. I'll be right out."

He jumped into his cutoffs and T-shirt no more quickly than Maude pulled on her scrap of a calico dress and the bikini underpants, which now stuck to her.

As soon as he came back, holding a Dannon yogurt his mother had given him—she was afraid he was too thin—and rolling his eyes, Maude announced, "I'm not going back to Bay Farm this year."

"What do you mean?" he said, licking off some yogurt that had gotten onto his finger. He handed the full carton to her. Raspberry, her favorite. It seemed a wonder to her, nourishment produced like that, by a mother, unasked for, as by magical hands in a fairy tale, or Mrs. O'Donnell. She looked into the little round cup, swirled with deep pink.

"Milt won't pay my tuition. My scholarship got reduced because he had more money, but he says it's really because I'm not smart enough, and he says he can't afford it anyway, that he's had to struggle and do without the whole time. He said he hasn't paid the phone bill in three months."

Danny immediately said, "I have savings. Use my money. That's ridiculous. The man should be shot. What's his problem?"

If a stranger had seen Maude at that moment, they might have laughed. Her mouth was a perfect O of stunned surprise. She couldn't believe she'd just gotten what she'd hoped for, for much longer back than she had wanted even Bay Farm.

"Danny! Can you? Do you really think you should? That's—I mean, your *savings*. I'll pay you back, of course." Surely he would hate her for it if she accepted and, after a while, wish he hadn't done it. "Do you know how much money it is?"

He swaggered across the room, picked something up off his young-suburbanite teak desk and tossed it to her. She fumbled but caught it with her elbow against her ribs. It was a passbook, in its plastic envelope.

"Go ahead. Open it."

She had to turn a number of pages to get to the current balance, but she got the idea. It was a lot of money. Six figures. It could pay full tuition for years at Bay Farm, more years than anyone could go there.

She hadn't known how exposed generosity—or charity—could make you feel. This might be the most personal act that anyone had ever committed with her. When that hairy senior had tingled her nipples and she had felt the shock of someone else's fingers in her labia, it was almost impersonal. This was the closest anyone had ever been willing to come. Money was private. It was unmentionable. It was bad form not to have it, because then you had to say things like, "I don't have the money for that." You had to have money to be able to afford not talking about it.

And her father had been venomous about it—as if she had set out to deprive him. She had always known better, before, not to ask for things, and she'd been right.

Milt would say the Sterns were vulgar and nouveau riche and that this was a typically vulgar nouveau riche thing to do.

She thought: I should be happier.

Because what she wanted was for Milt to want to make her happy, even if he couldn't. For him to say, I'm sorry, baby, I'd love for you to have Bay Farm.

And she wanted Bay Farm to want her. To value her enough to help her over this hump.

It felt surreal and furtive for it to be Danny, and when she still felt far away from him. She had always had reservations about Danny—secret, guilty, critical thoughts. She felt very guilty for them at that moment. Even for the reservations that were, so to speak, on his side: she would envision him with various girls, the ones she thought of as the "good girls," the ones who did well in unconnotative work like algebra and French grammar and took things like having eventual husbands and children as their right, just like their skiing vacations and Easter in Barbados; girls who had sunny, even expectations of life, who embraced it with cheerful enthusiasm rather than Maude's crablike wariness.

She would probe him now and then—didn't he think Didi Bates was a dish? Or someone else of his own healthy disposition. And he would surprise her by saying, "She's boring." The surprise was as much at her own lack of gratification by this as at the sentiment itself. Couldn't *he* see how wrong for him she, Maude, was? She had allowed herself to feel contempt for his lack of perception, as if loving her made him a fool (the voice of Seth she carried around in her, especially since his death-like disappearance, that said loving her made anyone a fool). She had taken it for granted that when Danny got to Harvard there would be some suave, confident Cliffie, and that would be that.

She had even suggested Weesie—she could imagine their sparky jokiness together. "Weesie? Are you kidding? Never!" he had said, as mystified that she could propose it as she was that he didn't see the beauty. *She* would take Weesie over her.

But anyway she was saved, saved for the time being, and Danny was her hero, though she inwardly squirmed to imagine how it would take place—would he hand her a check? How could she even bring it up?

Impatiently, Maude waited for Monday so that she could call the school. She didn't know if it was even possible for her to re-enter the class of '70. School started in a matter of days. Levittown Memorial High School started a day sooner than that. She had gone to the fortresslike brick building in June, to register. It felt like being drafted for the Army, to put her name down there, or like joining some list where an experiment was to be done on your body, where you were to be subjected to a disfiguring, possibly fatal disease, and this was wanted of you, wanted for you.

By Monday morning she was so anxious that she misdialed the school's number twice before getting the placid ringing. She listened to the tinkling trills as if they were the knells of fate. "Come *on*." The secretary put her through to the headmaster. It was all first names.

They had accepted a couple of new juniors, the headmaster told her. The class was full. Since she'd been a student in good standing, however—she could hear his discomfort in saying this; she knew he disliked her, and she felt hyperintellectual and *Jewish* in his presence—they could probably make room for her, he said, as they would not for an outsider.

She wasn't an outsider! "Re-prie-ved," she thought, in the tune from *The Threepenny Opera*.

That was the good thing about having parents like Milt and Nina, the very good thing: you were filled with the world's riches. You could have *La Primavera* as your favorite painting as a kid, because you sat around looking at your father's art books; you knew all the Brecht-Weill songs; you could think of a poem when you needed one, at least some of the time. You knew about Bay Farm and how to go there.

That morning, Milt looked at her as if for explanation. They were having toast and coffee, as always, over the *Times*. Maude was waiting for the front section. "Danny invited me on a bike trip," she said, so happy that it felt like a substance inside her that would come out, as she spoke, like light.

It was true that Danny had invited her—the night before. She was determined to let Milt know nothing until it was absolutely locked up. She smiled at him. She laughed. What she'd been given made her feel dangerously generous.

Milton grimaced, as if she were laughing at him. "What?" he said. She continued laughing. "*What?*"

She said she couldn't explain.

Then, as she went out the door: "I think I'm going to be going back to Bay Farm."

❀

It was an extraordinary day, perfect for their bike expedition, golden sun and just a hint of chill in the shade, like mint. What can he do? He can't do anything, she assured herself. He can't stop me. The bolt of fear through her chest made her eyes tear. "Danny!" She ran down the walk to her savior and, in the big car's front seat, clung to him like a little girl.

"What is it?"

"Nothing. I'm just glad to see you." She twisted to peer behind her. Milt stood in the pink doorway, looking grim. But he also looked bewildered. He looked abandoned.

Danny followed Maude's glance, saw Milt and offered his cheery wave. Milton started as if he thought he might have been invisible. He jerked his hand in a tentative wave back, a forced, self-conscious expression on his face.

Danny had picked their bikes up from school.

Maude thought Long Island the ugliest place, all commercial strips and "developments," as her parents called the grids of identical houses Levittown had spawned, spreading like mold across the landscape. It was always an amazement to come into the range of the estates. Almost surreally, you could turn off of the clogged ugliness that was Northern Boulevard and be on a shady lane with horses grazing, ponds glimpsed through willow fronds, lush fields.

They left the car off, at the entry to a track with a chain across it. Their destination was an estate that had recently been opened to the public. Here and there along their way, a twig of maple was precociously showing color.

"Are you sure you know the way?" said Maude. The car, left at the private road, looked like a friend they were deserting. She was well aware that what to her was a long, difficult ride was to Danny the merest little one-hand-behind-his-back exercise. She was the kind of rider who kept the handlebars in a death grip. Only with keyed-up, always-on-the-alert-for-fatality Weesie did Maude feel okay about her own relation to physical risk or exertion: Weesie was so anxious and nervous that Maude could almost be the normal one. "There won't be too many hills, will there?" Most of Long Island is flat as the landing strips, but there are hills on the North Shore. They had learned it in school: the terminal moraine.

Danny smiled. "Think I'd do that to you on this old junker?" He shook his head as he lifted out her beat-up Schwinn. "There are a couple of hills, but they're not too bad."

"Oh, great. Sure." She knew Danny's idea of "not too bad."

"Really." He was laughing—as well he might, she thought, looking at the gears and levers on his bladelike ten-speed racer.

She got her crotch over the boy-bike bar. "You should at least have a bike that's the right size," said Danny, not for the first time.

It was Seth's bike. Her previous bike, a tiny two-wheeler, had also been Seth's, at first too big for her and then too little. Before that, the tricycle. Nana Resnikov had given her that tricycle. It was red and shiny and new. Milt gave it away, to her best friend, who lived across the street. That was what he did: he made sure she didn't have what she wanted.

As if willful deprivation had enforced in her a need to do without, Maude shrugged: she wasn't wasting tuition money on a *bike*.

As she suspected, the way was longer and harder than Danny made it sound. He waited for her at the top of one long hill, at the end of which she wanted to pound him.

"It'll be great on the way back," he said, seeing her face.

"I hate downhill," she said through her teeth. "You *know* that." She braked all the way down hills.

They arrived hot and sweaty, Maude not speaking, not even willing to look at Danny. He followed after her like a well-trained dog that's been spoken to.

"I don't know why I agreed to come with you," she said, thunking down the canvas pack that held their lunch, without asking if he liked the spot. It was just such an outing when he'd told her about going away.

"Don't say that. Please, Maude. Don't ruin it."

"*Me* ruin it," she said, flashing ire at him out of those black-olive eyes.

Then she remembered what he was doing for her. "Sorry. Never mind." She began pulling packages out of Seth's old camp pack. She looked Danny in the face at last, at his melting eyes (baby seal eyes, she didn't stop herself thinking). She saw the muscles under his skin relax as he sensed forgiveness.

"Where's the blanket?" He was supposed to have brought the blanket. He wasn't carrying anything. "Jesus, Danny."

"And you've made such a beautiful lunch," he said mournfully, watching her lay it out. She tried not to make too great a show of distaste at having to lay plates in the grass.

It was the Pugh Picnic. Though it had been the dearest wish of the juvenile Maude and Seth to eat at every passing diner when on long drives, and they were clamorous in favor of Dunkin' Donuts and Jolly Roger, Pughs did not go in for such things. Too expensive, the children were sensibly told, and at the appropriate time, in the desirable spot, they would stop and have hard-boiled eggs, seasoned with salt from a twist of aluminum foil; tomatoes, and sometimes cucumber, that they would cut up on the spot; bread of solid character, buttered (not the Wonderbread the children craved); and a variety of cheeses, cut into slabs and wrapped in cellophane. There would be juice and milk in cartons, frozen the night before and still retaining jagged slivers, delicious to suck. Fresh fruit was to be cut into wedges, followed by cookies, disgorged from a ridged cylinder of foil wrapping.

At sixteen, Maude no longer saw any need for improvement in this except to add pieces of roast chicken, each preserved separately in tin foil, and the pretty enameled plates and cups Nina had once been given.

She herself felt pleased by this lovely plenty and her own providentiality, despite the missing refinement of a cloth to spread it on. It wasn't as if she could forget that; it irked her every second; she had to work at her enjoyment. But, gradually, the flame-throwing aspect of her irritation died away. Instead of irritation at Danny, there was merely something small but inconsolable in her at the lack of perfection in what so easily could have been perfect.

With a sigh of repleteness at the end of his feast, Danny lay back on the flawless grass with his hands behind his head. Maude felt free then to admire him. His gorgeous olive skin looked bronzed against the grass, the llama-lashes furring the tender lighter skin beneath his closed eyes, and a swag of black hair over a forehead that seemed to her now unequivocally manly. She didn't feel like a jerk for loving him.

Leaf shadows artistically dappled this prospect. Maude tried to imagine how she would paint him dappled by shadow. She could feel which colors she would use—she felt this in her fingers, as if she were squeezing the tubes. This was accompanied by an urgent feeling that had the savor of anxiety or despair, over whether there was any way she could get the arrangement of colors to communicate how it felt to be there and see him—that would make someone *her*, there, at that moment. It would always be another moment. She herself would never again be who she was at that moment. Customs, communication, culture would change.

She put a hand on his chest, its warm rising and falling. He loosed one of his hands from his head and placed it on top of hers, big, warm, and dry. He didn't open his eyes. "It's so nice to be in a place with grass and trees," he murmured.

"That's just about the most interesting thing you've told me about Africa," said Maude, who had found his letters frustratingly abstract, after the first one.

"Really? I thought I told you everything in my letters."

There was something about the way he said this. "It didn't seem like everything, Danny." She wasn't looking for anything in particular—just a filling out of experience. She'd wanted his letters to be like a novel or the kind of paintings she wished to make, so that she could feel what it was like to be there, at that moment. But then she knew there was something particular. Still as he was, he became stiller. He froze. His hand on hers was like dough. She slid hers out from under. "Danny?"

He heaved a sigh from the pit of himself, opened his eyes as if to check on the degree of danger in her face, and closed his eyes again.

Oh, don't let it be that, Maude thought. Let it be anything else. Let it be something he thinks is a big deal but I really don't. Something I don't care about, something bourgeois, convention-ally ambitious, some stupid nitpick over scientific ethics.

"It really wasn't anything, Maudlin. It was just a stupid—I didn't even like her."

Maude drew away. "Someone forced herself on you, did she?" she said. She was always self-possessed. She always had this horrible *poise.*

He let out air as if deflating and told her both more and less than she wanted to know. It was stupid. He described the girl well enough so that Maude could see it was true, that she had been the instigator, not that there was anything stopping Danny from holding her off. He had, at first. "But I just—I felt stupid."

"Yeah. You are."

Buxom. Blonde. Snappy as a firecracker. Johns Hopkins, not Radcliffe. There was that.

"I was going to tell you. Really."

She had plucked two blades of grass and was engaged in tying them together without breaking them. There. She plucked out two more. "Are you writing to her?"

"No. I was just—summer entertainment. She has a boyfriend."

"*That* seems to have been mutual."

"Maude. It really, really didn't matter. You're what matters."

"Well, if it really, really didn't matter, why do it?" She waited. In the face of his undenial, she added, "It matters. It. Matters. To me." She thumped her thorax.

Oddly, it was Danny who cried. But she could hardly spare him sympathy. First, there was that knife, or whatever it was, splitting her. It started in her chest and slashed down right through bone. It made it hard to breathe, but breathing was the least of her problems. Her problem was hurting so much, at his hands, and still wanting him to put his arms around her.

She began packing up instantly.

"Don't, Maude. Don't."

She wasn't moving with angry swiftness. She felt almost too weak to lift the trifling items. Nevertheless, she continued. Danny took the pack from her. Silently, she let him.

So urgently did Maude wish to get away and contemplate her hurt and confusion without distraction that for once she didn't brake all the way down the hill. She didn't remember the sudden turn at the bottom either.

Out of control, the bike swerved into a low stone wall, sending her somersaulting over the handlebars to land on the far side.

It was hard to convince Danny she was okay. The skin on one shoulder felt raw, but there wasn't any bleeding. Oddly, there would be a freckling of discoloration on the spot for the rest of her life; it would always look like a new abrasion.

The bike was mangled. It was still rideable, just, with the pincer of one brake squealing against the rear tire, its other half uselessly dangling.

2.

"**A**REN'T YOU INCREDIBLY *thin*?" said Weesie.

It was a rare afternoon that Weesie wasn't at school, when the days had gone from golden to gray—a Bay Farm "half-holiday," with no afternoon jobs or sports. You were supposed to use it to study. Maude was tagging along for Mary Jane's lesson with Milt to see Weesie.

"You should talk," said Maude. Weesie looked pleased and skeptical, as she did with all compliments, deflecting them. Maude added, "I just went off the pill, that's all."

Weesie raised her eyebrows and made a comical face: she didn't want to know. Maude was glad she didn't have to discuss her humiliation by Danny, and disappointed. She wouldn't have to reveal that particular confirmation of her unlovability, but she did wish Weesie cared. She wouldn't, however, supply Weesie with an added incentive to join the rats. If Maude was a sinking ship they were all deserting, she would damn well joke and laugh until the water covered her head.

"I wondered if you were still seeing him."

"I'm not." Maude didn't think Danny would give the reason away, since he and Weesie weren't the great buddies Maude thought they should be. With any other girlfriend, Maude would have been subject to relentless questioning, and there was, on Weesie's face, an uneasy look, as if she worried that she should do something. Maude realized it reminded her of Nina, this look—uncertain and dependent.

Weesie gave an uncomfortable Nina-ish little laugh and began telling Maude about something a mutual friend had done, a Bay Farm girl. Her reaction, weeks earlier, when Maude told her she wouldn't be continuing at Bay Farm, had been minimal. She had accepted Milt's reason, that he couldn't afford it, and it embarrassed her. It was clear she didn't want Maude to thrust the knowledge on her.

Maude had been dying to know everything that happened at school. But as Weesie went on, bringing in this person who'd done this and that person who'd done that, Maude felt worse and worse. The ground had shifted. A new culture had emerged, with conventions she didn't know. "Maddie?" said Maude, picking up on the mention of a girl none of them had liked.

"Sure Maddie," said Weesie, giving Maude a look as if she were being obstructive—a look of instruction, really; to keep Maude from her own uncoolness. To be cool is to know. "She's very *droll.*"

Maude wasn't missed, and not only was she replaced, but she was replaced by someone she didn't even like, someone *Weesie* didn't like. But she would justify rejection if she revealed how grudging and jealous she was. She mimed amusement, as if she too had always found Maddie Johnson "droll."

In a distant part of the house, the doorbell rang.

"Oh," said Weesie. "I meant to tell you. A couple of people said they might come by." The two girls were in Weesie's room, at Maude's request—Maude wanted to see what Weesie had brought back from her trip to Italy at the end of that summer. As Weesie rather helplessly pawed through this or that, it had become clear that she barely remembered and wasn't much interested. "Italy! It seems like five thousand years ago," she said.

"What's this?" said Maude, who had come across an etching leaning against the wall on Weesie's bookshelves.

"An etching."

"I know *that*."

"You *knew* I was taking art."

"No, I don't think I did. I mean, if you told me, I forgot." She turned away: "Not that I *would*." She turned back to the grayish little rectangle. "So you did this? You're talented."

"Oh, God, that's what my *mother* always says."

"That's not exactly aw—"

"We should go down."

Weesie ran out to shield her guests from Mrs. O'Donnell. Maude lingered, looking at things, as if her friend were there among the things—the little volume of *Howl*, the tiny Goreys (whose manner the etching somewhat imitated), the framed Pace illustration for a *New Yorker* cover. Voices came faintly from downstairs. She picked up the photo of Weesie from her days at Hills Girls School, where she'd worn a uniform. Weesie always joked, "You know how they say inside every fat woman is a thin one trying to get out? Well, inside me is a fat woman trying to get out." The real me, she'd called it. Pre-skinniness, pre-contacts. Pre-irony and febrile tension. There was the bud that made her upper lip like a beak, and the genial, direct gaze. She looked so easy to be friends with.

When Maude went down, surging into the living room were Isaac, who'd gone on the Italy trip—Maude used to think of him as her ally in the art room; when had he become Weesie's friend?—and a boy named Philip in whom Maude had always found an amusing sparring partner and enjoyable enemy. And there was the lumpish Maddie, whose only connection to these youthful aesthetes could be Weesie. It was a surprise to Maude that Weesie was friends with Philip, even more than Isaac had been. They were the art people.

"My, my, my," said Philip in his grand, cutting style, tossing back his greasy bangs. "So this is how the other half lives." Philip Neuberger was rich enough, but not the kind of rich that appears on the society pages. Donors to the American Jewish Committee didn't have balls at the Metropolitan Museum.

Isaac, sensitive and cultivated and almost overrefined, showed his appreciation of the reference with an upward curling on one side of his mouth.

"Lit ref," brayed Maddie.

Maude hadn't heard that term since Seth. It wasn't a literary reference. Jacob Riis was not literary. Just because it was a *book* title. "Lit ref." Good God.

In response to Philip's remark, Weesie wore her embarrassed-happy-disapproving face. It disclaimed the mortifications of wealth while firmly clutching the riches for her hospitality. She waved her long white arms like snakes, the bangle up above her elbow over a sleeve on her skinny upper arm. "Who wants wine?" It was a risqué offer. Always there was her keyed-up, heightened look of finding herself ridiculous, ridiculously funny, and expecting you to join in. And you did. Everyone smiled without knowing why. It was like a contact high.

Sensitive Isaac shrugged his narrow shoulders. "Sure," he said, closing his goatlike eyes. He had thick, ashy curls, as unfashionable at the end of 1968 as they had been for his whole adolescence. All the boy could do was manage a side part and let the dense mass bulge over one eye. With his skinny neck and full lips, he looked sprung from the 1930s.

He and Maude greeted each other with their usual half-suppressed smiles of being in on a private joke. The joke was that they were "intellectuals," a joke on them, that they couldn't help.

"So, I gather you're in college now," said Isaac, in his good-natured but ironically drawn-out way, his goat-eyes closing as he spoke.

College had been Milton's suggestion, surprisingly. He saw Maude come back from her bike outing, expressionless and saying nothing, as was her new mode in defense against Milt's new nastiness. "So what was that about going back to Bay Farm?" he'd mercilessly asked.

At dinner, apropos only of silence and chewing, he'd said, "Of course you could try community college."

"Com*mun*ity college?"

"Well, if it's not good enough for the Ice Princess, forget it. But I *thought* you might prefer it, since an ordinary high school is beneath Your Highness." He laughed at her expression. "If looks could kill."

"So, I could go to school with stupid older people instead of stupid younger ones."

"You snotty little snob."

"I think when something is shit, you should say it's shit."

Milt looked ready to come at her. He made a move such as a dog will make when it's offended but trying to keep its dignity, turning his head aside stiffly, so that she was conscious of the tendons and loosening skin of his neck. She wouldn't give him the excuse to hurt her physically. She had seen enough of that with Seth, who was openly rebellious. She had always been so pathetically super-good.

The next day, having inquired on her own, she told him that she would, after all, be starting there.

"I guess they'll take anyone."

"That's right, Daddy."

At sixteen, she was two years younger than the next-youngest in a very mixed class of former dropouts, middle-aged non-native-English speakers, prickly unwed mothers, and aspirants to private or state universities whose degrees might actually have some currency. Within a short time she was on something called the Dean's List that they posted in the hall, and then first in the class, a fact that caused her both pride and shame.

The grand Philip interrupted before Maude could answer

Isaac. "Yes—Miss Pugh, the artiste, is so far beyond the rest of us, she had to just skip two years of high school and go straight into the world."

Philip should have been widely disliked. He was plump and insulting, with dead-white skin like a slug and sharply articulated cherry lips. His greasy hair was always falling over his smeary glasses—but people tended to greet Philip's insults with smiles, as if they were love pats. He often had said to Maude, flourishing his brush as they stood at their easels, "*I* am an artist. *You* are an artiste."

Weesie responded for Miss Pugh, the artiste: "I don't think that place is brimming with artistes, Philip." Weesie thought it was pretty hilarious, community college. She didn't want to think of it as brimming with artistes. It ruined the stereotype. She hated Long Island too.

Mrs. O'Donnell brought a bottle of white wine on a tray with glasses. "I know you asked for the plain glasses, Miss Louise, but are you sure you'll not be having the white-wine glasses? Then I can bring you a bottle of red, at least, perhaps your guests would care for a wee touch of—"

Weesie beamed as if delighted with her, taking the tray. "No, Mrs. O'Donnell, really, you're too kind, not at all, Mrs. O'Donnell," managing her more in the lordly way Jock Herrick did—"Waiter, my chicken is not deboned." She would have been mortified to know of the resemblance.

The children heard Mrs. O'Donnell mutter from the hall, "Underage drinking. Bunch of young ruffians."

"You paid her to say that," said Philip, tossing back the greasy bangs and using his index and middle fingers to push up his glasses.

Weesie rolled her eyes. "She comes with the house," she said sotto voce, her eyebrows raised, and then shook with her crackling, generous laugh that people couldn't help joining in.

"Mmm," said Philip, tossing the bangs again and holding up

his glass of pale yellow wine, "tastes just like urine." He said it *you-rhine*.

Maude thought this the height of sophistication. Then Isaac said, "How would you *know*?"

"Touché, my boy, touché," said Philip, shooting the sleeve of his tweed jacket. Like every East Coast prep school boy, he wore jeans, in his case artistically dashed with a brushstroke or two, and an oxford shirt with his tweed. Isaac was nestled like a fuzzy chick into a fleecy shirt, rust-colored. He and Maude shared a love of autumn colors and artists who influenced no one. The first time they met, they practically clutched each other in their joy at encountering a teenager who cared about Emil Nolde and Ensor. Who'd *heard* of them.

"I think the wine is fine," said Maddie, hunched into a soft chair. Studious, somber, and defensive, Maddie always reminded Maude of a turtle drawing its head in.

Plump, white-faced Philip turned his back to her and said, close to Maude, "Remind me—why is our darling Louise friends with this cube?"

Maude, praying that Maddie couldn't hear—because, more than she disliked her, she felt sorry for her—responded, "But, Philip, don't you know? Weesie *aspires* to cubedom."

She'd never said it so flatly. It had always been a joke, because Maude didn't believe in Weesie's downward aspirations. As Maude spoke it, she felt defeated almost to the point of crying. Please don't be ordinary, she found herself praying as she looked over at Weesie. Please don't be like other people. As Maude looked at her, she realized that it was actually within the realm of possibility that Weesie might not be as exceptional as Maude believed. *Both* of them might not be.

More people arrived. I thought it would just be me, Maude thought.

As she encountered everyone, or they her, there was an instant of blankness in their eyes despite their polite faces, as if they could hardly remember her. Or else they thought she shouldn't be there. She thought she heard someone say, "What's *she* doing here?" But they might have been saying it about poor Maddie.

Weesie put on the *White Album*. Weesie was the first to get it. Everyone was picking up the unadorned jacket and opening the cover, studying it as if for clues. Weesie didn't care about pop music (or any music). But Maude had to admire her savvy. She herself hadn't heard of the album until this.

Across the living room Maude saw Mary Jane come out of the conservatory into the entrance hall, her head bowed, listening to something Milt was saying. Milt craned his knobby neck, looking for Maude. She thought this made him look like a goose. She thought it with satisfaction.

The lights had not been lit, and she could see Weesie's arms—even her *arms* were special, so thin, so white and blue-veined—waving in silhouette overhead, not exactly to the music but in mockery of her own pleasure. Weesie embodied irony. Maude was reassured by a familiar melting sensation in her chest, proof that she was not incapable of good feelings about people.

She sidled through the crowd to negotiate with Milt to stay later. Seeing her, Mary Jane took Maude by both shoulders and pressed her close, then set her back as she was. "You're so *thin*. You girls, you *starve* yourselves. You were beautiful before, Maude. You don't need to be a *skeleton*."

Maude was aware of Milt's uncertain expression, and pleased. She'd been waiting for Milt to notice. The whole point of starving was for him to notice. She cooked those fancy meals for him every night, complicated dishes, hollandaise, stuffed eggplant. She ate only the tiniest tastes. She ate a little to make it harder for him to notice. She ate to show what she was given. It was a demonstration, for Milt to see how little he gave her. She ate that much.

The starvation was easy to see, evidently, for Mary Jane. Mary

Jane didn't see the point, however; she thought it was for fashion. Maude imitated Weesie's beaming, generous grin that was like a shield. It was much like imitating Weesie's patrician disdain of satisfying appetite. It seemed valiant and strong to resist appetite's pull, like enduring an ongoing tribal rite of initiation. It was hard to say what this thin, indomitable tribe was. *Better people.* As the coolies had been. Better people: that tribe.

"Daddy, why don't I get a ride home later with someone else?"

Milt drew himself up. He sometimes used the presence of other people to say things that would wound in ways only Maude would detect. But other people also sometimes cramped his style: These kids were drinking. What if no one was going her way? And at what hour? Didn't she have classes tomorrow?

But he let her stay. Probably *because* kids were drinking, Maude told herself, on the theory that, in anything Milt did in regard to her, there had to be malevolence. He probably hoped they'd crash and she'd be off his hands, like Seth.

⚘

That evening, she'd been so happy to be with Weesie again, "as if nothing had happened," then hurt that others had been included, so casually, without even letting her know, without her being in on it. And then, when the crowd was there, it turned out to be soothing in a different "as if nothing had happened" way. But no one had mentioned Danny. It was as if he had been banished too, not that he had been part of this crowd, the art crowd. Still, didn't they look at her and notice something missing—an arm, her skin, her insides? Apparently not. It gave her a light-headed feeling. There was a crack in reality somewhere, and it seemed to run through her life. *Danny*, some voice in her beseeched—but, no, she couldn't. She knew he was waiting and hoping, that he *expected* her to be with him again. She could feel it. But to be with him again was to assent to being replaceable and insignificant. She couldn't consent to that—to even more of that than already oppressed her.

Painful as it was, it was easier to consider Weesie. Maude felt betrayed by Weesie too, but her sense of it was that it was her, Maude's, problem, not Weesie's. If Danny's infidelity meant the feelings Maude could compel were humiliatingly weak, it was her failure. That something of Weesie's feelings persisted must, then, be a credit to Maude's magnetism and Weesie's love. *Their* problem was elsewhere.

When Maude had asked, seeing something of Weesie's, early on—the signet ring from Hills Girls School; the photograph of a childhood drama production that looked like a Broadway set, only tasteful; the framed original of a *New Yorker* cover hanging in Weesie's room; the donation, published in the alumni bulletin, that Jock and Mary Jane gave Bay Farm—how rich *were* they?—Weesie had used her charming deprecatory smile, the one that creased her starved cheeks, and said, "We don't have anything. We live on air."

They'd learned about epiphytes in biology. The Herricks did not resemble epiphytes. Maude said she wished they, the Pughs, had that kind of air.

"My father has very good credit," Weesie said. Her tone, both scathing and comic, said this was ridiculous and shameful, more shameful than the lie. Weesie's smile was brightest when it was most false. She was angry at Maude for asking.

When Weesie went on her first Bay Farm camping trip, she wore green, sueded hiking boots that Mary Jane had had custom-made for her in Switzerland, the ones Maude had seen in Maine. Her lightweight pack was from Abercrombie & Fitch, as were the monogrammed nested pan-bowl-dish set, collapsible mug, and the fork, knife, and spoon that screwed together into a case like a brie wedge. This wouldn't have been so bad if the daughter of a professor, on scholarship, hadn't said, "Abercrombie and *Fitch*." Abercrombie's wasn't mail order; it was ritzy and Upper

East Side and breathtakingly expensive. Getting your camping gear at Abercrombie was a little Marie Antoinette as a milkmaid. Almost everyone else got their stuff from L.L. Bean.

Maude was the other standout. She, for instance, didn't know what L. L. Bean was until she went with Weesie to Maine. Her equipment came from a discounter in deepest Brooklyn, and all of it had been Seth's. She had an old wood-frame canvas pack that looked about as heavy as a doghouse; cheesy Dacron sleeping bag with pictures of hunters and deer on the flannel lining; and workboots that were so obviously too big, hardened in the shape of Seth's feet, and worn-down, the pale soles thin and uneven, that people wished they hadn't looked.

Weesie thought Bay Farm students were acting out a fantasy, in their blue work shirts and orange shitkickers, even if they did actually shovel shit in the Bay Farm chicken house, a fantasy of self-sufficiency, closeness to nature, and independence from civilization—a fantasy she had the sense of irony to mock, even while she took on chicken-house duty with her shovel, like everyone else. Her fantasy, after all, was to be a poor urban Jew. Her parents, on the other hand, didn't shovel shit even at a fancy private school. Though they wanted, in a general way, for everyone to live pretty nicely and were aware that not everyone did, they had no desire to experience that kind of life. They were baffled by Weesie's freak for Bay Farm and for what she called "regular" people. Though they indulged it, they liked their own well-padded life just fine.

Mary Jane Herrick had never been on a New York subway train. She hadn't even gone down to look. New York existed at street level and up. When they lived there she had never descended below the doormanned lobby. She had never seen a building's basement.

When Weesie went to the city, she promised Jock she'd use cabs, put up with the taxi money he stuffed in her pocket, and took the subway.

In a restaurant once when Maude was having dinner with them, Jock Herrick handed his plate back to a waiter without turning his head: "Waiter. This chicken is not deboned."

Weesie made him apologize.

Their address had no street number, just —— Estate.

When they stayed in Manhattan, they went to the River Club. Just for sleeping, and cocktails. They did not consider the club's food up to par.

Jock and Mary Jane's pictures appeared on the Food Family Fashion Furnishings page of the *Times*, with the name of the designer of Mary Jane's gown, at the Aqueduct ball. Jock Herrick III appeared on the business pages, with altogether too many zeros. When Weesie said their names, people recognized them. *Oh*, they said, their eyes getting bigger.

Not having the benefit of Drivers Ed at Roosevelt Field Community College, Weesie was taking private driving lessons. Ernie, the not-chauffeur, drove her to them. There were curtains on the backseat windows, and Weesie closed them, in case some stray Bay Farm person might catch a glimpse of her.

It would be easy to conclude that friendship did not tolerate difference; that it was little more than a convergence of conditions and convenience—an obsession with Barbies, houses near each other, a shared homeroom, a crush on Nureyev; you both had parents who were painters. You were the same age, you thought the other one was smart, which is to say, like you. What did any of this have to do with loyalty? What did it have to do with love?

The fact was, each time there had been a shift in schools, Maude had lost a friend. When her best friend had gone on to junior high, Maude was still at the elementary school doing sixth grade. That was the end of that. She had lost the next when she went to Bay Farm. That girl had treated Maude's departure from public school as defection, or personal rejection.

Maude had separated herself from Weesie by money. She had

said she couldn't go back to Bay Farm because of money. It was as if Maude had said, You're rich, I'm not. It was the sixties. She might as well have said she was the better person.

When Maude told Weesie she wasn't going back and why, Weesie had said, "*That's* fucked up." Yes, it was fucked up. It was so fucked up that merely saying it was fucked up was hardly a sufficient response, yet Weesie had instantly turned to other things, as if panicked. She was panicked. She couldn't afford to sympathize with outright deprivation or it would make her, too, helpless and victimized—and it would make them too unequal. Though everything had changed—they now had not only different presents but different prospects—clearly the way forward was for both to behave as much as possible, with each other, as if nothing had happened, to keep that appearance of confluence, hold on to what little convenience there was. It might be a kind of deeper sympathy and loyalty; it could be called tact. Disappointing though it was, it was more than Maude's previous friends had managed.

Philip drove her home, in his parents' boat of a car, gesticulating so lavishly, Maude was afraid he would drive them off the road and fulfill Milt's possible wishes. "Tough break," he said, "not coming back. But that doesn't matter to an artiste like yourself," he added, tossing his greasy bangs and smiling. In his view, the aristocracy of art trumped the privileges of material wealth. And she too had always believed that such trivialities as money were as nothing next to the kinship of taste.

He wanted to come in to talk to Milt, much admired by the Bay Farm art crowd, but the house was dark.

Maude made her way to her room thinking about this paradox: that the more she tried to hold on to or hold together what mattered to her, the less she held. It was like clenching ice. It just got smaller and smaller in her hand.

3.

THE CURRICULUM OF Roosevelt Field Community College was as unadorned as its architecture, an old Quonset hut on the perfectly flat airfield, left over from the war. The administration office was in a trailer on cinder blocks to one side. Many of the courses were remedial. Maude thought she would like that, something remedial. Remedial Familiality.

She amused herself. She wrote Remedial Familiality course titles down inside the black-agate-patterned cover of her Mead composition book, where it had a grid to fill in by subject and period, as if Mead expected her to be at Levittown Memorial High School.

Bay Farm sold its own notebooks—lined or unlined, with a tasteful silhouette on the plain cover of the refectory barn, the school symbol. Maude hadn't consented to use lined paper for the past two years. She wrote like an automaton, after all, in straight, even lines. You could draw on unlined.

At Bay Farm, a pale red-haired boy ran the store—a supply closet—open on certain mornings before classes. He leaned over the little counter that folded down into the doorway, hardly able to bear waiting for what you would ask for. He knew (two Bay Farm pads, unlined). He wanted to get on to the person behind you. He knew what they wanted too. He was so pale he looked as if he lived in the supply closet, and there was an impersonal angry impatience to all his motions and to the set of his unsmiling lips. He was like a creature out of Grimm in his closet, a tall, bony, angry gnome. He wore a visor.

Now she was on prole paper, with blue lines, sold in the supermarket or soda fountain, next to Crayolas and Scotch Magic Tape and Bic pens. Of this last, hers had to be black, Extra Fine. Good for cross-hatching.

Milt hadn't found the school store so fairy tale-like. He had been furious going over the bill, which came at the end of terms. But, after all, you needed pens and notebooks. She didn't even buy textbooks, after the first term; she used the ones on the reserve shelf. Milt got angry in a different way when she got the library job to help pay expenses: "Ungrateful kid. You act as though I don't support you."

Why think about this, she told herself, sitting on a tube chair, its Formica desk made to look like blond wood, curving around parameciumlike and one-armed where the composition book rested. She was beautifully dressed. Somehow that was a big deal for her, to be beautifully dressed every day. She wore dresses she made, which, with the amount of time she now had, became more fanciful with each creation, veering away from the Simplicity and Butterick tissue templates. Demure Jackieish cap-sleeved affairs with glass buttons like crystal globes; something Morticia-like in black crepe an ancient beatnik friend of Nina's once gave her, along with chiffon she had tie-dyed in the thirties. Premature capitulation. She had a figure out of the thirties, that woman, a bolster bosom and no hips, with a permy frizz of "bob" to match. Her eyes looked rimless, demanding, and angrily disappointed, though she could be coy too, in a flapperish, baby-talk kind of way. A semi-failure.

Maude wore shaped suit jackets and pleated linen pants from the forties that she found at the Hadassah Thrift Shop near the train station. Worn with her balletish Capezios. Her all-around-the-eyes brown kohl. Her hair hanging to her waist or in a braid.

The other students all but cleared a space around her. The girls had made a fence around her at that first Bay Farm graduation, because of her clothes, her look—too special, too different. But it was mere garden edging compared to this holy fence. There was no cool crowd here. She was it. She pitied them for thinking so and went out of her way to be friendly. Starving, she felt ethereal and gorgeous.

She felt the men and boys look at her too, which really seemed pitiful. Didn't they see the sign that said Do Not Touch? They did, really. They were painfully respectful, if obviously horny. She recognized her teachers as her affine group. They were smart, mostly, and grateful for her. She and they were mutually grateful. But they weren't going to come over to play. They weren't going to invite her over either.

She spent as many hours as possible studying. She read Nietzsche for the hell of it. That was cheering: she really was the last person on earth. Sitting in the spectacularly ugly library of the college, reading these works, led to a sense of exaltation hardly distinguishable from desolation.

She tried Jung. She turned pages and realized that, after the first few paragraphs, she had forgotten she was reading, her mind occupied by other things, though her eyes continued to scan through the lines and stimulate her hand to move at the end of a page. She felt as if she were underwater. She felt as if she couldn't wake up. She stopped.

She watched old movies on TV. They were the movies her parents would have grown up with. In some hidden, inward sense, she lived in her parents' generation as much as in the excitement that would be called "the sixties." She identified with grown-ups. She thought she was one. After Milt was in bed, in his kingdom upstairs, she would put on a plain black silk slip from one of her twenty-year-old evening dresses to watch women in swell clothes enact passion with men who lit their cigarettes and wore suits.

She called the two people she knew in Manhattan, a Bay Farm girl who had graduated and another who had fucked up so badly she never would. Milt said these calls were too expensive. She was calling from 516 to 212. Fine, she said, slamming down the greenish old black telephone. I'll get my own.

She did. A white Princess phone with its own separate number, PErshing 7–5864. The bills came to her, in her name, fifty cents extra for the Princess phone. What was great about the phone was that the dial lit when you picked up the receiver. This was so pleasing. You wanted to make calls in the middle of the night, with the lights out, just to dial by the greenish luminescence. She could imagine lying on her bed talking by this friendly, personal light, like the burning end of a cigarette, like a firefly. Murmuring. A boyfriend would have come in handy here.

Looking at the compact phone, so new, so white, in her dingy black room where the warm-hued African rug covered some of the ugly seafoam, it occurred to her that, rather than just paint in her room, as she did these days, she could paint the room, as she had threatened to do when Nina was plotting her escape.

The worst part turned out to be lugging the cans home with the wire handles cutting into her fingers. Or how much they cost. That hurt too.

Milt had once said he'd pay. Forget that. She'd never ask him for anything again.

No, the worst part was sleeping in that smell. She didn't mind the odor—there was something pleasurable in its insistently chemical nature, its antagonism to nature, like a medical disinfectant. Like modernism. A smell that took the art out of artifice. It was just that she thought the fumes were probably killing her. Giving her a brain tumor or eating her lungs.

Or maybe the worst was trying to get the chemical effusion to cover the walls, the chipped walls on which the dark paint had faded to deep gray. The chipped spots were white. The new coat of white went on in curving, wild swaths that looked like some modernistic abstract lace, flurrying shawls over the black.

Milton came in and told her *not like that.* That was a pretty bad moment. She tried not to mind his instructing her. He exercised so much power over her that one ounce more—no, what's smaller than an ounce?—the weight of a postage stamp more was as if he squeezed her under a press. One of those things that made the frozen-stringbean John Chamberlain sculptures, out of cars crumpled to dense cubes. She felt herself becoming compressed and tiny. "Not sideways—you don't roll the damn thing in *curves.* Up and down, for God's sake." And that look of disgust, that angry, dignified cat look that *disdained* to fight. "Go ahead. Show me."

If she said no, she was pitiful: she behaved like a child and revealed how great she felt his power to be. But it was horrible to do what he said.

She could disdain to fight too. She didn't look at him. She rolled the fuzzy cylinder in its ribbed pan, caked in black underneath, and made a swath up, a swath down, sizzle, sizzle.

"That's more like it."

Who needs your approval, anine? Fuckhead.

It still took four coats. Five, in spots. Then—

Then she had a white room. A white room. Like blank canvas. It seemed to expand and pulsate around her. Even the thin first coat had. It was like night and day, you could say. Anything can be done on white. It asked to be filled, but it was beautiful in itself: it was pure possibility. It was possibility incarnate. It was every morning at Bay Farm, where the wonderful thing might happen that day, where the wonderful thing was expected.

She wondered if it was possible to paint linoleum tile. Red would be nice. White would be great. Off-white, "oyster" white, as the cans say. But she couldn't face another trip back from the hardware store: not the handles cutting her palms, not the cost. Especially the non-money cost. She wouldn't be able to go into her room, her wet-floored room. It would be like blocking the rear hole of your burrow while the hunter waits at the front.

The rug looked beautiful, if incongruous, on the black tiles with their uneven waves of white. The tiles had an unpleasant rubbery give and sheen. She thought about giving the rug back. She'd have to arrange it. She'd have to deal with Danny. The rug looked right with the Navajo blanket Nina and Milt had bought on their honeymoon. She'd removed the prim turquoise bed-spread Nina had once put there in one of her surprising reflexive bows to convention. Maude had made some plain white curtains, though nothing could be done about the squinty windows, high on each side of the corner, near the ceiling. Horrible.

Seth's room across the hall had a glass door to the cracked patio out back and a big window facing the unbuilt-on field beyond. Seth's room had always been light blue. It wasn't as if she had never noticed. She had complained about it for years. She pointed out the unfairness, for which she got no explanation. She didn't need one, really: Seth was Milton's. Milton only had one child, only one that was visible to him, and Milt was the adult who counted.

But Maude would have liked to know why *they* thought they did it, or why there could be just one of anything in their family, as if it were the family rule, the Rule of One. That's how she would structure it if she wrote a Pugh ethnography: In this rigidly binary system, members are either *this* or *not-this*. There can be only one man, one woman, one boy, one girl, one artist, one person who counts.

No one had ever tried to stop Seth from hurting her. Nina let him do whatever he wanted. Milt would say, "You two cut it out," as if it involved two. Nina made Seth breakfast but expected Maude to fend for herself. She brushed Seth's hair but left Maude's tangled: she promised to do it when Maude got older. Seth got new clothes, and Maude got his never-fitting boy hand-me-downs.

Yet it was Seth who hated Milt. Seth who would whisper to her—"Watch—look how he walks. He looks like Mr. Machine." Who would go into ecstasies over how *stupid* Milt was: "He thought Joan Baez was a guy. He thought it was a boy's name!" And Maude would be careful not to say, "Maybe he was thinking of Joan Miro, or something." Because then all the rage and disdain would turn on her.

You could never say anything bad about Seth to Milt. Milt would refuse it: I don't want to hear, he'd say, holding up a hand.

Sometimes Milt would gang up on Maude with Seth. They came into her room and made fun of her dolls, of how her clothes didn't fit, of how she'd covered the cracked paint of a hand-me-down night table with a towel. "It's like a bathroom in here," the two males had said, breaking up, clutching each other, weak with laughter. "Maude lives in the shitter. She lives in the *john*."

When Seth disappeared, not even the good things or neutral things could be mentioned. His big room—built as the master bedroom before another was added upstairs, with the studio—sat there, inhabited by air. Aside from borrowing his records, Maude rarely went in. If he was dead, which was perfectly possible—she had no way of knowing—it was his mausoleum.

There was one other thing she went in for. She went in there to cry. It felt better to mourn Seth's life than her own—*she* was still there. True, he had always done his best to hurt her, almost all the time. But he had been her hero too. He was cool before she knew what cool was.

Logic was no help to her. Logic was her enemy. She *should* hate Seth. She should be glad he was out of her life, and sometimes she was. But it wasn't the same as not feeling a connection, the oldest part of herself, like the thick wood of an otherwise supple green vine, the green parts easily snapped off and regrown and hardly missed. Hard wood, central stem. You can't justify it to yourself when you love people who are inimical to you. You can paint your room white and still be locked in the black house. It's shaming, loving them, and no path is right. Because it wouldn't be better, particularly, not to love them. It would be convenient. But it isn't, really, an option.

4.

AT THE COMMUNITY college there was someone who hung around, who liked Maude and who she wished didn't so much—more than the other merely reverent students. A guy. A young man about twenty, she guessed. A cute guy, some would say, if you like the beefy type so musclebound they walk as if they have a full diaper. Someone who clearly did not see the Do Not Touch sign. This was almost a relief, except that around him she really did feel like a glass object that might break. He kept asking her to come for a ride on his motorcycle.

What was it about guys and motorcycles? That had been such a thing at Bay Farm, the way boys talked about Harleys. They all wanted Harleys. That was how they said it, *Harley*. They didn't say Harley Davidson. They were on more intimate terms. They said *Harley* and it was like saying *orgasm*, or having one, they looked so pleased. They discussed them. It was like locker-room talk. It would have been less offensive if they had talked about girls. At least girls were alive. These boys were so smart and so dumb. Even Danny let himself be pulled in. Motorcycles were a magnet. For boys. What Maude thought was: there is a total identity between motorcycle rider and idiot. What was the point of the damn things? Noise, speed, and danger—some of Maude's least favorite things. Boys thought they were penises, that was what it was. Had to be. *She* thought, thank God they're not: penises are so much nicer. Padded, pink. Satiny. Animal. At least the one she knew.

One vacation from Bay Farm—she would always look forward to vacations, count down the days and then, after a few museum visits or days spent sewing a new dress, the vacation would yawn: no Bay Farm society, no network that gave meaning to the stray remark or drawing or school paper, no teacher pat on the head or appreciative coolie look that made a whole day or week or year worthwhile, life once again on the shelf—on one of *those* vacations, she had bought a *True Romance* magazine. She was curious, never having read one, but with a sly edge to her curiosity, as if beyond it was something she could use to impress and, yet further, that aspect of American commercial silliness—the giant molded boy on top of Big Boy restaurants; the smiling, glittering earnestness of country music stars—that simply filled her with a pleasure like laughing gas, a pleasure fuller and happier than mockery.

And indeed it was that way. She read straight through its dull-colored rough newsprint pages, looking intently at the coarsely reproduced photographs as if for clues, as if they would augment the sparse and clichéed details of the stories—"sooty" lashes and eyes in code colors that signified trustworthiness (brown) and danger (green). She enjoyed these stories the way she had loved reading the stories in *McCall's* when Nina subscribed to it. She used to grab it first thing the day it arrived, when she got home from third grade. The stories were about on that level in *True Romance* too. But there was one she loved.

As a story, it was as dopey and full of hackneyed conveniences of circumstance and authorial conniving as any of the others. It was its closeness to her own milieu, or something that passed for alternative or superior, that made it particularly piquant. "I Was a Motorcycle Mama." That was the title. It never failed to make her laugh, however often she looked at it. The picture showed a girl who looked like, well, a Bay Farm girl. Like

Maude, really. In all the other stories, the women were abjectly aspiring—they had their one good dress (taffeta in one story, in which the romantic lead was blind; he liked its audible swish) and led threadbare lives the poor men were supposed to light up. They had hairdos. The motorcycle mama had long, straight, dark hair parted in the middle and slithering to her jeans. Her particular folly was Vince, of the sooty lashes and green eyes, who conformed to stereotypes of the high Romantic period, which meant, actually, that he was incompatible with the kind of romance *True Romance* considered true: he finally loved his motorcyle gang more than his girl.

"Motorcycle Mama" was, in a way, the Bay Farm girl translated into Levittown imagery, a vision of the street that the street could understand. Finding your own weird affine group, the subculture you recognized as yours, and trying to do well in it, by its terms. Maybe that was why Maude nearly wept with hilarity and why she brought the pages to school, hectoring everyone to look, no, but don't you think it's great? And maybe that was why they didn't get it. They didn't grow up in tract housing and they couldn't see the weeping hilarity of it. Even Weesie just smiled faintly, with goodwill, until finally, fed up, she said, "I don't really understand why you like it so much."

And now here was a motorcycle, what, papa? Wanting her to be his motorcycle mama, anyway. It was only because those dopey coolie boys gave such cachet to motorcycles that she even considered it, as if they would see her and know about it and she would be a proxy coolie, preening for an audience that wasn't there.

It was one of the first warm days, the meteorological rather than equinoctial beginning of spring, but optimistic all the same. She'd never been a spring person. She thought autumn was the beautiful time, the reawakening, the quickening and enlivening time after the torpor of summer, the true beginning of the year, when things stir again—when school starts. But she had never experienced a year like this. At one wintry point recently, she had gone into Seth's room to look out the window. In her room, you had to stand on the bed to look out, and then what you saw was only all the other houses, like a row of posted bills where your eye keeps going to the next, seeking new information but finding only the same thing.

She had sat on Seth's bed and looked at the pitiful twigs of skeletelized winter saplings cutting the white sky like the frailest black lace, the stiff stalks of the field with its creepy wall in the middle, meant for handball but now decrepit, and of course the houses edging the field like plastic monopoly houses, with their roofs slanting at her like turned backs. She looked out and didn't feel anything. Not anger or impatience, not yearning for something better, not even sorrow. Just nothing. What was left was barely a pilot light, just enough vitality to experience this as not a good thing. She had sat long enough for a star to appear. I wish, she thought—I wish I may, I wish I might—. Nothing came up. I wish I could want again.

Something clutched at her when this formulated itself, a swirl of horror at her own nullity. It was hardly even an effort anymore not to eat. What was the last thing she had wanted? She had to think. The lack of calories must be affecting her brain, though schoolwork continued to be easily mastered, even physics, even calculus, which she had expected to be trouble, taking the extra tutoring sessions offered in anticipation. The last thing she had wanted . . . Milton had asked what she wanted for her birthday. Number seventeen. It seemed the age of ruination. He looked sour and impatient when he asked. I don't know, she had said. Can I think about it?

And the image that insistently presented itself, when she did think about it, was flowers. She imagined pressing her face into the fragrant embrace of a silky bunch of lilies, roses, narcissi, stock—the soft-petaled flowers with deep, nourishing scents.

When she told Milt, he had looked at her suspiciously.

"Flowers? That's all?" He couldn't stand it; he couldn't stand anything about her; he could hardly stand to look at her; and he was furious at her for not demanding something exorbitant, the expense of which he could hold against her.

When she came home from school on her birthday, a sheaf of stalks was stuck into a pitcher on one of her yellow dressers. The stems were wide, flat, and ridged like cactus, and along them were papery, rattling, narrow furls of purple—a fingernail paring's width of color. It was something called statice, apparently. Florists used it to fill out bouquets of real flowers. This wasn't from a florist. Florists would have added baby's breath and ferns. It was one of those bunches commuters could get for a dollar at the station, with a rubberband at the bottom, along with daisies dyed unnatural colors or rosebuds that drooped the next day and never opened.

Maude felt like such a sucker. How could she have set herself up like that? And she would have to thank him. He would know she had to, and he would know she was thanking him for a slap in the face.

She did also get a card (All best wishes for birthday cheer, To a girl who's sweet and dear) and a ten-dollar check from Nana Resnikov, a card (airbrushed kittens, a sprinkle of glitter) and a smaller check from a great-aunt, and nothing from Nina, who forgot. ("Oh, well, you don't really care about that sort of thing, teehee.")

She had thought she'd buy herself the bouquet she wanted. She would wait a couple of weeks, so it wouldn't be so obvious and inflame Milt, and then she'd go to the florist—she knew just the one, where flowers were like a misty rainforest behind the glass—and get those giant lilies with raised pink spots, with that deep, sweet scent, and pale roses, and cinnamony white stock; baby's breath and ferns all around; maybe white iris, because she loved irises. They'd wrap it in tissue. They'd tie it with a ribbon.

However, by the time two weeks had passed, she couldn't bring herself to do it. It wasn't the money. She'd spent ten times that on Christmas presents. She just felt a kind of limpness about it, as if her muscles couldn't manage it.

That was the last thing she could remember really, really wanting as she sat on Seth's bed, her seventeen-year-old hands useless in her lap.

Every morning she tried to imagine how she'd feel if she were waking up about to go to Bay Farm. Every night, she missed Danny. Every day she thought about hearing from Weesie, but didn't expect to. Sometimes she did. But it was as if Maude had used up her wanting muscles.

So spring this year had an altogether different feel from what it had in any year she could remember. It wasn't as if she hadn't always thought it beautiful. La Primavera. But this year she was grateful for it. She felt her inward self had locked and that, like underground shoots pushing from kernels, and fiddleheads unfurling, she too might strengthen, lift up, and, in a creeping manner, imperceptible except to stop-action photography, feel the snap of life.

On this first warm day, she was wearing a dress she hadn't had on since junior high. It fit her again. Sturdy cotton in ridged pink stripes, with an empire waist and straight, narrow skirt. When she wore it at thirteen, it had made her feel fashionable and grown-up. Now it felt more like a memory of safety. Sometimes she thought she would have been better off if she'd never gone to Bay Farm. Then that would scare her. Even though she could get into the pre-Bay Farm dress, it was constricting. If she stretched her arms out, the cuffs would pop. By the time Stanley Delaney stood in front of her again, in all his burly beefiness, her muscles were stiff by force of involuntary demureness.

He had a round head and shiny face wreathed in ripples of smile and squint as he stood before her, in front of the Quonset hut and trailer, with a motorcycle helmet in each hand. He was squat, not really much taller than she was, but twice as broad. "So, is today the day?" His grin might not have been a grin, just part of the squint.

She had told him "sometime." She shrugged, squinting back, thin and weak as an invalid. "Sure. Why not?" she said, feeling not unlike the girl in the motorcycle mama story—she'd be doing something really different, that none of her friends had done, with the kind of guy they'd never even talk to. She wouldn't do it either, though, if she had more congenial options. She was doing something none of them ever did, that she could almost make herself believe in as racy, except that it still seemed pretty stupid and pointless.

He handed her the helmet and adjusted it on her. She adjusted the helmet after him, as if to erase his touch. It was clearer suddenly, the antipathetic nature of the venture. It wasn't just the speed, noise, and idiocy; this involved bodies. She would have to embrace the huge bike with her thighs; she would have to touch Stanley Delaney.

They would think this was so cool—that got her through it. Climbing onto the damn thing, having to let the narrow skirt wrinkle right up to her white panties—*they would think this was so cool*. "No, you have to put your arms—what's the matter? I don't bite." *They would think this was so cool*. It was an actual Harley, which he had to tell her. She never would have noticed. Boy, was the noise unpleasant. The thing started off with the stench of gasoline, a clobbering machine fart, and then she was being shaken the way babies get killed, like a balky saltshaker in humid weather, no rice grains. Her back teeth knocked together. The noise and vibration were mind-annhilating, but somehow she did have enough brain function left to feel angry at what was being done to her and what she'd allowed.

At the same time, she still felt: hey, look at me. She tried to enjoy it. Holding his large, too intimately sweaty middle. And suddenly feeling, as they veered along the old runways where he took his joyrides, as if she were falling off. "Lean, lean!"

"What?"

"LEAN. Lean into it," he shouted. "Like bike riding."

She leaned, a little. Now she really felt as if she were falling off. "Don't go too fast!"

The old runways were riddled with zigzags of burgeoning weeds through widening cracks. The motorcycle bumped and hiccupped over them. The scenery was comically minimal. There was no scenery. Just flat to the horizon, scraggly grass, cracked runway, and in the direction of the Quonset huts, to which they were at last heading, two saplings in bandages that looked like sticks a child had jammed into the ground and called trees.

They came to a gravel-scattering, shuddering halt. He put out his squat legs on each side, steadying the bike for her to get off. The shaking stopped—there was a sudden, dramatic silence—but her legs still shook. She stood up like a wobbly fawn, removing the bowling-ball helmet and rolling it through her palms toward him, to take back.

"So?" He peered into her face. He had a deferential, almost courtly air, like that sports director at Bay Farm who'd had a soft spot for her and given her the easy jobs. "Not going to be a biker chick, huh?" he said—so disappointed, and working so hard to be good-humored about it. He had to turn his head away and summon a smile before he could look back at her with his round, shiny face.

"I'm sorry. I guess it's just not my thing." She pulled at the pink-striped skirt, trying to get it uncaught and hanging.

He asked if he could take her to a movie sometime. "Not on a bike," she started to say, but he got there first: Not on a bike.

As it happened, there was something crucial he hadn't told her about himself. She guessed what it was when he called her up on her new number, though that in itself turned out to make the guessing almost superfluous.

"I thought you might have the same number as this old buddy of mine who had the same last name as yours." That's what he said when he called.

She looked at the lit-up, translucent dial of the phone that bloomed around the label with her number on it. "You're not *Stand*, are you?" Stand and Deliver. Big joke nickname among the big, rowdy boys.

"You *are* Seth's sister," said Stan Delaney. "Man, what the hell happened to that guy? He like really did a vanishing act, didn't he?"

No one who knew Seth mentioned Seth to her. It was the first time anyone had even by implication allowed that she had a right to care about him.

5.

THAT NIGHT, THE phone rang after Maude was in bed, in the dark. She knew who it was. Maybe it was the hour or the awareness that college admission letters had arrived that day, hers included—two wait-lists, both wanting her to finish high school—but she always knew when Danny was calling. She used to say she could tell from the sound of the ring. But why had he taken so long? Who on earth, if he loved you, would be stopped by being told not to call?

It wasn't her phone. Danny didn't know about her phone. It was her father's, and he had picked up, upstairs. She heard his footsteps. It always seemed as if they were on her head. She went into the black hall and called, "Tell him I'll call back on my phone" before Milt said anything.

"All right." Thump, thump, thump.

"I hope it didn't wake you up," she called up to him.

"It's okay."

There were these moments, like truces, like love showing up in the middle of the battle.

She got back into bed and lifted the gratifying receiver. The little gizmo sprang into light.

He picked up during the first ring. "Maude?"

"Hi. Congratulations." She knew Harvard had accepted him. Danny was the only person who had ever been in any doubt.

"It's not what I wanted."

Maude knew he meant her, that he wanted her. "Oh, Danny, don't be a . . . Yes, it is. Anyway. It's not as if I could have gone with you. I never would've gottten into Radcliffe."

"Yes, you would. Of course you would!"

"I don't think so. Not the way I was struggling in math. And anyway, they have like zero studio art. Just art history. I hate art history. I mean, I don't hate the actual history of art, but it's so arid the way they do it. That Clement Greenberg person is there, who Milt thinks is hot shit. It's all formalism."

"I have no idea what you're talking about. Maudlin, it's so wonderful having you say stuff I don't know what you're talking about."

She could just about laugh at Danny's enjoyment of the novel sensation of ignorance he could receive at her hands.

"You remember what formalism is."

"Like painting in a tuxedo, right?"

An old joke. She had always loved it.

"So, what I'm calling about is—Maude?"

"I'm here." She could see the ridges of her legs under the covers, like a mountain range on a relief map.

"I wondered—you know, I don't have any paintings by you. You are still painting, aren't you?"

"Of *course* I'm painting. Jesus, how could you ask?"

"I don't know. I don't know. Anyway—I'd like to have a painting of yours. To take with me."

"To Harvard? Well—I guess you could come pick one out. In August or something."

"Hey, as soon as that, huh?" It was mid-April.

"You're right. Maybe that is too soon."

A silence ensued, one of the expensive, ocean-in-a-shell wired kind that happens between people connected by mutual injuries.

"What I was hoping was, you'd do a picture for me. I mean, just for me."

"A commission. Huh." He was approaching her as an artist, not a girl. Safe, wasn't it?

"Kind of."

"What would you want in it?"

He reeled off what amounted to an anthology of her style. It always surprised her—sometimes like doom or fate—how Maude her pictures always looked, how irrepressibly her touch and perceptions insisted on their recognizable identity. She might have liked to subdue them. Maybe that was why Milt painted squares. You could not derive *Milt* from a set of squares. She painted from imagination. There wasn't much outside for the paintings to look like.

He wanted a nude, in a room, with a plant or flowers. She did stuff like that all the time.

"Okay."

"You'll do it?"

"I've never done a painting to order before."

"You don't have to—"

"I don't have to anything, Danny."

"Sorry." Why was he so obedient? Why didn't he rescue her, overcome her refusal? Overcome her. Court her, beg, apologize and apologize, call ten times a day, appear with flowers? She knew he wanted her, but not enough to *do* anything about it. Or he thought of himself as so without standing that he couldn't. He left it all to her.

"I like the idea."

"I'm glad."

Another expensive succession of message units passed in silence. That was what they were called on the bills, message units. "Danny?"

"Yes?" he said eagerly.

"I want to hang up."

"Maude—"

"I'm going to hang up. Do you want to say good night?"

He didn't say anything. Slowly, so there would not be any harsh sound, not even a click, she depressed the button that controlled the circuit. About halfway down, the light went out. The lovely light. The mountain range of her legs disappeared.

6.

STAND LIVED IN his grandparents' backyard, in what was more or less a garden shed. His grandparents' house was in a rundown prewar lower-middle-class community, with bigger backyards and bigger trees. The houses had porches. If you were generous, you could call the shed a small barn. Stand had run a heavy yellow construction-gauge extension cord through a basement window out to his barn so he could have electricity, even though he lived semi-camping style, with a portable stove that burned Sterno.

Inside, the walls were mostly sheetrocked but unpainted, with the nailheads gleaming. Maude found it attractive and even domestic. It had a feeling she craved, of being almost secret and handmade—a hideout, but better than the forts she used to build in the field with scraps from Milt's studio. With Stand's clothes and records strewn around, and a ridiculous transparent plastic chair that was inflatable, like a pool toy, it felt more domestic than Nina's dome.

Stand offered her a beer, pulling one from a Scotch cooler. Maude had only tasted beer once and thought it was horrible. She sat on the pool toy. She wasn't going anywhere near that bed, which sank when Stand sat on it, curving like a hammock. He reached to one side, to a little decorative box on the metal trunk that was his night table, and took out a joint. He took a deep, practiced toke and held it out to her, his forehead wrinkled in his round, shiny face. She shook her head. He jerked the joint insistently in front of her face, but she turned her head aside, feeling like Miss Priss but thinking, He's trying to seduce me. She knew Milt would say she'd asked for it, going home with a boy.

Stand, however, seemed to give up at this and leaned back against his one thin pillow, half hanging out of its jungle-print case, and enjoyed his joint. "Man, you don't know what you're missing. This is good stuff. Uptight outasight."

"I know what I'm missing. Pot just makes me feel uncoordinated and tired. It's supposed to make you happy, but it doesn't make me happy. It makes me feel as if I can't do anything. It makes me *more* uptight."

"You're weird, Pugh."

"Yeah. I'm weird Pugh."

He thought that was very funny. It's hard not to feel contempt for people who are too amused by mild humor, but of course he was stoned. She took out what she smoked these days to keep herself company, little cigars. She felt they made her special, even though that was pathetic—something Weesie would never stoop to—but she had convinced herself she liked the taste. Her mouth felt like a garbage pit. Stand duly made the appreciative remark about the little cigars, which looked like brown cigarettes. He was only more impressed by her: wow, a girl who smoked cigars. She wished her skirt weren't quite so short. It was a child's skirt she had found at the Hadassah Thrift Shop that happened to look fabulous on her. Oh, well. She looked fabulous. She'd have to live with it.

Stand put on a record, one of those reiterating-the-obvious I'm-a-MAN blues kind of things that boys seemed to get off on (I'm a MAN; I'm a backdoor MAN; MAN sounded like MAIN). The album covers scattered around bore illustrations familiar to her, but she didn't know the music, because she never played popular music, except a little on the brittle white-plastic clock-radio Seth had left behind, but never albums. She still had her old Tchaikovsky and Rimsky-Korsakov records, from when she made up ballets in the living room, and she had the singer they all worshiped. She had listened to a certain twenty-minute song for hours this year, all about a woman who was so special, no man would ever understand her or be able to approach her—a song that made Weesie scoff. Now it was Weesie who found the alleged poet's lyrics *ungapotchkeh*, only she said *de trop*. Anyway, the last time she had talked to her, ages ago.

This was what she'd come to. Maybe she'd found her level.

Maude looked up. Then away. Stand was wearing frayed cutoffs and, as was evident from his lounging with one foot up, no underwear. She could see straight to his balls. It wasn't the kind of thing you could tell someone, like that their slip was showing—um, excuse me, sir? Your balls are hanging out.

"You don't much go for this music, huh?"

"I—"

"I thought with Seth being your brother and all—"

"I like *old* blues. Like, you know, broken-down old guys with regular guitars, not electric. Sad guys, who are really blue."

Stand looked at her a minute and got up, his balls mercifully retracting behind cloth, and put on a hymn plinked out on guitar strings. *In God there is no East or West*. She rewarded him with a smile.

"Yeah, Seth kind of liked *girls'* music." "Pack Up Your Sorrows." "Thought I Heard Somebody Call My Name." No wonder she'd cleared the pop hovel.

In Stand, Maude could discern the outlines of Seth's old crowd, the crowd one step below the brains—the brains being the serious, smart, hard-working kids destined for good colleges, who were popular, who starred in the school plays and ran the literary magazine (*Metamorphoses*). Seth's crowd worked on the literary magazine but didn't run it. They played the maid or Third

Gentleman; they were in the guitar club but not the debating society. The girls wore long bangs and serapes; the boys wore their hair like the Beatles, which most boys didn't, yet. Seth's hair was so long he got kicked out for it once. The square kids said, "Girl, girl," in the hallways.

Maude had looked on this crowd in admiration, slight fear, envy—and with an undertow, as she got older, of disappointment, a disappointment, she now realized, Seth may have felt himself. They were "underachievers," the officialese word Seth preferred. He loved words like that, the very kind that made Maude wince.

It sounded important to Seth just because it gave what he was a name in the new "value-free" lexicon—a name that replaced, for instance, "bad student," not to mention "self-deceiving slob." He was "unmotivated." He was "conflicted." That was true enough. Typically, this group got C's and D's in school but high scores on standardized tests, which was what alerted the officials, who otherwise wouldn't have bothered to consider these deadbeats intelligent—just a kind of vaguely beatniky variant on hoods, who were universally seen to be dolts. Seth bragged about the double-eight-hundred P.S.A.T.'s of his friends who were juniors. He complained about how easy the school was, and how boring, but not about his own mediocre grades. He must have feared they were just.

Stand was one of those with a perfect score on his college boards, eight hundred verbal, eight hundred math, which was a lot better than Maude had done when she took them this year, as you could arrange to do whether you were in school or not. Stand had flunked out of high school. Maude felt judged by these tests, even though she rationalized her performance by saying they only showed how good you were at taking tests. It was hard to imagine how much crummier Seth felt. He was contemptuous of everyone else and had talked about himself as if everything were possible, whatever he chose. He didn't realize he was contemptuous. He thought he was nice. After all, he was only contemptuous of people who deserved his contempt. Like Milt.

Maude was disappointed in herself, but she struggled not to buy into Milt and Seth's view of her. When she took her S.A.T.'s, she had been told she should take an "achievement" test as well and had selected biology, mainly on the basis that she had Danny's old thick, oversize paperback on how to study for your biology achievement test. She had come closer to eight hundred on that than on her verbal. Her biology teacher at Bay Farm had said she didn't have "a biological mind," which was amusing, from a verbal perspective. But she knew what he meant, even if he was a clod at articulating it. She didn't think literally. In fact, she had an ax to grind with literalism. The mere isness of things could be beautiful and soul-enhancing in the physical world, but as an object of thought: inert.

Physical reality didn't have to be literal either. Stand's apartment was poetic because it was the embodiment of metaphor. The old shed stood in for a house, was poetically like a house; the camp trunk stood in for a table; a cooler with a spigot, where he kept his water, was a gently satirical suggestion of plumbing. It was beautiful the way a dollhouse was beautiful, the way using an acorn cap as a bowl, a handkerchief for a sheet, a fancy matchbox as Barbie's jewelry case was beautiful; the way Picasso's monkey head made out of a toy Volkswagen was beautiful.

What was the point of reality if one part of it didn't suggest another part, and if parts couldn't be captured and framed so that you felt you could contain it? That it didn't just contain *you*. Seth had once said to her, as if he had discovered her besetting flaw, "You think everything's connected."

She found it hard to care what reality thought of reality—that did seem to be the "biological," the scientific perspective: *no* one's point of view. What mattered really, she thought, was where you stood and how you put everything together and what it felt like, and finding a way to come out of the isolation of your view so someone else could recognize it—or just have an even bigger as-if experience, come into your experience *as if* it were theirs.

The point of view of formalism was to turn art—so deplorably unsystematic! so unimpressive compared to nuclear bombs and hydroelectric plants—into science. Paint should not be made into houses or faces or trees; red was just red, a square was just square. That was what Milt strove for: no meaning. Isness. Literalism. "You're so literal-minded," Maude would hurl at him, and Milton would smile his thin-lipped, luckily-I-know-better smile. His paintings were "experiments" intended to measure the effect of one color against another, the effects of color on edges and angles.

If there was anything beautiful in it, Maude had lately come to think, it was the very fact of not really being an experiment. The beauty was in just playing with color. The artists who believed their paintings were science were like great big children, quite young children, in a big game of let's pretend. Let's pretend to do science, using mud and sticks and leaves from the garden. Because what measured the "success" or "failure" of these experiments? Pure subjectivity. Appeal. There was no sense in which they could not work, except by looking bad. At best, these "experiments" were metaphors for some romantically conceived purity of science. Or just metaphors of purity.

It was virtually impossible for paint not to mean, unless it was just the coating of a wall. And even then, it told you a lot, it told you what the person who chose it thought that place ought to be—institutional, original, ritzy, feminine, whatever it was. Cool. It gave you a feeling. And she loved that about it. It was what Milt's black walls were a denial of, that there was meaning. Like that awful red canvas at the Whitney that time. Which even Milt hadn't liked. But he wouldn't like anything contemporary in a museum. Not unless it was by him. Maybe he was the most jealous man in the whole world. Maybe only he could have things, or if he couldn't, no one could, no one could be allowed to deserve anything.

What did Stand's unpainted walls mean? That he couldn't be bothered, which was that whole crowd, in a sense, in a nutshell.

"So did your folks, like, tell the police?"

Maude put her winglike brows together. "I can't remember police coming to the house." She looked full at him. "I guess I don't know. It kind of wasn't as if there was this moment he was gone. I mean, it seemed pretty bad when he just didn't show up for dinner and didn't call and didn't come home that night and wasn't there the next morning, and never got there. They must have called the police. My mother was frantic. Not that my father wasn't upset, but he was mostly trying to calm her down. She just shrieked the whole time. My father was saying, He's probably with a girlfriend, he's probably with friends, he probably just forgot to call. Which he couldn't keep saying after like a week. Of course, my mother was just imagining all the stuff I've been imagining for years. You know—"

"It's okay. You don't have to say." But they both had to stop and process the tabloid-style pictures that pressed themselves upon their inner vision—hideous mutilations, Seth in pain or terror, moaning in a ditch or tossed, about to land, seeing his death before him, his face twisted with fear. Maybe those things were less likely to happen to a boy, but he had been only a kid, even if he was a man-size kid, a year younger than she was now. You hoped for the best, but you imagined the worst.

"I like to think of him living in the East Village or something." This was where the girl who'd screwed up at Bay Farm was living. "I like to think I'll just be walking down the street one day and I'll just run into him. Sometimes I imagine him, like, picking apples and peaches—you know, working his way up, crop by crop, from Georgia to Canada—did you know he did that once? Maybe lumberjacking in winter. And sometimes—I mean, imagine he just sort of became someone else. He could be like living in the Midwest. He could have *kids*; he could just have this whole other life where nobody knows. But whatever I imagine, it's always this life where he never even hears the word art."

Stand smiled, benign with pot or memories. That couldn't mean much to him, never hearing the word art. "Man, we thought it was cool when he disappeared. Like just, how cool. I thought he joined a motorcycle gang."

"You mean 'cause that's what you would have liked."

"Wow. Yeah. I never thought of that."

People were amazing. Just amazing.

"What else did people think?"

"Aagh. I don't think anyone was like giving it a whole lot of thought. It was a fun scandal for a while, that's all. I'll tell you one thing, everybody figured he was in pussy heaven—begging your pardon."

"Oh, sure. I'm sure that's just how the girls were thinking of it."

"Nah. You're right. Who knows what they were thinking."

"But did you have any idea? I mean, did anyone see anything about it, see it coming? When they thought about it later."

Stand sucked at his roach until it nipped his finger with heat and he had to drop it into a dish. "I'll tell you one thing, he thought you had it really easy. He thought you had it so great 'cause you were a girl. The apple of Daddy's eye."

"You don't know how funny that is. And I thought he was so great, even though he practically ripped my arms out of their sockets—that was just his way of saying hello. Still—don't tell me I'm any reason he left. He didn't like me, but it's not as if I *mattered*. He had the world's most horrible relationship with our father."

It came back to her, as it always did when she thought of this: Seth red-faced, yelling at Milt—the color of raspberry sherbet, desperate, cornered. He fought with Milt every day, he did everything not to comply, to make life hard for Milt; and he demanded to be loved for it, and his wide-eyed, challengingly staring, angry face, quivering, looked always ready to flinch. He had a naked face that didn't know how to be closed. "You rotten kid," Milt would say. "You rotten kid." Then Seth would turn to Nina. Milt's face was stiff with reproach but about to collapse into bitterness and disappointment. Nina would cling to Maude as if Maude could save her.

"So, anyway, they hire a detective?"

Maude liked the way Stand talked. It was reassuring—paradoxically, his own sheer literalness made things solid and defined. Nothing was slipping around here, assuming new identities. He wasn't a doubled person like Milt or her or Seth or Weesie, a person with versions of himself behind other versions of himself, struggling toward the literal. Or not. He was easy with himself. He didn't hate himself for flunking out or doing drugs and scaring his parents, or feel demeaned by his circumstances. He loved his Poppy and Gram, as he called his grandparents; he was proud of his fifty thousand brothers and sisters. (She couldn't keep track, but there were a lot of them.) His world was solid. He told Maude she could take a high school equivalency exam and have a degree and apply to colleges like Cooper, if she still wanted. She hadn't heard of high school equivalency.

"I never thought of a detective. I don't think so. But, I mean, they wouldn't tell me. I mean, you can't say Seth's name around them, pretty much. I thought detectives were only in movies!"

"Nah, where you been, Pugh? Get with it! I got an uncle's a P.I., used to be a cop."

Private investigator? "A detective! Really. Huh."

7.

HER MOTHER DID not look happy, but when had she, really? Nina's face was puckered and defensive, as if expecting a blow, and yet she looked ready to administer one if Maude said the wrong thing. It was Maude's first visit since Nina and Rod Patrick had moved from the geodesic dome: it had proven impossible to heat. The couple were now in an apartment in what looked like an old farmhouse. Maude found herself saying, "I have to admit, you've improved your living conditions." To herself she sounded like Weesie—as if she had a secure, lofty perspective and weren't subject to anyone.

Then Nina did look happy, as if she'd at last gotten the approval of her stern mother, seventeen-year-old Maude. Fleetingly she thought of Danny; her mother's daughterliness raised the specter: how dare Danny be obedient to her spoken wishes! Like a *good little boy*. How could he do that to her, put her in charge?

Maude fielded Nina's childishly naked "You like it!" with a stingy "It's very nice."

As soon as she was with her mother she wished she weren't. Even more, she wished she didn't wish this, didn't wish Nina away. She set herself to give Nina what Nina wanted.

"We had such a time moving in here. The landlord did nothing, *nothing*. We discovered a leak in the bathroom wall and had to get a plumber in. You wouldn't believe what these guys charge. He pulled at this, he potchkied with that, and what happens? Rod has to find the leak. No kidding, Rod just looks at some—pipe, I guess, and says, 'What about this?' And that was it! Unbelievable. Unbelievable, these guys. Isn't Rod great? Isn't he?" Nina's look connected hotly. She nodded, to indicate to the unresponsive girl the correct reply. "Oh! Did I tell you I'm painting again? Rod thought it was criminal I gave it up, criminal, and look—" she gestured toward the wall over the sink, to a delicate rendering of the living room visible through a door—"a breakthrough," Nina said. "Don't you think?"

Nina was talented. It *had* been a shame she'd given up. "It's really nice, Ma. Really good." Not quite enough. "You're talented."

Nina nodded some more, her smile brightening.

"And look at what Rod's doing." Nina brought a picture in from another room, and another and another.

"Do you mind if I sit down?"

"Oh, sorry, baby. We should go into the living room. Come into the living room."

"Can't we stay in here?" said Maude. She would be more committed farther in. But she was letting Nina see . . . "Or, but—"

She let Nina lead her in, as she knew she had to. "You have to see the furniture we've gotten. It's amazing what people throw out. Perfectly good stuff, beautiful stuff."

"You always said I shouldn't buy clothes from thrift shops. You said they had germs. Aren't you worried about germs?"

"Look at this, is that amazing? Is that a marvelous piece? Cottage Victorian, that's called."

"It's beautiful. It's much nicer than—"

"Oh, well. Bauhaus has its place too. Don't you go knocking your father."

"I don't think I can give him worse criticism than you have," Maude muttered. She looked up warily. Across Nina's tired, soft face, guilt battled anger. "Do you know what we sacrificed for you to go to Bay Farm? Huh? Huh? Do you know what I've had to do without?"

Maude just looked at her. "You mean I'm the reason you left Daddy?"

"You wanted for nothing, nothing. Ya spoiled rotten, that's what you are."

"Spoiled!" Maude laughed miserably. "I wish."

Nina, standing, was all helpless rabbit's paws, and yet her face was menacing. She took a step toward where Maude had sat, in the instability of a rocking chair. Maude felt herself in danger of wincing. She froze her face. It didn't matter that they lived apart, that weeks, months went by and they didn't see each other. As soon as they were together, they were in the thick of it. They both wanted the selfless sympathy of a mother.

Nina stood over Maude, could almost be said to tower. Nina's hand shot out. Maude couldn't help flinching. "Oh, oh, oh," Nina wailed. She bent over, tottering.

"What is it, Ma?"

Nina put the back of her hand to her forehead and rolled her eyes up. "Oh! Oh!" she yipped some more. "Get a wet cloth. I need to lie down." She sank onto the studio couch, knuckles still to forehead.

Maude stood. "You mean like a maiden in a Victorian novel?"

"A cloth, a cloth," Nina breathed, as if she could manage nothing more.

Maude quickly found the bathroom—indeed, panels of bulging melamine siding had been removed, revealing brown darkness and lengths of pipe—grabbed a washcloth, wet it, and brought it back to the living room. She could not bring herself to lay it on Nina's forehead. "Here," she said, flopping

it onto Nina's hand like a dead fish. Nina arranged it on her
forehead and closed her eyes. They looked like the eyes of the
redwinged blackbird Maude had wanted to draw and that Milt
had tried to chase from the house—bulging and endangered,
thin membranes over jelly.

Maude sat again in the rocking chair and looked around at
Rod's not-bad charcoal drawings of nude models and landscapes,
at the clumsy handmade pottery and amateur mosaics, and
at the armchair covered by an Indian cotton bedspread. Her
mother, with her eyes still shut, began speaking as if with the
voice of the dead, droning and gravelly. Maude wished she'd
clear her throat.

"Did I tell you I'm taking chorus?" the strangled voice came.

"What, you mean the madrigals group?" Maude could afford
to hang her mouth open and shake her head in incredulity:
Nina's eyes remained closed. Maybe more like a frog's than a
bird's.

"That's what I *said.*"

"You sing with Weesie?"

"That girl can't carry a tune. She's very nice, your friend, but
a voice she hasn't got. Not that she cares. She's like Milt."

"What do you mean?"

"Oh, you know. Thinks she can do no wrong. She's nice, but
it's, what's the word, noblesse oblige."

Maude shook her head some more, but differently. Weesie
was like a princess, but the Sarah Crewe kind, not a spoiled brat.
Maude was glad Weesie was nice to Nina.

"Did you know the speakers committee asked Daddy to
address Friday Meeting?"

"Oh, yeah." Nina loosed the nugget of a laugh. "I think that
was Rod's idea, a thousand years ago."

"It hasn't been that long." Maude fiddled with her hair, soft and
comforting, dangling on her thigh as she hunched forward.

"You're like a grown-up now. But it's true, you always were. When you were three, you were."

"Why was it okay for Seth to go to Bay Farm and me not?" She had spoken the forbidden name. Nothing happened. The earth did not open up and swallow her.

"Seth didn't go to Bay Farm. What are you talking about?" Nina's voice came alive, plaintive and irritable.

"I mean you wanted him to. That's why we visited, remember?"

"You and your memory—a steel trap, you've got. He needed help. We thought it would help him, you know, academically."

"But how were you going to pay for it? He wasn't going to get a scholarship. I mean—why won't Daddy let me go there now, when he's making all this money?"

"First of all, it's not all this money, Miss Know-it-All, and second of all—" Nina's voice became dead and gravelly again, "he has expenses you know nothing about."

Ordinarily, Maude would not have questioned further. She knew her family too well. She knew it was a warning, not a state-ment, and that she wasn't meant to ask. "What do you mean?"

Nina shrugged, her eyes closed, still lying with the washcloth like an Indian band across her forehead.

"Do you know where Seth is?"

What made her ask? The words seemed written in light-ning. "Is he in trouble? Are you paying for lawyers or bail or something?"

"No. Nothing like that."

"You do know where he is! You're in touch with him. I always thought—"

"Enough. Enough. Stop asking questions. He doesn't want you to know."

"He who? He Milton?"

"He ya brotha. He doesn't want to see you."

It took a while for Maude to absorb this. The rest of her life. She absorbed enough to say, after an interval of whirling blankness, "Where's he living?"

"Don't ask. I told you, I can't tell you."

"Is he in New York?"

"It's none of your—"

"Is he all right? Was he in trouble?"

"He has an apartment. He's fine."

"You see him."

"We talk."

They talked.

"And that was all right with you. It was all right that I thought he might be dead." After a little while she added, "I don't know why I think I'm a member of this family."

"Don't say that, Maudie." Nina spoke in her dead voice, as if the battery were running down. Maude would get no more out of her. If she tried, Nina would say horrible things to her, about her. Maude felt she shouldn't care what her mother thought of her, but she did. She couldn't live with herself when Nina disapproved of her. Yet she spoke anyway; she risked a little more, so great was her bitterness.

"I don't know why *you* think I'm in this family. I've been outside the whole time."

"Maybe you wish you were. You have such contempt for us. You despise us for being poor."

"That is crazy! When have I despised you?"

"You didn't want to be seen with us. When you were at that school, God forbid anyone should know you had parents."

"No kid wants to be seen with their parents. Are you kidding?"

"All you wanted was to get away from us."

"Well. How ironic." She wiped her palms across her cheeks. "I don't understand why you hate me," she aspirated. "Why didn't you ever stop Seth from hurting me? Why do you protect him and not me?"

"We don't hate you," said Nina. Furiously.

This was funny. Maude could see it was funny. Even if she failed to be amused.

8.

IN THE FAIRY tale, the condition that must be kept in order for the sister to break the spell on her brothers, which made them leave her and made them into flying fowl, is that she must be silent the whole time. She must not speak. She cannot explain why she is gathering nettles, why she is weaving them into thread, why she is weaving the thread into cloth and cutting the cloth into shirts, which she will sew, one for each brother. She cannot defend herself when she is accused of witchcraft; she cannot explain herself because, if she speaks, her brothers will remain under the spell of being swans forever. So she is just bad, too weird, and she is tied to the stake and the fire lit.

Swans appear out of the sky as the fire burns. Handily, she has the magic shirts with her; handily, her hands are not tied, and she throws the shirts, one over each swan and, lo and behold, there are her brothers, restored. But she has not had time to finish the last sleeve on the last shirt. That brother forever after, where one arm should be, has a beautiful white swan's wing.

The fire was already lit. In all the versions of the story, the fire is already lit. Surely the sister was pretty burnt by the time those brothers metamorphosed. How did people even get to the sister to get her off that stake? Did they run for buckets and water? They'd be way too late. She'd at least be shriveled from the heat. Asphyxiated. Prospects for happily ever after just don't seem that plausible at the end of that story.

Fuck nettles. Not that she had anyone she could talk to anyway. Danny would listen. But she'd have to forgive him. Weesie would not listen to criticism of Milt. She should tell Stan Delaney, at least. For what that was worth.

And another thing. The brothers and their sister, they are living in the woods when the boys get turned into swans. They are there because their father is afraid that his wife, their stepmother, wants to harm them, and he is right. She's the witch who puts the spell on them. Later, when the sister is accused of witchcraft herself, it is by her husband's mother, her mother-in-law. There's a lot of bad family feeling in this story. There's a lot of unmaternality and husbands being more loyal to malevolent women than they might be, which is much the same as being malevolent themselves. Bad family feeling. It is surely a story about loyalty and the rewards of loyalty. And the cost.

Since her talk with her mother, Maude had served Milt three dinners. That night, she cooked chicken tarragon. She skinned and deboned chicken breasts, following instructions in a book, and braised them in cream. "So, how's Seth?" she said as Milt put the first morsel in his mouth, wondering if her father would choke. No bones—too bad! Waiter, this chicken is deboned.

Nina must have told him by this time. Milton stopped chewing. "You're cruel," he said, squinting right into her eyes.

"Me? Me?" She got up from her place, her face as red as the chair. "Me?"

This would never do. She sat back down. "I learned from masters," she said coldly. Icily. Call me the Ice Princess, go ahead.

Just the sounds of chewing, chinks of plates and knives and forks. Maude ate chicken and broccoli, did not allow cream or rice. She ate to disguise her starvation, to hide the rebelliousness of her hunger strike. Milt was not going to notice. Nina was not going to say "Darling, are you all right? You're down to bone." They wouldn't care, they didn't, it was proof. This was the only time she ate, sitting opposite Milt at dinnertime. If she actually starved—but it seemed you could survive on amazingly little—if she starved or collapsed, they'd just hate her more. The Germans will never forgive the Jews for Auschwitz. Still, she waited for them to notice. It was a test. She had the pleasure, every day, of knowing that, as parents, they flunked. No scholarships for them!

She was so angry. She was going to burn herself up with it, tied to the stake of her own indignation, above the pyre of her fury.

Milton pushed out his chair with an ugly scrape and lounged off. QXR went on, cigarette smoke furled from behind the white brick chimney, from the black living room. She got up and cleared the table; she left the dishes for Milt. That would surprise him! A daring act of disobedience, to leave dishes to clean! Oh, she was rotten.

In her white room, still faintly antiseptic with housepaint smell, she picked up her expensive, extravagant white Princess phone, that she paid for, and dialed Stand.

She got "Gram," of course, who was able to summon Stand from his den of pot smoke and crashing music. Maude imagined stocky Stand next to his little Gram, patting her shoulder or something. She imagined them easy with each other. Accepting. It wasn't that they were gooey-gummy lovey-dovey; it was that they didn't judge each other. It was relaxing. It seemed to be connected to lack of ambition.

Lack of ambition was not something Seth had shared. It would not be possible, from this house. He had wanted to *matter*. He had wanted to be first lead and to be chosen editor. He needed to prove himself as much as she did. Maybe he just couldn't. A houseful of failures, each feeling terrible and trying to make the next one feel worse.

Stand got on the line. "Hey, Pugh," he greeted her. She

envisioned him, in cutoffs and a sleeveless sweatshirt. The image of his balls dangling out intruded, as if he'd never be able to have them out of sight now that she'd seen them.

"Hi, Stand. Guess what. You know how I didn't know if my parents had ever gone to a detective or anything? They know where Seth is. My father pays rent on an apartment for him. I thought you'd want to know."

"Jesus shit. Jesus shit. You must be feeling pretty burned."

Maude laughed. "I'm feeling pretty burned. And my parents are both pissed off at me."

"That is like *nuts*."

"It is, isn't it?" This was pleasing. "So, anyway, if you want Seth, Seth is to be had. Somewhere."

"Jeez. You don't want to see him?"

"He doesn't want to see me."

"Pugh. You give up too easy."

Easily she thought, correcting his grammar, as if she were Milton—as if it were her job to find fault. She winced with self-hatred. "But he would just be horrible. He'd slam the door in my face. I mean, I don't even know how I'd find him. It's not as if they gave me his address or anything. They won't tell him he's hurt me—they never have. You see? I'm evil because I even *asked*. I questioned them. I'm just supposed to roll over. Seth was supposed to too, really. That's why he was always getting punished. He objected."

"Seems like it worked out pretty good for him. Maybe you shouldn't try to be so good."

"Once, when I was like nine or ten, my mother said about this woman they knew, 'She acts as if she has to apologize for living.' And I was so amazed. Because that was how I felt. As if I should apologize for living. As if I'd committed a crime by being born or something. And Seth, who was bad *all the time*—who wouldn't do his homework, who wouldn't wear what he was supposed to to Thanksgiving dinner, who left the dishes when it was his turn, whose room was a pigsty—I would always be told he had a hard time, I should be understanding. Even though they did awful things to him, that's what they would say and let him do awful things to me. They didn't want to hear about it.

"Maybe I do give up too easily. But, you know—if I ran away, they wouldn't end up supporting me, you can be sure. They wouldn't subsidize some New York apartment for me. They'd just disown me. Or maybe they'd send Seth to beat me up." She laughed. Actually, the awful thing was, Milt would hurt her *and* cling to her. And not see why she didn't like it. And she would be unable not to mind. Unable not to think in some way he was *right*.

"You know," said Stand out of nowhere, "Seth's not that smart."

"Really?" said Maude, though she realized it had half occurred to her, in a forbidden kind of way. He must be, she thought reflexively. He always knew about things. He was the one who told her about Milt, pouring poison in her ear really. *Look at how he walks*—and then she would notice the unevenness of Milt's gait, the peculiar stiff-leggedness. *That laugh*, he would say, and suddenly Milt's laugh would emerge as hyena-like and embarrassing. Or Milt would be putting down Nina—How could you do this? Huh? Huh?—about something trivial, like parking badly, and Seth would go *Listen to him, listen to him. What a prick. What a shitheel.* Whispering in her ear, gleeful. It was undeniably exciting. *Shitheel. Prick.* About their father! About a god.

But almost in the same instant she saw his face, Seth's, with a certain expression he had, a certain superior way of talking that she thought of as his "sacred" voice. His face would look the way it did before he flinched, with his chin pressed into his neck, looking straight at your eyes, only his lips moving, as if animation would invite insufficient seriousness, and if you looked away, you'd be a traitor. He could talk this way about Lightnin' Hopkins, but also about the proper way to roll a joint or the deeper significance of *Night of the Living Dead* or the meaning of the worm in the bottle of mescal—in other words, become a blowhard of solemn credulousness and earnestness. Well, he didn't want to be a failure any more than she did. Who could bear that, in front of Milt? Who treated even your best efforts as failures. Who always told you everything you did wrong.

"They're all jealous of you, Pugh."

"What is there to be jealous of?"

"Ah, come on, kiddo. Ya talented like Picasso or something, and smaht. How's that make your old man feel, when he's supposed to be the big cheese? And he's getting on. Your old lady, from what you say—well, forget it. Maybe they just don't like it that anybody else should love you. Maybe they want you all to theirselves."

Who of them loves me, she thought; who can he be thinking of? And: He's completely right.

As she worked it out, it must have gone something like this: if Maude outshone Seth, she made Milt look bad—or Milt thought so—so he let, or encouraged, Seth to hammer her. And he must have felt bad about that, so he had to blame her, find something to justify the hammering. Maybe the better she did, the more she tried to be what she thought he wanted, the more he would hate her.

This seemed true and yet impossible. "Oh, you think I'm better than I am. You do. But I'll give you this much. I do think Seth was jealous. But I don't think it's what I am or anything I've done. Though probably trying to be perfect was the worst thing I could do."

"You're right there, kid."

"Did they call you *Stand* for *Stand by me*?"

"Nah. It's just Stan D. You know, for Stan Delaney."

It was too bad she couldn't fall in love with Stand. He was so reassuring—and smart! He was so good. He would protect her. Except that Milt would skewer him in seconds. She could imagine the mockery. Stand might not care, but Maude would.

9.

"THE WALLS ARE black—the whole inside of the house. Even my bedroom was black. I wore black leotards and tights—I took modern dance from the age of four. You know, those footless tights, so you can dance all Martha Graham and barefoot. So, even the bottoms of my feet were black."

Maude gleamed brilliantly up at Bruno Heim, the artist who had been pointed out to her as the teacher who taught the cool class at the art school that advertised night classes on groovy posters in the subway. She had taken a night course in sculpture for the sake of doing something different. It turned out not to be so different; it was depressingly reminiscent of the community college. Though the students were dentists and accountants or graphic designers, professions her day classmates could only aspire to, collectively they had a similar air of resignation and adult fixedness on these inertial Tuesday evenings, with their exhausted quality of work begun at too late an hour. The students had no swagger. They didn't believe they had any special destiny. They seemed unmoved and immovable.

But Concepts class, Bruno Heim's class, was in the day curriculum. Day students were kids, as at a real college. And if the groovy art school selected purely on the basis of who could pay its fees, Bruno Heim's elite workshop—in what, exactly, remained unclear—was selected purely on the basis of Bruno Heim. What was clear was that this was the thing to go for. The cool class. She'd talked to some day students, and this was obvious from eyebrow-raisings and private looks at each other.

She didn't have much swagger at that point herself. The black veil that had started separating her from things when she was four, around her brother's eighth birthday—and which had grown transparent and almost lifted at Bay Farm—had been, since that winter, since the bad birthday of the bad bouquet, thicker and more encumbering than ever. She walked from Penn Station to the art school in the evenings, aware of the sky and the changing light as the season progressed and equally aware of how detached she felt. When the term of night classes started, it was dark for this walk; but by spring, the sky at the western end of each cross street was a parfait, indigo at the top, coral at the bottom, changing over the course of the journey to cobalt bordered by strips of pale yellow and lavender. She merely noted the change, and her own flatness. She thought with a kind of dull wonder of the person she used to be, for whom the colors would have melted into her core, thrilling in ecstatic yearning.

Having to tell the potential new teacher about herself—needing to charm him—awakened something. Describing her life in that disowning, ironic way—it was like making a picture or tabulating an ethnography. It put it to one side as an object, apart from her. This put her, strangely, in a place where she could begin to experience again. It almost willfully pushed aside the black veil.

Bruno grinned back at the prospective student, exposing a gap between his front teeth. His cheeks glinted with pale stubble. His blond hair fell to one side and covered his collar. He looked both dangerous but—if you were careful—strong and powerful enough to be benign. Above his hard and knowing grin, his eyes gave the impression of being round openings that revealed, inside his head or behind it, like a Magritte, cloud and sky. "You look likely," he said, and laughed and laughed. "Yeah. You'd be good in the class."

❦

She took her high school equivalency exam on the first day that promised summer heat. As a Nassau County resident, she was assigned to a school just over the border in Queens. This was fine on a map. Or by car. But to get to it, she had to go away from it, taking a commuter train into the city, then the subway almost the same distance in almost the same direction she'd come from. Two hours.

As she held a strap, swaying, looking from the elevated subway into the walled backyards of Queens, crossed with laundry lines and pocked with raised swimming pools, it struck her that this would be the first day of Selected Work Week. She felt Bay Farm tug on that shoulder, the one poking east.

The test was held in one of those city high schools for several thousand, vast and aspirational, built of brown stone, with a wide staircase intended to be magnificent, over which the disaffected student populace sprawled. Some of the black kids sprouted Afros, and there was a straw-haired hippie in a Hawaiian shirt, but most of these kids were of the Add-a-Pearl type and their consorts, still teased and, amazingly, greased. Their hair seemed like an emblem of a sad premise, that nothing in their lives would be better than this, their adolescence.

She made her way up the many steps through this army, through glass doors and down wide, brown hallways echoey with mad shouts and clatter, to an office where she was directed back outside to the glare and around to a quiet side entrance at street level. A piece of paper was taped to the door: GED candidates, with an up-arrow colored in with magenta Magic Marker.

General Education Diploma? Maude was never enlightened as to what the initials signified. Gutted Edification Drivel. Gelid Energy Derivatives. Geriatric Enemas Divided. They used to play this, she and Danny, she and Isaac and sarcastic Phil; passing a VFW hall on their bikes, it was Vaginitis for Winifred. Vicious Flying Worms.

The Gelid Energy Derivatives or Geriatric Enema aspirants were exactly the community college population: parents and grandparents, overworked immigrants for whom English was a second language, a swaggering dropout in his twenties, people who looked anxious, as if they might not pass.

Since this was the period of her life when she looked into everyone as into a mirror, it occurred to Maude that maybe she wouldn't, herself. She had no idea what you were supposed to know at the end of high school. She was years younger than anyone there. It was reprehensible for her to think she was different; she was a snob, just as Milton said.

It was just a few hours, this test, but they were to stay in her mind forever, hours utterly, almost brutally, prosaic—the stubby, mendicant diploma candidates, the unnecessarily stern yet robotic proctor, a school librarian who noticed that Maude carried a paperback of *I And Thou* and, with a meltingly indulgent, embracing look, remarked that a reader of Buber seemed an unlikely candidate for a GED; the teeming front steps wall-to-wall with strangers her own age, the unexpectedly quiet, tree-lined street in which she found an empty luncheonette during the break.

The test questions were grievously easy, with their sets of four answers, of which only one was to be selected by filling in with No. 2 pencil between the dotted lines. With outrage hardly distinguishable from resignation, she thought, I could have passed this test in seventh grade.

It was administered in sections, verbal and math, morning and afternoon, three hours each. Which was short for all of high school. Maude finished the first, even with checking her answers, with more than an hour and a half to spare. Everybody looked at her as she stood with her test form. There was almost a gasp.

Maude looked through the pages again, just in case: every sheet, every numbered question had its dully shiny graphite mark. She proceeded apologetically to lay the form on the proctor's metal desk. The heads went down, their glances reapplied to the test, with expressions painful to see.

As she did to the classes that made her feel déclassé, Maude wore a dress too proper for the occasion, one of her carefully sewn A-lines of rough Mexican cotton in eye-popping shades, and eyeliner all around her eyes. She never developed a repulsive starved look, a Rosette look, but her movements were careful, conscious, almost prim. She was always aware of being looked at. She carried a picture in her head, like a tiny television monitor, of how she must appear, as if, by imagining what people saw, she could remember who she was.

At the luncheonette, she sat on an old-fashioned steel revolving stool and ordered coffee. That was her usual lunch. She was very hungry. She counseled herself to wait for the deeper hunger, a booming, thudding set of pangs like the ringing of the big schoolbell at Bay Farm. On the counter was a metal cakestand holding, under its suave glass cover, twisted crullers or beignets, dusted with sugar. She indicated she'd have one of these.

The cruller was of the puffy, light school of fried dough rather than on the crusty-solid end of the spectrum. It was celestial; mythical. Nothing had ever tasted this good. Nothing ever would again. She'd never be this hungry again. Every cell called out for sustenance; every cell cooed with delight over the morsel.

The counterman, an old fellow in a white cap like an envelope, like an army cap, leaned back, in his white apron and white short sleeves, and relished her pleasure, his arms crossed over the bib.

10.

MAUDE GOT AND lost several jobs over the summer. Nothing dramatic was involved, but she felt her deficiency, though even that seemed an aspect of her distaste for the roles she had to play, which felt false and distorting. For a while, she was a mother's helper on Fire Island. All she wanted to do was lie on the beach, reading, and, in the evening, flirt with boys among the gangs of well-off teenagers who hung around the gratifyingly honky-tonk strip of bars, crabcake stands, and boutiques near the ferry landing. Instead, she was meant to be pleasing Dr. Shapiro's healthy, self-delighting boy and girl, who were most greatly entertained if they could perform for Maude, or get her to watch *Batman* with them when they were in their summer pajamas, laundered by her. Everything about them expressed complacent self-satisfaction, not least the expensive pajamas. Taking care of Baba and Russell, so greedy for attention that they excluded her, was uncomfortably like being with small, good-natured, but voracious Milts and Ninas. She didn't like the sand grittily underfoot on the floor, which she was expected to vacuum, or the embarrassed way bald little Dr. Shapiro looked at her in her bikini on the weekends. Evidently big, warm, buxom Mrs. Shapiro didn't love it either.

In those weeks, she walked on the beach while a man walked

on the moon and, really, she couldn't have cared less. She could not participate in other people's excitement about it.

The next job was in a dark, unsuccessful bookstore that was like summer in a tomb. No walks on the beach. Despite the lack of customers, Maude was not allowed to read, as though reading—advertising the product!—were a bad thing. Mrs. Reeves, the depressed but not defeated proprietor, always found something for her to do that didn't involve books at all—sorting through unsold ornaments that got peddled at Christmastime, neatening untouched stacks of bookmarks. Let go without rancor or explanation, as with the Shapiros, as she was handed her pay, Maude went back to her old part-time library job, where she had the pleasure of order—the double pleasure of both books and order—but only at the ass-end of August, while the regular girl was away.

At least it was the ass-end of August. It was a matter of days now, and she would begin daytime classes at the groovy art school. All year she had felt stunned, in a state of suspended animation, but summer was as if all of life was in intermission, not just her own. *She* walked on the moon.

Weesie's life wasn't in intermission, though. Weesie had been away, in Maine; not at her family's place, but working at a camp a former Bay Farm teacher had started. Much of the staff was from Bay Farm. You had to be asked.

Weesie called during the interlude of after-camp, before-school. "You've got to come over. I'm dying of, like, sclerosis from a diet of rich people. My father's got this English *lady* here—Lady Goodfellow, can you believe it? And my mother's got Father Penleigh. Remember Father Penleigh?"

Maude had not thought of him, but she did remember. Mary Jane sponsored his art program for street kids. There'd been a picture in the metropolitan news section of the *Times,* grinning kids on the sidewalk with their poster-paint artworks. Weesie started mock-singing, "In the ghet-to, in the ghet-to," and burst into embarrassed, mocking laughter at the radical chicness of her mother, this lunch, their lives.

Ernie, the not-a-chauffeur, met Maude at the local, deserted train station and deposited her on the gravel of the Herricks' drive, so clean it looked washed and bleached. Weesie came bounding from behind the house, in a striped bikini. "Oh, my God!" said Maude, standing back after the initial shrieks.

"Isn't it amazing?" said Weesie, looking down at herself. "Gazongas." She laughed as if her body characterized her as little as her parents' way of life did.

"You've gone from Audrey Hepburn to Sophia Loren." Weesie had gained about ten pounds, but somehow all in the right places.

Weesie pretended almost not to hear. "It's the fat person in me, trying to get out," she corrected.

A silver-haired man of great height, with icy eyes, wandering by in white pants, roared, "You look *wonderful*, Louise. Don't lose an *ounce*." He ran a corporation that made instruments for NASA and the Pentagon. Weesie rolled her eyes and shook her head, pretending to be droll but compressing her lips sternly.

"I think my mother's about to have lunch served," Weesie told Maude, as if this were the most damning and ridiculous thing yet. "I'd better put something on."

There was a flurry of introductions as they entered the screen porch, where two square tables, covered in linen cloths splashed with poppies and cornflowers, were laid. Jock and Mary Jane sat with the Lady, with her carefully styled gray hair that looked colored in in one shade, and her big sparkly rings. The scary ice-eyed man sat at that table too.

At their own table they had Father Penleigh, officially and heartily interested in Young People. Celibate unnecessarily and unnecessarily publicly, he was also an appealing and tremendous flirt, in his collar and short sleeves. Mrs. O'Donnell served: herby veal, scented rice, watercress salad, white wine and rosé in decanters and iced tea in crystal pitchers.

As usual, Maude felt intimidated and, as usual, no one would have guessed. It was a relief when the girls were free to run off to the beach.

It was so different from the beach at Fire Island, where she'd watched little Russell and Baba in the wide swath of fine white sand stretching to the horizon, fringed by seagrass and rust-red storm fences slatted into the minimal rise of the dunes. In that dark sea, the waves could grasp you and toss you down you knew not where, waves that reared up like thunderheads, curling and foaming. No matter how far you walked down that endless beach—passing women in hairstyles and golden bikinis fastened by bangles, whose frosted lipstick contrasted with their leathery tans—it was exactly the same. That was the ocean beach. This was the North Shore. There was a strip of sand, but then mostly pebbles; waves barely lapping, hardly more turbulent than a lake; and dunes and cliffs topped by shrubs. Thick, mowed grass came right down to the beach. No smell of Coppertone. No other people at all. It was like the crescent of beach at Bay Farm, except that the grass there was allowed to grow into a meadow. Maude had often gone there between classes, to sit in the intensified quiet made by the plashing wavelets. And she'd gone there with Danny.

The girls settled on towels. Or not quite settled. Weesie, with her typical restless energy, couldn't. She rearranged her towel, lay on it squirming, and rearranged it again. She ran back to the house to get a drink. She came back, threw herself onto her stomach, began reading the paperback she had with her and almost immediately cried out, "Is this incredible! Is this incredible!" and had to read a passage out loud, and then, "Oh, my *God*, listen to what he did next."

At last Weesie lay on her back, to sunbathe or talk. Maude turned her head to look. Weesie's face wore the expression of a puppy caught in a child's grasp, defeated into quiescence. The beaky bead of her upper lip was like a pout within a pout. It seemed part of her charm, her exceptionality, that—coexistent with her enthusiasm, mockery, and jokes—was this persistent, chafing dissatisfaction, her restlessness. It was what led to the enthusiasms—for Milt and high-toned art, to wanting to live "like poor Jews in the West Thirties"; it endowed dull Maddie Johnson with a sheen—and, because Weesie didn't hesitate to be judgmental, made her attention, however brief and restless, feel like grace.

Throwing her arm over her face, Weesie said, as she often had before, "You're so lucky. You're so lucky you know what you're going to be."

Maude let loose a bark. "How would I know that? I don't even know if I can go to college."

"You know what I mean. Being an artist and everything."

"I *don't* know. I might rather be an anthropologist."

"Do you know you got the only A in anthropology for our year? In fact, you and Lizzie Eldredge got the only A's in it ever."

"How an earth do you know that?" Bay Farm gave grades, but only for college transcripts. They were secret grades. To discourage competition. You got descriptive reports, called comments. It was more personal.

"Didn't you hear? Parker Knowles and Steve Pearl broke into the office in June and got everyone's records."

"Oh, God. I must have pretty bad grades in algebra and geometry." B-minus? The comments had commended her sense of logic.

"D's. And C in French."

"D's!" They listened to the tiny waves, sip, sip. "I'll never get in anywhere."

"We all did shit, that was what was so incredible. Almost no A's. *Boys* got A's, go figure that. Your friend Mr. Danny. And, you know, Francie Perkins and Melissa Ciro."

"Them! The grinds?"

"Exactly. Who would've thought being a grind—I mean, they're not that smart, those girls—who would've thought *that* would pay off?"

"It's not as if I *didn't* work. I *knew* they hated intellectuality. They hate ambition. Think of that stupid Rod Patrick—do you know the first thing he said in my first class, 'No one here is going to be an artist'? And you would never guess from the comments. My comments were always *great*." She had gone to Bay Farm to become an underachiever, like her brother!

"They're punitive puritans. And hypocrites. *We're* too cosmopolitan." Weesie flopped over onto her stomach again, uncomfortably, because of the gazongas. "There goes Radcliffe, anyway."

But Maude could see Weesie didn't feel judged. She felt secure in her restless Weesieness, and Maude helplessly continued to admire her. She would never get what she wanted from Weesie. Okay. Maybe she'd never get what she hoped for from anyone. Maybe she wouldn't have known this if she had continued at Bay Farm. Maybe she would never have had to.

Weesie was cackling that Lanie, of the former teased hair and falsies, had dropped the divine Boy for Ed Platner; it seemed that the Boy might prefer boys. Not a ripple. Weesie didn't recognize self-doubt.

Maybe it was okay to accept a lesser fate. Maybe it wasn't lesser. Maybe it didn't mean you were a failure.

11.

THE LAST HOT days of August she spent answering want ads for jobs in the city and looking at apartments. This led to men who interviewed her breasts and, after leering at her for some requisite time, showed her out. She didn't wear a bra, on the one hand, and she was a seventeen-year-old dropout, on the other. The apartments always were in neighborhoods that had her nearly choking with fear just to walk down the streets to them. The metal stanchions of their police locks extended halfway across their cramped kitchens, and still hadn't kept the burglars out.

Her G.E.D.—Get Educated Dearly?—scores came: passing, but less good than they might have been. And that was all she would ever remember of them. The damning Bay Farm grades Weesie had told her were emblazoned in some hot place in her chest. But this document from the Board of Regents of New York State, which represented a lost, damaging, unframed part of her life, a time that both defined her and didn't seem part of her, dissolved from her mind instantly like tissue in water. She cherished her difficult-to-unfurl June '68 student-body picture from Bay Farm, with its two hundred tiny faces, hers among them, but the 1969 document that purported to represent the equivalent of a diploma disappeared. She must have sent a copy of it with the college applications she made that winter. But she had no memory of ever seeing it after unfolding the flimsy pale blue-and-white sheet, perforated down one side.

Bay Farm diplomas were illustrated, by a committee of artistic students, with icons of the particular graduate's abilities and tastes, suitable for framing.

⚹

It was fall of 1969 and then it was 1970. The end of the sixties. The bland round of the zero seemed to say, with parental repressiveness, Enough now. Settle down. But, "The sixties ended in sixty-eight," Maude insisted in a high-handed way. "They ended when Nixon was elected." To bolster this, she cited the Weathermen and the Panthers, the way they overthrew the we-shall-overcome spirit of a peaceful peace movement and the ideals of race blindness and brotherhood: those were the sixties. Nixon was elected because Robert Kennedy was shot. Brotherhood went down with King. Spring '68, the Negro kids at school turned black and stopped talking to the white kids; they sat apart at their own table in the refectory, introducing segregation where it had never been.

Of course, other things had ended in '68 in Maude's own particular life. That may have influenced her view.

In the artworld, however, it had always been the sixties, it always would be, and this it had in common with Bay Farm. There was that fizzy atmosphere of *anything is possible, you can be whatever you want.* In the artworld this meant freedom that would not be called license; an open invitation to experiment and go as far as you could. This was always the atmosphere of art, but it was more so in the sixties. The sixties squared it, you could say; took it to the next power.

At the groovy art school—among the day students, who were normal college age, her age—she could impress her classmates, if she wanted to, by saying she was a high school dropout, as if she wore a leather jacket, as if she were a Jet or a Shark. She always added, "Not really. I just started college early." Either way, it sounded done by choice. It didn't sound as if she were in her own private 1950s, locked into a grid with limited, stilted right-angle options for movement, as if stuck in one of Milton's paintings. Compact and square, his paintings were always grouped in fours. A quartet of them made a single work—like their family. That was how they were sold, in units of four. After the gut-eviscerating terror of her apartment search, she was still living with him, commuting from the G'Island.

Bruno Heim got visiting artists to teach Concepts class for him. One of them, a woman—the only time a woman came in—showed them a picture of herself from the 1950s. "That was when I was old," she said, giving it to them to pass around. Peter Pan collar, worried, serious smile, lipstick, bangs cut high so that she had the forehead of a cretin—a proper coed. For the class she appeared in tight jeans and wild frizzed-out hair to show them slides of her monumental, immaculately rendered gray paintings of screws and nails and corrugated steel. She seemed as wild and jazzed as her hair. She had left the fifties. She invited all of them to come visit her loft. She brought two clear little plexiglass boxes. One was filled with her own dark pubic hairs, gathered from sheets and shower; the other contained fingernail parings—as if, if you meticulously saved what your body shed, you would see yourself. The parts of your body that are really dead, the parts that weirdly keep growing when the body is dead. You would know. The self you would find would be the person invisible in the compliant, unhappy coed. As if self-discovery meant, not finding your limits but seeing that there were none.

The artist pointed out that the little boxes made abstract sculptures, the airy calligraphic squiggles of the dark curls, the pearly repeating crescents piling up against the clear walls.

Bruno wore his grin throughout this presentation, sometimes with a derisive little wheeze through the gap in his front teeth.

He laughed at anyone, just a little but quite openly. This seemed more pointed, though; nastier. "She's crazy," he said to Maude after class, in his office. There were four of five of them in the class who were privileged to hang around his office, eating chicken legs on the rocking chair there wasn't really room for, lounging on the couch. None of the others were there, though. It was only Maude for the moment.

"She doesn't seem any 'crazier' than _____ [the artist who plucked out his body hair, naked in a gallery, while viewers came and went] or _____ [the artist who cut himself, photographing the bleeding and healing]." Both had visited Concepts class.

Bruno snorted and shook his head. "She thinks I'll want to sleep with her."

Maude's black-olive eyes assessed him—short-legged, with a belly, balding like a tonsure, with those long blond strands, the pale, pale eyes ringed by stiff lashes, and that half-open mouth showing the gap, that life-is-a-big-joke look. The visiting artist was beautiful, sparky, and fun. Fortyish, if she went to college in the fifties. Maybe Bruno only wanted them if they weren't interested, or were half his age, like Maude. "She *would* have to be crazy, to want to."

He loved this. He crunched Maude around the shoulders, swirled her around, and stopped with a big thwack of his wide lips on hers. She gave him her coolest, most sardonic look. This made him laugh more and reach for her again. She stepped neatly out of his way.

"What a cliché," she said. "Doing it with the teacher!"

He gave a deep ha-ha-ha from the belly. "Come on. Let's go to the bar." He sometimes invited a student to the bar. If you went to the bar, you were in the really serious teaching part of Concepts class.

※

"Even the bottoms of our feet were black, from dancing barefoot. The funny thing is, when I see my mother these days, she complains, 'Oh, Maudie, you're always wearing *black*.'"

The famous artist Maude was talking to laughed.

"Huh, that's interesting," he said, the only one at the bar who worked something as old-fashioned as paint on canvas in this avant-garde and very recently successful crowd, a group whose idea had been to repudiate success. The one thing Maude had been surest she liked about their work was that it couldn't be sold, couldn't even really be shown. Not having a product tricked the art world out of its ugly categories of success and failure. Now, it seemed, this was a selling point.

The painter's paintings were, however, in a sense, as null as they could be. The only color used was white. "So he's really like a total idealistic Bauhaus modernist, your father?" he asked.

"You know, I *like* the idea of better living through design," said Maude. "I always did. It's just that I have a different idea of better living."

The painter was older than most of the men, with tired skin and a forbearing expression that suggested he was less impressed by his own success and avoided people who were impressed.

"It's the thing I hate about abstraction," she went on. "Most abstraction. It's about taking things away, including meaning. Some pictures, you look into them and you think, if that were my life, I'd be happy. But—. It's about reduction. You wouldn't feel that way about Mondrian. He reduced everything to verticals and horizontals, but his idea was to include all of reality. Most abstraction—it leaves out what counts. Or you're not allowed to consider the emotion in it."

He gave her a measured look. "Yep. Formalism is a straightjacket. The funny thing is, though, I'm in love with the medium. I'm so in love with its textures and forms that color can feel like a violation of something. Too strong. Kind of violent." He leveled a pale look on her. "You and Bruno have to come by sometime. Visit my studio." He assumed she was Bruno's girlfriend. As Bruno had said, she "looked likely."

They were sitting at a long table, or rather, all the little tables had been pushed together along the banquette to make one. A long double row of artists. All male. Someone had an *Arts Review* in which Bruno appeared, looking as if he'd been snapped unaware, looking crazed and goggle-eyed. The whole idea of the press in depicting these guys was that they were *far out*, willing weirdos, the Yippies of the art world, people who staged stunts (tweezing chest hair! self-mutilation!).

Nonlinear: that was the big word. It was interesting to hear these guys, in an oddly boring way. The guy who did paintings that were words—not painted, actually, but produced through some photolithographic process whose impersonal technological finish was also in its fashionable favor, some commercial print process, in a factory—sat at the row of tables in the bar saying, "My work is nonverbal." He closed his eyes as he spoke. Which did offer the opportunity of studying his blond-bristled eyelids and pudgy cheeks.

A short, intense man, sitting across from her and the white-painting guy, who'd been listening too intently to Maude, added his two cents. He spoke in a rushed monotone, not meeting anyone's eyes. Maude felt sorry for him, although he was tremendously respected. The other men fell silent to listen to him. But she could see he didn't know how to receive their respect and remained enclosed.

"You become an artist because the world doesn't match your needs. You need to create something to make the world habitable for yourself. That's one side of the equation. On the other side are the people who can afford art. They also want to make their world habitable, but they don't know how to create what they need. So they try to buy it. But nothing quite matches. And they're nervous. Unlike artists, they forget that they're doing it for themselves. They worry about whether they're being made fools of, and whether it's a good 'investment.' They don't have the courage of their convictions. So they pay for experts—gallery owners, critics—to tell them. But if the owners and critics make it too easy, they put themselves out of business. The business side has to keep moving the line. And the artists, half the time they don't know what it is they want—to sell, to please the rich people and become rich themselves, or to go for what they started out for—saving themselves, making the world bearable for themselves by living in their art—and besides, what they make never makes the world habitable for them anyway, or only for about two minutes. You always feel outside and disappointed. So even the artists collude with these jerks. They lose sight of their own real interests. Then everyone is second-guessing."

What if the things you made to satisfy your own needs pleased no one, and the things you made that pleased other people satisfied nothing in yourself?

"That's too fucking teleological," said the word artist who claimed that his work was nonverbal, chomping ice, from down the table.

The man next to Maude sat up suddenly, like a full-figure erection. He had straight hair down to his waist and an aquiline profile. "I know that girl," he said, his eyes fixed on one of the waitresses, undernourished-looking like all of them, big-eyed; like walking wet dreams, they wanted nothing other than to please. He slumped as if embarrassed by revealing enthusiasm. "I think I fucked her once." He turned to Maude, speaking to her directly for the first time. "Do you know her?"

Maude didn't know what to say. He was loathesome. He should notice *her*. She swung back to the intense little man everyone thought was a genius, who looked as if he had a crush on her.

Someone mentioned Hegel. They loved to say "phenomenology." "What do you mean?" said one of the men.

"Well, that there's this straight line to history and that it's all leading somewhere, in one direction, and that direction just happens to be the art that some critic, who buys up a lot of this stuff, likes. And what he understands about it is what's most literal about it—that there seems to be no subject besides paint, besides two-dimensionality, besides color, composition, and line. Sure, you can look at Piero della Francesca that way, in terms of color and composition, but that doesn't mean that's all that's there. It's not all iconography, but it's not all formal effects either. Who was saying that before, about stuff being too reductive?" He looked around the table, his glance skipping her. He might have a crush on her, but she was a girl: she couldn't have spoken that way.

She could feel her skin tighten in that way that meant she was about to volunteer herself.

"So what else is it like being an artist's daughter?" said the white-painting artist, with his comfortable nothing-to-prove manner, with his tired skin.

Maude laughed through the blush of nearly having addressed this crowd. "I never had a lot to do with his work. He did once ask me to pose . . ." She described that long-ago experience, so strangely hurtful. "And I don't know why I was so disappointed. What did I expect? But I really thought I was going to look at his picture and see me." She reflected a moment. "It looked like a pile of sticks."

Conversation meandered on, and on. A lot of shoptalk about commissions and dealers and who got what. Leaning so elaborately on one elbow that her head was nearly in the puddles and bent stirrers and ashes of the wobbly pedestal tables that had been pushed together, Maude looked past Bruno's active profile, down the long row of artists.

There was the excitable Italian with the big international reputation who was winningly jolly and unpretentious about his mathematically determined constructions, which were probably a great success because they were really pretty. You weren't supposed to think things like that, *pretty*. *Beautiful* was only marginally more acceptable. His little teeth were even and neat, like corn kernels, and always on display in his search for mirth. Next to him was the guy who did light sculptures. These too were regarded as austere and rigorous and were in fact whimsical, sweet-colored, and, at their best, beautiful, and Maude liked this man because he would say as much. She liked the light sculptures—which had disgusted Milt, outraged him. There was the man who did white paintings.

※

She gave in to Bruno's importunities. They went to his tiny Greenwich Village walkup, where a water tap was allowed to gush unrepaired—a New Yorker's tough joke of a fountain. She called Milton and told him she was at a girlfriend's.

Sex with Bruno seemed like some necessary, chastening part of her education. But it made her lonely. Each impact of Bruno's flesh or limbs was an absence of Danny, who otherwise she mostly managed not to think about. She pressed herself against Bruno all the more determinedly. The memories and images seemed to slide themselves between their bodies.

She felt a wound gaping inside her chest as if it were an apple, fallen in the grass and gnawed by insects, a wide crescent exposed, only it was the meat of her, dark red and glistening. She had never stopped wanting Danny. You were supposed to get over things. It seemed as if she never got over anything. Each new loss only deepened that gnawed, hollowed-out place.

In that inverted, cutting way, then, sex with Bruno, whenever she consented to it, became a memento of what she had to recognize now as real love, however flawed. Sometimes, to heal the gnawed place or dull that ache, she pretended Bruno was Danny all around her and inside her. At other times, his not being Danny made sex something ordinary, as if it really *were* just a transaction between bodies, the spasm at the end no more exciting than rubbing against your own finger.

That night, she was nearly trapped in the city by the blizzard that began in the early hours. But trains were still running. By the time she returned to the city a day later, the deep snow had already been plowed to the sides of the streets, where it made icebergs, a Great Wall of packed, slabby snow. The next few weeks were cold, so the icebergs stayed, stained by dog pee and human pee and gradually accumulating, like black snow on a cliffy, mountainous landscape, the soot of the city. By the time Bruno and Maude visited the white-painter's studio, the snow was black. The streets glistened with snowmelt.

While the men talked at one end of the long brick-walled loft, she wandered off, still too cold to take off her coat. The brick walls bore a line of white pictures around three sides of the loft. Stepping sideways, she inspected them—slow, intermittent steps, long pauses. The paintings spoke of the viscid, supple lusciousness of paint. They also seemed to say that there was something here that was about her. It was intimate and important. But it kept slipping just outside the lit area of her brain.

While the men's voices murmured, while they sat in the far kitchen end, she went back along the walls and studied the paintings again. They weren't really white, in the sense that there were several shades of white. She loved to look at the tubes in art supply stores—titanium white, ivory white—the plenitude, the cornucopia, the seductions of color. But there was another seduction, each time she finished covering a painting panel with gesso. The gesso was white and gloopy, too loose and shiny to have the sensuality of oil. Even so, she had loved making patterns with it when she first started using it, at Bay Farm. There was an unaccountable feeling of loss when she smoothed the patterns out—flattening one painting, in effect, a white painting, to make the humble, submissive surface for another. Philip, mean, amusing, sarcastic Philip Neuberger used to watch her at it, pushing up his glasses and tossing his long, greasy bangs, with that happy look he had when he was able to be provocative. "Have the courage of your convictions, Pugh. You love it! You love action painting, admit it, leave it that way, leave it alone." But she wouldn't. She was anti-abstraction. She wanted it to mean something.

These paintings, the white-painting artist's paintings, not only meant something but seemed to mean what *she* meant. If only she knew what it was. She stopped before one in a single shade of white, with horizontal brushstrokes thickly incised at the top and bottom covering an overall scumble. She almost laughed, as if to recognize herself.

She thought again of her gesso paintings, the squiggles of white on white. She'd been at Bay Farm when she did them. Of course, she thought: etchings.

What she found particularly wonderful in making etchings was, you could print them at every stage. Each time you made a line or a mark, you could make a print of your composition just to that point. It was preserved forever. It wouldn't be lost under successive marks, because even if it was lost on the printing plate, in the paper print you'd still have it. Even if your etching plate got *ungapotchkeh*, you'd still have that pristine print, your beautiful white imprinted snow, that you could keep if your choices proved wrong or something went awry in the acid bath. The simple line drawing that got rounded out with cross-hatching and then the flowered wallpaper you scratched in behind it and then the way you'd tried to shade the background that made it all look busy, you didn't have only that, the mess you'd made.

You could never make more prints like the ones before those bad decisions, but you could still see the picture when it was full of possibilities that hadn't yet been chosen. They vibrated in the bare spaces, in the whiteness, as new snow cries out for your footprints.

Her own gesso paintings in her eyes were representations of

pure fluid possibility. The white had more in it, through the eyes
of her imagination, than any picture she was able to realize. She
had almost never been satisfied with anything she'd made. And
it now struck her that, in making her way to Bay Farm—and she
had *made* that; it was entirely her own—she had made her way
into that open white field. It felt like infinite possibility. Every day
she went there or expected to go, something extraordinary might
happen, and did. Anthropology class. The lecturing raccoon by the
compost heap. Weesie. The snowy apple blossoms. Danny beneath
them. Being alone in the wind with the Long Island Sound.

Bay Farm connected to a wider world than she could reach
from the little black Levitt house. It was, in itself, a world. She
had said something about this once to Weesie, walking along a
path between classes; that it was like a snowglobe. "The micro-
cosm in the macrocosm!" Weesie had shouted in her excitable
combination of enthusiasm and irony, throwing her arms wide
to the landscape dotted with figures moving along the paths.

There has to be some narrowing as you go along, she thought,
staring into the rectangles of beautiful white. Even in a white
painting, making the stroke *that* way instead of *that* way—it
determined what possibilities were left. Not just in paintings. It
was like playing tic-tac-toe, all of life. If you put an X on Radcliffe, you couldn't X the box for Cooper, and if you got D's in
algebra, those boxes were going to have big O's in them and you
couldn't X either one. If you were sucked out of your path, out
of what you thought was your life, into a different, unintended
one, the expected choices possible were blocked or dropped away
forever or were unrecognizable from that vantage point.

But if that happened and you stood in that strangeness and
operated from it, were you the same person? Could you get back
on the path at some point? Would you get to the same destination? Or would your way be blackened with cross-hatching,
grimed like the snow, *ungapotchkeh*, too trampled to be found?
Or just different?

12.

MAUDE SMILED AS she made the tiny, brightly colored pictures. The suitable-for-framing Bay Farm diplomas were designed on the model of illuminated manuscripts. They were hand-lettered, by seniors selected for their abilities with the flat-ended nibs of calligraphy pens. After the lettering was stroked onto sheets of buff parchment and proofread by other members of the diploma committee, they were passed to the illustrators, also on the committee. With the lettered parchments the illustrators got lists, communally compiled, of each graduate's propensities and preferences. These were supposed to be iconic qualities. No faculty member invaded this committee, so a particular coolie, for instance, was shown reading *The Doors of Perception* and with an ashtray among his books, as if smoking and drugs were officially acceptable. And this might be executed by a sweet-natured senior who favored smock dresses, had smiles for everyone, never did drugs or smoked, and generally had a disengaged air, beneath her frizzy hair, that suggested beatitude.

The committee members, chosen for their talents, had dispensation from other non-course school activities from April onward, until the fifty or so diplomas were complete. Like the girl who had to spin thread out of nettles, they accepted an implicit vow of silence for the duration. You were not allowed to reveal what iconic qualities had been named for illustration. You were not allowed to reveal who was illustrating whose diploma.

Maude would have been on this committee. She would have had Weesie's diploma to do, and Weesie would have had hers: it was regarded as a plus if you had inside information, a possibly deeper sense of what mattered to the recipient. In March, Maude wrote to the school, asking if she could be an illustrator. She expected to be turned down. What a privilege, to be part of something *Bay Farm*. Instead, a parchment arrived in a big envelope, lettered Louise Agatha Herrick.

Weesie wouldn't know Maude had done it until it was handed to her by the headmaster on the dais in the refectory in June. She would have been sent from the meeting while this decision was made.

Maude drew, colored, and dreamed wishfully. When she was done, she put the leathery sheet back in the big cardboard envelope, pasted on a label, addressed it to the committee, sent it off, and waited.

It is a misfortune to place your love in an institution. With what, what organ, is an institution going to love you back? Here she was, big sophisticated artworld person—who consorted with famous artists, who slept with one; who was in her second year of college!—wanting nothing more than to be handed a parchment lettered by her friends, with less than professional little pictures on it, and hear her name called, in alphabetical sequence with the others in her former class. It was for this she found herself still waiting, as if she'd had the other years '68–69, '69–70. As if it were possible. She didn't get over things, but she would if she heard *Maude Pugh* between Francie Perkins and Ellie Raines in the roll call of graduates. She imagined she would. She imagined her love requited. Her divided lifeline would come together.

13.

WHEN MAUDE COMPLAINED about life class to Bruno, he laughed, as he did at most things, including her reluctance to sleep with him. "Charcoal! Why do we have to use *charcoal*?" she complained, just as the Levittown housewives had in Milt's class. "It's impossible to get a clean line or clarity. It's muddy. It isn't even *black*. You can't even make it opaque. And newsprint—it makes my skin crawl to touch it. It's like raw wood." She grimaced, closed her eyes, and shuddered.

Bruno, in the swivel chair at his desk, showed the gap between his teeth. "Why not just take a photograph?" he said with his hard grin.

"Very funny. What do you know about visual art?" Bruno had arrived at conceptual art, as it was lately being called, by way of beatnik bongo poetry and then happenings. She unrolled an abomination she'd committed, of the nude model, sub-Immerman. "*Look* at this. I could always *draw*, and look at this. Penelope"—the drawing teacher—"says she has no idea what I'm doing. As if I were from the *moon*."

"You are from the moon." He enjoyed her glare at him and the dangerous jungle look she had lately adopted, braiding her hair at night to bush it out into a wild cloud that jiggled and floated when she jerked her head. But he saw that she might really be upset. "Come on, moon maiden." He pulled her onto his knee. He patted her back—pat, pat, as if someone asked you to pat their dog and you didn't believe anyone could like doing that. "I know you can draw."

"You've never seen my drawings."

Life class, Maude thought, was deathy. It was silent except for the scratching of charcoal on newsprint, and the pacing footsteps of Penelope, prowling from easel to easel. The twenty of them straggled in, set up their pads of newsprint, got out their little boxes of fragile, brittle charcoal sticks and grimy gum erasers, eased onto stools, and sat stolidly while the model—they were professionals who seemed dulled to everything except their own desire for physical comfort—shed his or her robe and began posing.

The one-minute poses were the worst. You could get down only the ugliest, most approximate scrawls, nothing you'd ever want to see again. Then five-minute poses, not much better. Then twenty minutes. Even these ended too soon for Maude. She was always just discovering some complicated mismatch of profile and ear at that point, finding that the left side didn't connect with the right.

It was a good thing she had the titillations, worldly connectedness, and acknowledged superiority of Concepts class and Bruno—supports thin as an eggshell but with a reassuring suggestion that all potential in the universe had not been sucked away. Because, otherwise, not being able to draw was like the final loss of potency. She had sustained herself for years by enacting her fantasies on paper. They had even, her drawings, seemed too alive sometimes, like the "monsters of the id" that made a certain sci-fi movie from some lonely afternoon's television viewing indelibly scary. That was one reason it had begun to look attractive to do something else, anthropology, something.

But that would be making a choice. Simply being *unable* felt as if her father's unconscious evil wishes for her were magic far stronger than what she could muster, as if Milton's jealous desire to drive out everything from her life, so that only he remained, controlled the universe; as if she couldn't move so much as a literal finger without drawing his cosmic fury and punishment. At this remove, it was even as if he had driven Danny and Weesie away and claimed Bay Farm—where he had been lauded! as a lecturer!—for himself. She was scared of him. He had killed her cat, poor Ghostly, her greatest love, then, in the world. White fur with black blood congealing.

But that was ridiculous. Magic didn't exist. That was stupid.

"Class," said Penelope, her lank ponytail twitching down to her ass, "from next Monday, you can use whatever materials you like—black conté crayon, pencil, charcoal, any kind of paper, so long as it's at least eighteen-by-twenty-four. We'll be doing long poses—one-hour, two-hour, and at the end, when we work with color, the same pose for several classes. Okay. See you next week." She swung one skinny arm up, in an olive-green sweater, by way of waving to them, while looking down at her shoulder in the aversive way she had, as if they were too much for her.

Maude fell in with a serious girl she had talked to a few times, Myra. "I'm going down to New York Central. Want to come?" Myra offered. New York Central Art Supply, where Cooper students bought their supplies.

They walked downtown together through the just-beginning New York spring, the trees still bare but an occasional daffodil showing on a playground border or in front of the big, white apartment buildings at the edges of the Village. The girls' hair blew in their faces. There were still a few weeks of germination time for the envelopes from colleges applied to in January, thin if bad news, thick if fruitful.

In the narrow, stock-crowded store, with its rainbows of Windsor & Newton tubes and square pastels sold by the stick, Myra introduced Maude to compressed charcoal, "nothing like what we've been using—you have no idea." The compressed charcoal was cylindrical and solid; the hardest grades had a sheen; the softest were velvety and left promising smudges on her fingers. There was special paper, striped by watermarks and with a furred nap to catch and hold the charcoal powder.

With these tools, at the next meeting of their life class, it was as if Maude regained use of her tongue, and more than regained it. "God, that's photographic," said a classmate, not altogether approving such retrograde naturalism.

It felt uncanny that she could do this suddenly. It felt as if she'd unwittingly learned French in her sleep. Penelope stood a long time behind Maude's easel. "It's interesting to see," she announced to the class. "Some of you just needed to find your own medium."

Maude didn't mention to anyone in Concepts, oh, by the way, she could now capture reality, nor did she show her drawings. If it felt like evil magic possibly emanating from Milt that she couldn't draw as she'd always been able to, it felt equally magic that she suddenly could draw better than she ever had. It might not happen again. Not that the Concepts people would care. In Concepts class, they had been working on an exquisite corpse. The Dadaists had made exquisite corpses on paper, one person starting a drawing, folding the page over so only part of the scribble showed for the next person to continue, and then that person would do the same. The one the class was creating began with a sound tape, which the rest of them would hear for the first time in that day's class. The clue Maude had gotten was a nonsense word written on a strip of paper. You were at the mercy of the level of talent or intelligence of the person before you. That day, the rest of the corpse was to be revealed. The exercise turned out to work more like a game of telephone than like the Dadaists' experiments, each clue worse than the last, the continuations uninspired, including Maude's, degenerating from zingy juxtaposition to vapidity, corpsily devoid of spark.

Several days onward, when Maude had "spoken French" in life class again, and more than once again, she brought her drawings to Bruno's office. She knew he was a bad audience for anything in this line, but she was bursting. She unrolled one on his desk. "Hey!" he said, his circle-of-sky eyes lighting, as if the magic of representation were, finally, irresistible. "Shitass. That's Pink Pearl," he said, using the nickname the students gave to a certain slack old model. "It actually looks like her. Shitass. I don't know if I've ever seen one of these drawings of models with a *face*."

Actually, there was a girl in life class whose drawings were always accurate, recognizable, and poetic in the way they captured light. They had faces; they had everything. But Maude was pleased to accept the compliment.

Maude sat on Bruno's desk, elbow on knee, chin on hand. "You're just supposed to care about light, mass, shadow, and the composition of the page. You know, for it to come out, you *do* kind of have to kind of forget what it is and just draw the shapes of the shadows."

"You drew the shapes of the shadows, all right."

"I did, didn't I?"

"Hey, if you're going to draw so graphically, do one of someone sexy. Do me one of you!"

"I suppose *you'd* want full beaver." She just didn't like him enough. She didn't believe she could like anyone enough. She missed Danny as if they had parted that minute.

Bruno showed his gap, but he looked differently at her, as if nervous in the presence of a spell that worked, even though it was no more than a competent life drawing. "What? What is it?" he asked.

Her festive air was gone. He saw a thoughtful absence. She spoke into her lap. "I promised someone else a picture. Ages ago. It just occurred to me he might really want it." She had never really believed Danny's request until this minute, until Bruno asked for a sexy one, of her. Danny really wanted her. Suddenly, she felt sick with the need to undo the wrong. She had punished him above and beyond what he deserved. *She* had been cruel. He hadn't asked for much. It was just that what she'd wanted was to give him everything.

"You'd better not be doing *him* a full beaver."

"How do you know it's a him?"

Bruno sat back heavily in his chair. She was not going to sleep with him again. He was sure of it. He wished he couldn't tell. He would rather not have noticed. He picked up the drawing of Pink Pearl. "Let me have this one. Just sign it."

14.

S HE READ THE letter three times, in case her eye had skipped over something, some crucial "not" or "no," in case she'd misunderstood, still standing by the pink front door where the mail had slopped through the slot, fanning onto the black seafoam linoleum. Milton was filling the percolator for a pot of coffee, careful not to let water touch the electrical prongs.

"Daddy?"

"Mmm."

"I got into Sarah Lawrence."

"Good."

He continued his task rather than turn toward her. His back appeared to sizzle, though the tension might all be hers. "It's four thousand dollars."

"You could commute," he said to the cabinet above the sink.

Then it would just be tuition. "I really couldn't." A rescue came from a phrase remembered from the college handbook. "You have to live on campus the first year."

He sighed, skinny and tall in the doll-like kitchen, in jeans that bagged around his storky legs. His white hair came down over the collar of his corduroy shirt. She could see how soft it was, like feathers. She could see, from his back, his struggle.

"I'll get a college loan." She was old enough to sign for one.

"No." He turned around. "You'll do no such thing. Don't be ridiculous."

She looked at him. Her face ached with not showing fear.

"I'm paying."

You *are*? she wanted to say—Why *now*, when all this time . . . But she knew better than to set off such a process of fission in the mystery uranium. His face was deeply disappointed, somehow. Was he going to say he'd be glad to be rid of her? But he just walked into the next room, lighting a cigarette, leaving the white ceramic percolator to begin its long, sucking gurgle and pop. He'd done everything he could to hold on to her, if only as a captive and slave.

She too retreated, to the white cell of her room, to fill in the forms and send them off before he changed his mind. Not that he would be able to stop her now. Maybe that was why he'd given in. She'd never believed he'd pulled her out of Bay Farm because of the money. It was to keep her from getting away. It was to keep her.

Maybe she'd become a person for whom it was too easy to leave, to leave people behind, to leave men. Maybe she'd lost her own meaning, become an abstraction of herself, become her own exquisite corpse, something someone else started and finished. Maybe she couldn't love, or believe in it, or it just seemed too damaging. Milt's love took the form of enslaving—who wanted that? And she was like him. She was not unlike him. Danny had loved her but she had proposed for him Didi Bates and Weesie, of the tribe of *better people*: people who knew how to love, who would stay with it. Anyone would be better at loving than a Pugh.

As she was getting ready for bed, she caught sight of herself in the big round mirror that was a hand-me-down from Nana Resnikov. There was something Oz-like about its shape and the blond, deco-ish crescents that held it top and bottom. It made a picture, that flattened circle, with her in semi-dimness, her naked torso, her hair. That was the picture she would give Danny. Looking at herself, she felt herself to be him, seeing her. Danny looking at someone he cared about. Someone he forgave. She would capture her own reality, for someone else.

She got out the wooden box of pastels Milton had given her one day, at random—"Here. Want these?"—three tiers of chalk, almost all the gradations of color.

She would be the model and the artist. It would not look like a bunch of sticks.

A week or so later, Bay Farm's spring break, Maude talked to Weesie. It had been a very long time. They hadn't seen each other since the Father Penleigh and blue hydrangea day the past August, and now it was spring again. There had been a postcard from a skiing vacation, with amusing descriptions of Swiss people and, before that, in September, a discussion of their respective courses. ("*Concepts* class! Oi-oi-*oi*." As Maude had described some of the artwork involved, Weesie said, sounding both humorous and as if she thoroughly expected her implied command to be obeyed, "I think that's a little *too* far out.")

Then, radio silence. In the first year, Maude had made the mistake of calling Weesie and catching her distracted, preoccupied, and uninterested. It was better to wait. When Weesie called, Maude told her news.

"So it looks as if I'll be going to like a regular college next year."

"What? No more"—and Weesie put on the spooky voice kids used if they were saying *The Twiiliight Zone*—"*Concepts* class."

"No more Concepts class. I hope there'll still be concepts."

"So where?"

"Sarah Lawrence."

"Sarah Lawrence!" Weesie screamed. "Sarah Lawrence!" she screamed some more.

"What?" said Maude.

"Guess where I'm going."

"No!"

"Yes!"

They had to spend a while screaming together.

When they had calmed down enough, Maude said, "We can be roommates."

"Roommates!" said Weesie in her excitable way, as if roommates were a high-camp notion.

"I mean, if you want. I don't think I have to have a roommate. As a junior."

"Junior! Oh-my-*God*. Life is so incredible. Life is *so incredible.* Isn't it? Isn't it? A junior." As an afterthought, Weesie remembered to say, "Of course we'll room together."

"Oh, great. I'll fill that in on the"—Maude adopted Weesie's intonation—"*housing* form." They giggled. "I'd rather be a freshman, really . . ."

Still, freshman or not—fresh or slightly spoiled—when Maude hung up the little white Princess phone that she would soon be returning to the phone company, she hardly knew what to do with her happiness.

15.

ANDERING AROUND THE tiny, empty house while Milton was out, and knowing that she would not be stuck there forever—that she would never live there again, in all probability—let Maude appreciate its jewel-like quality, with the squares of color glowing out of the blackness. It was not unlike the afghan that lay over the arm of the black couch, squares of concentric color within bright color, each outlined in and joined by crocheted black. She had never had trouble loving that.

She was thinking about what she'd do for the final Concepts class. It was a self-imposed task. Bruno wouldn't care and the class wouldn't care if she did nothing, which was what most of the class would do. Why not, if an empty gallery, presented as a show, could still make a splash, even though it had been done. For her, though, showing the empty gallery again was like telling the same joke over and over. It lost its punch.

Outside the wall of glass, redwinged blackbirds rose from the field in a group, the heartlifting vermilion on their wings flashing as they swerved up and disappeared. From the cracked patio behind the living room to the row of houses visible on the far side, the field was soft with wildflowers—buttercups, clover, the first pinks, tiny at the end of the stiff blades that were their stalks, and the dandelions that so angered the other homeowners. The field was slated to be shaved and tamed that summer into an official park, with playing fields and metal swings.

She'd been thinking about an ethnography of the artworld but couldn't come up with a way to present it elegantly—the affine group of the men who could sit in the bar night after night, who knew the right things to say, the right people to know. The glossary—*visual verbal linear dialectic Wittgenstein Gertrude Stein Duchamp.* A glossary of forbidden, uncool, embarrassing words: *feeling expression beauty universal transcendence.* The forbidden qualities of prettiness, decorativeness, lack of sophistication, traditional craftsmanship.

Though the atmosphere of the artworld might be a perpetual sixties, in art, it turned out, not all that much was allowed. At first conceptual art had seemed to bear out the atmosphere of freedom. Visual art at that point forbade all narrative elements— anything except color, form, composition, mass, any representation at all, even of emotion. Visual art was to be scientific, to make progress, in the exploration of its pure components. Maude put Milton as a dot on that timeline. But conceptualism, in its way, wasn't much different. It was just that its mandate was to reduce art to its intangible elements—the framing that turned whatever was framed into an object of commentary or contemplation, whether it was a urinal, a soup can, or the knowledge that the artist was listening to your footsteps and masturbating under the gallery floor. It was still about what made art art.

But the artist covertly under the gallery floor, under your feet—it did give you a feeling. And something else they talked about at the bar, in class: blurring the line between art and life so that art *wouldn't* be something framed, on a pedestal, apart, but something *lived*; and, likewise, your life could be redeemed by becoming, itself, art. How exciting *that* was. How—romantic. Hence the boxes of nail parings and pubic hair, the exhibited electrocardiograms and medical charts, the videotapes in which an artist comes and goes, doing dishes and forgetting his keys but not talking of Michelangelo. As process, okay. As product—maybe pretty boring.

She could imagine acceptable things she could make. Wearable sculptures of coiled twine or strips of rag or feathers, in non-body shapes; cubes covered in real growing grass; rooms with a grass floor, or filled with artificially made fog—if possible, a cloud floating in the middle of a room. A joke about containing the uncontainable, nature; about the puniness of artifice. Ungrandiose, antigrandiose art. It would appeal to the senses; it would be beautiful, in fact. And, therefore, probably uncool.

For, above all—so it seemed as she stared abstractedly out at the soon-to-be-paved and replanted field—art had to be exclusionary to succeed. It had to make an in-group and an out-group. She had even seen a gallery piece about that, this year, done with masking tape on the floor. The way art could do this was by special knowledge, the kind of initiation where you betrayed nothing (no goofy handshakes or pins and insignia). It was straightfaced but never earnest—you just wore shades. The work couldn't be too accessible or easy in its appeal. It must not be for everyone. You had to be one of the initiates. The knowledge required had to change frequently, be an ever-moving target. And that was what was wrong with traditional art—with representation. It was a magic no one really understood, and it was powerful magic, with deep effects; but anyone could learn to read it in two seconds. Everyone could like it.

You would think, she thought, that people could stop worrying about being cool once they got out of *high school*.

This ramble of thought was interrupted by the clank and clatter of the front door, and Milt was there with her, unavoidable, throwing his raincoat onto one of the red kitchen chairs. "Well," he said, as if she had asked a question. He'd been in the city, she knew. "They're dropping me."

This was not going to be good. "Who?" she said. If only she'd been in her own room when he came in. She couldn't help it: she wanted to hide.

"The gallery," he said bitterly, as if it were her fault, and as if she ought to know.

"Your gallery? Your gallery is dropping you?"

"I'm not selling well enough." His hands and shoulders made a wide W of a shrug. "They have better uses for their space." He looked at her face. "Don't worry. I can still pay your tuition."

"I wasn't even thinking about that." A stronger feeling overcame her fear. "Daddy—I'm so sorry."

"Aagh"—he made his classic tossing-away gesture—"it's just fashion. That's all it is. It's just fashion."

"You're right. You're absolutely right," she said as he loped past, on his way upstairs to his studio or bedroom. "Oh, Daddy. You're a real artist."

He paused at the bottom step. He didn't look at her, and she saw he couldn't. "Thanks, honey. Thank you, Maudie." He looked at her quickly. "I never thought you liked my work." He took one step, disappearing into the walled stairwell, so that just his voice was in the room: "You're good to me, kid."

16.

*T*hought *I heard somebody call my name—thought I heard
somebody call my name; painting a picture, across the amber
sky, of love, and lonely days gone by* . . . The "Somebody's
Gonna Miss Me" song kept going through her head, the song
from her brother's record, stolen from his room to play at Bay
Farm, the first time Danny smiled at her, in the pop hovel. She
thought of how the list of graduates was called from the dais
in the refectory for each senior to come up and get his or her
diploma at graduation. My name will not be called. I will not
hear someone call my name, she warned herself: don't hope.
Don't kid yourself.

*Painting a picture, across the amber sky, of love, and lonely days
gone by.* Bay Farm graduation was in three weeks. She was going
to go. It was her graduation, her class. She wouldn't miss it. She
had had to ask someone when it was.

The drawing for Danny was rolled to go into a picture cylinder.
With only its back showing, the rolled-up picture looked like a
big, dirty diploma. She slid the dirty diploma that was her mirror image, her other self reflected and caught, into the mailing
tube and taped on the label. Danny Stern, Harvard University,

Cambridge, Mass. It wasn't much of an address. She hoped it was enough to get the thing there.

If not, after all, it would come back.

He had it anyway, whether he knew it or not. Her real self, some essential aspect of herself, her loving self, what there was of it, had stayed with him. She dug her bare toes into the yellow rug from Africa that looked like sunshine on the floor. She had tried to wrench that self away for her own freedom, but she couldn't, not with Bruno, anyway. She felt as if Danny watched her, even now as she sent him this coded message of herself, in a tube. She needed someone to see her.

If it were actually her graduation, she thought, she'd invite Stand. Who'd done a pretty good job of seeing who she was. Stand had gotten into a better college, a real one, but it turned out he wasn't going to go. He was doing construction work with an uncle's company and making huge amounts of money. More than Milt made at his most successful. He said he couldn't be bothered with college.

Three weeks later, on the morning of Bay Farm graduation, Weesie called, "just to make sure you're coming."

"Of course I'm coming." Not that it had been mentioned between them before.

Some things never change: Maude asked what Weesie would wear.

Just a summer dress, apparently. Maude planned to wear the white net antique thing from her first year—Miss Havisham in her wedding dress, carrying the torch for Bay Farm.

"It's hot," said Weesie, meaning the dress had sleeves (even if they were net, transparent, and as substantial as spider web) and that she disapproved. *She* had moved on. You wouldn't catch her in that old Pucci, dated and embarrassing in 1970. Already an antique dress was hippieish in a discredited back-to-nature, back-to-the-old-ways way.

"It's good hot, not bad hot," said Maude, meaning not sticky oppressive heat but the kind that makes you want to lie in the sun.

"It has sleeves," said Weesie, coming as close as she was going to to mentioning sweat.

Why, Maude wondered, was Weesie always so sure she was right, so that if you differed it meant you didn't, in some crucial way, get it? She felt her usual helplessness and inferiority. Then she didn't. She turned around and mentally looked at Weesie instead of feeling Weesie's disapproving gaze on her. This was a weakness in Weesie, a blind spot. Weesie's disapproval didn't mean Maude should disqualify herself. Maude didn't have to accept the rule of her judgments. It was possible that the tribe of *better people* could accommodate both of them. "Well, I'll be the one who's sweaty, not you," said Maude finally, as if exempting Weesie from responsibility.

The dress, probably from the teens of the century, was a little tattered, a little yellowed. But still beautiful, Maude thought, examining the effect, that afternoon, in the Oz-y mirror, with the tan of her shoulders and upper chest dark through the white net, above thick white embroidered flowers. She pinned her hair up. She remembered how the girls had insisted she get the dress, because it was so her, and yet it had made a fence around her as being too special. Well, maybe it was like her—different after all and a little the worse for wear.

She had had to ask Milton to drive her. When they got to the car, he went to the passenger side. She had gotten her learner's permit in Drivers' Ed at the community college, but still had no license, from lack of practice. This was unexpected graciousness. He handed her the keys and faced forward. This is so *normal*, she thought, though really it wasn't—her in her elderly costume, driving her father, who had pulled her from school, to her non-graduation. She wondered: by dragging him there, did he think she was trying to rub it in? She maneuvered the little stick-shift down the trafficless streets of once-identical houses, to the commercial strip and, nervously, onto the highway. "You can go faster," said Milt in his imperturbable way. He certainly wasn't hoping she would crash.

There was a big silence on the way. She wanted to ask about Seth, about what went on between them—Seth and Milt, Seth and Nina—about why they so totally left her out. But she couldn't. It would make everything horrible again. Milt seemed, momentarily, almost to approve of her, and she knew he would consider it an attack if she asked any questions on *that* subject. She knew how precarious and provisional it was for him to accept any feelings in her that were independent of his wishes—to allow room for any of her desires at all.

At school, Milt did not get himself over to the driver's side but got out with her.

"Are you staying?"

"Sure," he said, as if it were a foregone conclusion—as if it really were Maude's graduation. "I'll find your mother." Milt and Nina were on better terms with each other than Maude had managed with either of them. They were in it, so to speak, for the long haul. When Milt had his show, Nina had even helped with the invitations, addressing envelopes. Sometimes Maude heard him talking to Nina on the phone. Never Seth. She imagined Seth communicated with and through Nina. Seth had always hated Milt. He'd wanted Maude to. But she didn't. Part of her did, but she didn't. This was who they were. Maybe everyone's family, if you scratched the surface, was as weird. Maybe this *was* normal.

She strolled with her father to the refectory very much as if it were. As he spied Nina with her Rod, he bent to peck Maude on the cheek and loped off toward them, as if embracing your estranged daughter and attending her non-graduation with your ex-wife and ex-wife's lover were also the most ordinary thing in the world.

It was still sunny at this June evening hour, after Bay Farm dinner. The Pughs had come only for the climax of the day's events, the handing out of diplomas. Milt seated himself with the faculty and staff, down one side of the refectory, next to Nina. Maude sat with the students, facing the dais, in the main body of the old barn, under its high, beamed vault. There were lots of unfamiliar faces—two years' worth, all the freshmen and sophomores, though there was a certain generic Bay Farmness to them: a complacency about being there and, naturally, the Bay Farm look of long hair, cutoffs, or fabulous, fanciful versions of elegance and polished dress. Time might make new cultures, but this was still Bay Farm culture. The kids were the same blond and Nordic gene pool too—high WASP—with a smattering of Jews, Catholics, and black kids, the groups that got the preponderance of abundant scholarships the school prided itself on.

There were a few alumni around, as there always were at graduation, recent graduates who still missed the place, and possibly always would. She noticed a particularly attractive young man, dark, like Danny, but older. He must have felt her eyes on him, because he turned and looked at her quizzically, tilting his long head to one side. Her face heated as if she'd been caught in the act, and her eyes pricked as she smiled at him and almost instantly looked away. It was Danny. His smile was so exactly the same that she didn't see how for a moment she'd mistaken him.

The commencement speech began—by the Senator uncle, from a liberal northern state. The headmaster came up afterward, shook the Senator's hand and thanked him, leading some more clapping, and began the roll call. In Bay Farm's egalitarian no-grades way, there were no valedictorians or any of that kind of thing, just Abbott, Beals, and so on through Wells and Zapandreou. Louisa Agatha Herrick. Weesie got up in her to-die-for simple French cotton frock. Maude watched to see Weesie's expression when she unrolled her diploma. Meanwhile the names went on, mounting into the P's. Steven Michael Pearl. Francine Shaughnessy Perkins. *Now*: Ellen Susanna Raines.

The person next to her made a joke. Maude took pride in turning and smiling, her eyes maybe suspiciously bright, but that could be just ordinary sentiment. Almost everyone was a little teary.

She'd kept hoping. She'd held on to the stupid fantasy that special dispensation would be made.

After Zapandreou, there was prolonged clapping, stamping, whistling, and shouting. The headmaster held up his hands for quiet, but finally shot his hands to the side in exasperation and gave up. As people around her stood, Maude looked for Weesie, to congratulate her and other old friends. At the borders of the crowd, seniors were shrieking and jumping up and down, embraced by family and classmates.

From the other direction, Maude heard Weesie's voice say her name and turned. There were Philip and Isaac, holding their diplomas and advancing on her. "This is great!" said Weesie, brandishing her diploma. Maude started to explain, in her painstaking way, how she'd contacted the diploma committee and so on and so forth. She was interrupted by the sarcastic, self-mockingly pompous Philip, who had washed his hair but still needed to toss his bangs off his glasses and jab the glasses up his nose. "By virtue of the powers vested in me as head of the diploma committee—"

"Blow it out your heinie, Neuberger," said a smirking bystander.

Philip ignored him, with the happy smile with which he always gave or took insults. "By the powers vested in me as head of the all-important diploma committee"—he shoved one of the parchment rolls toward Maude—"we thought you should have this."

Weesie's face was split by a wedge, her biggest to-the-back-teeth grin. "Open it," she said.

Maude unfurled the parchment. It was just like a Bay Farm diploma only, instead of being signed by the headmaster, there were the signatures of Isaac, Philip, Weesie, and the other committee members, and there was no gold certifying school seal. There were four little pictures, arrayed in a square, like Milt's picture families. One showed Maude so realistically, it was like an old-fashioned portrait miniature.

"You each did one," she said, recognizing the styles. "But this . . ." she pointed to the beautifully rendered portrait, her finger wet from wiping her cheeks.

"My mother helped," said Weesie. "And Milton helped *her.*"

"Oh, God," said Maude, unable to pretend she wasn't crying. What a sap, to cry like Miss America.

She felt a field of heat at her back. A hand reached over her shoulder, pointing at the miniature, and a tenor voice said, "I prefer the one you sent me."

She whirled to face Danny but didn't get to look, because he gripped her too tightly. She held out the diploma so it wouldn't get crushed. But *she* was. For a while, she couldn't speak.

Acknowledgements

Many and grateful thanks to:

Huguette Martel, Mark Belair, Amy Rosenthal,
Tom Mallon, Ellen Pall, Vicki Barker, Caryn James,
Alice Truax, Tina Bennett, Alice Quinn,
Katie Herman, and Matt Seaton.

❧